PRAISE FOR GR

### *Beach Rental*

DOUBLE WINNER IN THE 2012 GDRWA
BOOKSELLERS BEST AWARD

FINALIST IN THE 2012 GAYLE WILSON AWARD OF
EXCELLENCE

FINALIST IN THE 2012 PUBLISHED MAGGIE AWARD
FOR EXCELLENCE

"No author can come close to capturing the awe-inspiring essence of the North Carolina coast like Greene. Her debut novel seamlessly combines hope, love and faith, like the female equivalent of Nicholas Sparks. Her writing is meticulous and so finely detailed you'll hear the gulls overhead and the waves crashing onto shore. Grab a hanky, bury your toes in the sand and get ready to be swept away with this unforgettable beach read." —*RT Book Reviews 4.5 stars TOP PICK*

### *Beach Winds*

FINALIST IN THE 2014 OKRWA INTERNATIONAL
DIGITAL AWARDS

FINALIST IN THE 2014 WISRA WRITE TOUCH
READERS' AWARD

"Greene's follow up to Beach Rental is exquisitely written with lots of emotion and tugging on the heartstrings. Returning to

Emerald Isle is like a warm reunion with an old friend and readers will be inspired by the captivating story where we get to meet new characters and reconnect with a few familiar faces, too. The author's perfect prose highlights family relationships which we may find similar to our own and will have you dreaming of strolling along the shore to rediscover yourself in no time at all. This novel will have one wondering about faith, hope and courage and you may be lucky enough to gain all three by the time Beach Winds last page is read." —*RT Book Reviews 4.5 stars TOP PICK*

## A Light Last Seen and A Reader's View of Cub Creek

*From a reader about Cub Creek and A Light Last Seen:* "'In the heart of Virginia, where the forests hide secrets and the creeks run strong and deep,' is a place called Cub Creek. A place that has meadows filled with colorful flowers and butterflies to chase, and dirt roads and Cub Creek to jump over and disappear into the woods. A living and rural place that draws the reader to the setting and the characters who have stories to tell. A place with light and darkness and as unique as the characters who live there. When I opened the beautiful cover of this book, I stepped into the Cub Creek world and met the main character, Jaynie Highsmith. This is her story."—*Reader/Reviewer Bambi Rathman, February 2020*

# A DANCING TIDE

BAREFOOT TIDES SERIES ~ BOOK TWO
AN EMERALD ISLE, NC NOVEL

# A DANCING TIDE

## BY

## GRACE GREENE

BAREFOOT TIDES SERIES ~ BOOK TWO
AN EMERALD ISLE, NC NOVEL

Kersey Creek Books
P.O. Box 6054
Ashland, VA 23005

A Dancing Tide

Barefoot Tides (series name)

Cover Design by Grace Greene

ISBN-13: 978-1-7375486-0-7 (eBook) (Release Oct. 2021)
ISBN-13: 978-1-7375486-1-4 (Print) (Oct. 2021)
ISBN-13: 978-1-7375486-2-1 (Large Print) (Oct. 2021)
ISBN-13: 978-1-7375486-3-8 (Hardcover) (Oct. 2021)

Printed in the United States of America

# DEDICATION

*A Dancing Tide* is dedicated to my aunt and uncle who introduced me to Emerald Isle, who had their own love story and love of the beach, and whom we lost this year. Thank you, Sallie and Ronnie, for the love, support and encouragement you brought into our lives—and for the memories made.

# ACKNOWLEDGEMENTS

My sincere thanks to everyone—the beta readers, Jill, Terry, Amy, Amy, and the editor, Jessica Fogleman, and to everyone who contributed to *A Dancing Tide*, as well as to *A Barefoot Tide*.

Grateful thanks to the readers who read *A Barefoot Tide* and asked for more about Lilliane and Merrick and the other characters. This book, *A Dancing Tide*, came into being because of you.

# BOOKS BY GRACE GREENE

**Emerald Isle, North Carolina Series**
Beach Rental *(Book 1)*
Beach Winds *(Book 2)*
Beach Wedding *(Book 3)*
*"Beach Towel" (A Short Story)*
Beach Walk *(Christmas Novella)*

**Barefoot Tides Two-Book Series**
A Barefoot Tide *(Book 1)*
A Dancing Tide *(Book 2)*

**Beach Single-Title Novellas**
Beach Christmas *(Christmas Novella)*
Clair *(Beach Brides Novella Series)*

**Cub Creek Novels ~ Series and Single Titles**
Cub Creek *(Cub Creek Series, Book 1)*
Leaving Cub Creek *(Cub Creek Series, Book 2)*
The Happiness In Between
The Memory of Butterflies
A Light Last Seen

**The Wildflower House Novels**
Wildflower Heart *(Book 1)*
Wildflower Hope *(Book 2)*
Wildflower Christmas *(A Wildflower House Novella) (Book 3)*

**Virginia Country Roads**
Kincaid's Hope
A Stranger in Wynnedower

www.GraceGreene.com

# A DANCING TIDE

*A Dancing Tide,* the second book in the *Barefoot Tides two-book series,* continues the story of Lilliane Moore of Cub Creek in rural Virginia, who accepted a temporary companion job for ninety-year-old Merrick Dahl of Emerald Isle, North Carolina—and discovered it's not always so easy to go home again. That if you do, you'll find your life has changed in unexpected ways.

*How do you put the pieces back together? Should you try?*

Lilliane accepted the temporary job because she needed the cash, but the biggest payoffs were the new friendships she made and the realization that she is more tied to protecting her family history and homeplace than she'd ever understood. Now she wants freedom to travel and make changes in her life, but she is torn between that desire and needing to do right by her deceased parents and their memory—most specifically, protecting the numerous sculptures her father crafted in his workshop before his death twenty years earlier. The workshop can't stand forever, and she, herself, is almost forty. What will become of her family home and treasures if something happens to *her*?

She can't be in two places at once—helping Merrick at the beach and in Cub Creek protecting the homeplace. Lilliane wants to make the right decision, but whatever choice she makes, she risks failing everyone— *her friends, her family and herself, and her future.*

# A DANCING TIDE

## Chapter One

I woke in the dark, disoriented. It was near dawn—I knew that instinctively—but where? I lay in bed listening to the night sounds through the open window and heard the restless rush of waves.

Was I back at the beach in Emerald Isle?

But the scent that came in on the breeze smelled of woodland and greenery.

Listening more closely, I understood the sound of ocean waves was only the wind tossing the boughs of the tall trees in my backyard. It was summer. The branches were heavy and the leaves rustled against each other as the trees swayed.

This was Cub Creek. I was home.

I touched my coverlet and smiled. I should've known where I was by the bedding alone. My thread count here was more like *threadbare* and nowhere near the quality of the down quilt and fine cotton sheets back at Merrick's house.

Moving my hands across the coverlet, I felt paper, then many sheets of paper, and I remembered the rest. I'd been reading Merrick Dahl's latest manuscript. I must've fallen into a restless sleep. Merrick, Davis, and Gwen had been at my house that very day. Merrick's voice echoed in my head: "Lilliane, please read this and give us feedback. We need your help." He'd said that to me, a woman who rarely read—and had never read for fun until I'd met him and become ensnared in his words.

Between this story he'd written and the crazy, unexpected day I'd enjoyed with them here in my home, my normal world had been seriously disrupted—but in good and happy ways. It wasn't surprising that the unaccustomed excitement would creep in and disrupt my sleep too.

How much of the surprise visit from Merrick and Davis, then Gwen showing up to join us for dinner, plus what I'd been reading when I'd fallen asleep, had made it into my dreams? Dreams that had then transitioned into this present, half-awake, fresh-from-sleep reality. No wonder I was confused.

It didn't take long to orient myself. By the moonlight streaming in through the nearby window, I could see well enough to gather up the manuscript pages scattered around me.

So, yes, I was home in Cub Creek. My parents' home. In fact, it had been my grandparents' home and, before that, home to earlier generations. In short, the house was old and looked like most every other two-story, white-painted (now peeling), oft-abandoned homeplaces seen along country roads—houses still upright and holding on against time and gravity, but barely. Yet while this particular homeplace—mine—wasn't in great shape, that condition was improving. I'd earned good money working as a companion for Merrick Dahl in Emerald Isle—coastal North Carolina being a world away from my forest clearing at the end of a dirt road in rural Louisa County, Virginia. I loved my home. I also loved Emerald Isle, a place of sunshine, fresh ocean breezes, and inviting water, and I'd been invited to return there by Merrick himself.

And I would. For temporary stays, at least. When? I had no answer. Merrick had an aide working for him right now—though not the rather stalwart-looking aide in a nurse's uniform who'd replaced me. Apparently, she hadn't lasted long. And Merrick wasn't satisfied with his current aide either, and maybe she was leaving too. Merrick said she'd given notice and was only staying until the next replacement could be found. Davis had stated that was the reason Merrick had insisted on making the trip here. Merrick, with his own special wit, had declared they'd come to kidnap me.

It was flattering to be missed, but I couldn't go back yet. For one thing, it was a five- or six-hour drive. Not something I could undertake on a whim. Soon, though.

More immediately, my friend Gwen was coming to my house this morning and bringing her camera. Our purpose was so potentially terrifying to me that I could hardly acknowledge the idea of it, but it pushed into my early-morning thoughts, chasing away any hope of going back to sleep.

Leaving my bed, I went down the stairs, navigating by night sight, then crossed the living room to the kitchen. My slip-on shoes were next to the kitchen door. I picked them up and shook them by habit, in case a spider or a mouse had tucked in snug for the night, then slid them onto my feet and unlocked the door. I was already wearing my amethyst key pendant, and I clutched it now as I walked through the backyard, moving toward the shed and Dad's workshop.

The moon and stars were bright overhead, making the shadows in and around the clearing solid and distinct. As the trees moved in the fitful wind, so did their shadows, while the distorted shapes cast by the firepit and chairs remained as still as statues. Like things left behind. Forgotten by life.

Behind me stood the bulk of the house. Ahead of me the shed loomed—a building that had been preceded many, many years ago by the original log home, which had been reconfigured into a small barn and then "improved" by my father for his workshop. History everywhere. And memories. Along with the night, all those things came together, forming almost a cocoon, and I moved within it. The rest of my known world was sleeping, and I was out here alone, yet I felt safe, as always.

A sudden gust bent the trees and stirred the boughs. I stopped to listen because the sound was, as I'd thought while half dreaming, like that of ocean waves. Fleetingly, the tang of salty air came back to me, along with the gritty feel of the warm sand against my skin. I was almost there again.

A cry in the night—likely a coyote—was answered by another and another, and their calls moved me forward.

Even in the dark, the key was easy to finagle into the lock. It opened smoothly. I removed the lock, then flipped the door's metal hasp and slid the left panel aside. Inside, despite the dark, but before I turned on the overhead light, I pulled the door closed again. I'd tried to explain my secrecy to Gwen, and she *thought* she understood, but she didn't get the full picture. She believed it was an emotional reaction on my part. The emotion, the wish to protect my father's memory, that of both my parents, really, was true enough, but the practical fact was that I didn't want thieves or despoilers to notice.

A light in the night would shine like a beacon through the trees. Someone wandering the dark woods would notice a light, especially an unaccustomed light. They might wonder what I was up to. They might think I was hiding something here and get curious. What might I be protecting? Already, over the past few days, this door had been opened and the contents exposed more than in the intervening twenty years—the two decades that occupied the space in my life between losing my parents when I was only eighteen and now, the present day.

I'd done my best to safeguard my father's metal art and other projects, the house, and everything, but I couldn't guard the property 24-7, year-round, being ever-present and always ready to run off people of poor intention. Even way out here, you'd find them. Or they'd find you. Sometimes I wondered if there truly were no secrets. Were we just fooling ourselves? Seemed like just thinking something in your brain could put the thought into the air—into the still spaces above and around us—where it circulated. You never knew who might pick up on that info.

This was not something I discussed with anyone. Certainly not with sensible, regular people like Gwen. She'd think I was superstitious or crazy. Truth was, I was probably a little of both. I'd certainly come by my quirks honestly from my parents and forebears. Besides, there were enough real-world risks to fret over.

But I was also lonely. As much as I loved my home and all that came with it, if I had to be here all the time . . . the loneliness could be overbearing. It was another reason why the fun yesterday had been disruptive—I'd loved having my friends here. I'd enjoyed the laughter.

Despite the dark interior, I found the corner light switch, and yes, it worked. It was always a question, since rodents thought nothing of chewing through wires, live or not. The electric bulb did what it could, but the shed was huge, and the interior—a conglomeration of old barnwood, metal, and fiberglass sheets—was vast, so the room was shadowy, and the corners were dark. I stood, breathless, stunned, as I was each time I saw the light glinting off the metal art. In and among my father's tools and more mundane things like bike tire pumps and old carburetor belts, the metals and shapes and textures arrayed on the walls stole the show. Some of the items on the walls looked like shields an Iron Age warrior might've carried, some looked futuristic, and others just . . . were. But there in the middle was the airplane with the propellers attached to the nose. Only a partial fuselage was behind it and nothing else, yet within the confines of the shed, it was still a massive reconstruction that overwhelmed, and introduced, the rest of the building's contents.

Less than twenty-four hours before, Merrick had stood here. I'd never forget the expression on his face when he'd caught his first glimpse of the bomber, with its propellors up front, bold and unmistakable. It had been the exact expression I'd anticipated. I would've been disappointed with less. And Davis had been the same. Even Gwen had been astounded—and had made some on-the-nose points about what kept me here.

Caretaking, she'd said. Essentially no more than that. Gwen had said I was the keeper of the memories, of my homeplace, and of my father's creations.

And now I was considering making these strange and amazing creations known to others? Perhaps to the world? Maybe even offer them for sale?

My heart tried to thump right out of my chest. I put my hand on one of the propellers and moved it, thinking of Dad working in here throughout much of my growing-up years. He and Momma. Usually together. Occasionally, he'd let me help. "Hold this, Lillie," or "Take this cloth and polish this up." I looked at my hands. They'd worked alongside my father's hands whenever he'd allowed it—which hadn't been often enough for me.

But Gwen and I had a plan.

Gwen would be here to photograph Dad's metal art in the morning. After we were satisfied with the pictures, I would contact Susan Biggs for advice. I'd known Gwen for years. I knew Susan too, but I'd only known her for a few weeks, and in a business capacity, because she'd hired me to work for Merrick for the first time. Our common interest was Merrick Dahl, she in her role as his business manager, and me . . . my relationship with Merrick had begun when I accepted the temporary job at the beach as his companion.

Merrick and I had hit it off almost from the start. The professional obligation had quickly become friendship. As for Susan, she and I had an understanding and I trusted her. The problem was that by asking Susan for help, I was giving her permission to share my private business with anyone and everyone, as needed. That was a huge leap for me; I might as well be launching myself into a wormhole without any idea of what I'd be traveling through or what might lie in wait on the other side. The only sure thing? Doing this would throw my life off its even keel. Perhaps worse. I might take that leap, disrupt all that I loved and had worked for, and find myself no better off.

Possible heartbreak, however it went.

Gwen would be here in a few hours. Before that, I had to shower and dress and find a more positive attitude. Not yet, though. First, I wanted to stand here in the midst of my father's work and allow the memories connected to it to surround me. Soon, whether this idea worked or not, my father's legacy would no longer be private. There was no way to know what that would bring into my life—big or small—but I was pretty sure that if I went through with this, my life would be forever changed.

CRSO

Gwen drove up the dirt road to the house and parked her car near the tall oak. Through my open door, I heard the car tires crunch on the last of the gravel in the driveway. I'd wondered if she'd really show. Not because she was unreliable but because she'd think better of this craziness too. What we were about to do seemed so . . . foolish? Hopeful? If we succeeded with this, a lot of things could change for me. Decisions would be required. Was I ready for that?

I paused at the screen door as her car door swung open. Gwen was a nurse, not a photographer or a marketer, and she was about ten years older than me. She and Susan had been college friends. Susan wasn't in the art market, but she worked as a business manager for Merrick and other clients. Gwen was sure that Susan would be happy to offer advice and guidance.

Gwen believed great things would come of this. A part of me believed along with her. But a big part disagreed and was whispering questions at me, like why was I exposing my personal business, my *family's* personal business, for no good purpose? With the whispers came panic, which I did my best to hide.

Gwen saw me in the doorway and gestured at me to join her.

"Good morning," she called out. "Can you get the tripods from the back seat? There's a shop light too."

As I descended the porch steps, I asked, "Have you had breakfast? Want some coffee?"

"Thanks, but I'm good." She grinned at me. "I'm eager to get going. You know, I half expected you to change your mind about all this."

"I have doubts, but I'm willing to see how it goes. For now."

"Last night I was thinking that we should bring in a real photographer. Maybe one of the photography club kids from the high school. Some of them are quite talented."

After replying with a loud, immediate no, I said, "This is good enough."

"I understand your concern. You're still getting used to the idea of sharing this publicly." She added, "I'm proud of you, Lillie, for coming this far."

*Lillie.* Gwen was one of the very few people who felt free to change my name, and from whom I allowed it. Most of the time, I corrected everyone who tried. My name was Lilliane. But for some reason, maybe simply because I'd known her for so many years, I didn't fuss. Plus, she was a nurse. Always helping people. Seemed wrong to be petty about what she called me, so long as it was friendly.

We toted the tripod and shop light and some other odds and ends around the house to the shed. I unlocked the door, slid it open, and moved to pick up the tripod again.

Gwen said, "Not yet. Let me get a video of the inside as

it is—and has been for so many years—before we clutter things up."

"Maybe this is a mistake."

She handed me the tripod. "Right now, we're just taking pictures. After you see how they turn out, you can decide whether to proceed."

My hands were shaking as I set up the tripod. Gwen noticed.

"Just taking photos, Lillie. That's all we're doing. It's all good."

"Thank you." I nodded. "I do appreciate your help."

CRSO

We were silent as Gwen recorded the video on her phone but then, as she snapped pictures of the more impressive pieces, she kept up a contant chatter. She took lots of photos, both close up and panoramic, with her digital camera. It was obvious the chitchat was intended to distract me, to keep my nerves from getting the better of me. Most people saw me as a cool, capable person, and generally I was, but not when it came to exposing my private family matters to the public.

"Did he give them names?" she asked.

"Names? For the metal art? No, not that he admitted to, but Momma and I did. We had names for some of them."

"Which?"

"Well, I named this one *Warrior Shield*. Don't laugh. I was a teenager at the time." I gestured at the features as I spoke. "It looks like a shield, doesn't it? Like an ancient warrior might carry? Until you look closer. Then you see the hubcap, plain, but circled with the chain and embossed with bolts and the angled flanges arrayed around the outer edge."

"I see that."

Farther along, I said, "Momma called this one *The Rosette Stone* because the parts Dad added looked like big flower petals—rosettes—to her. She said the flat sheen of the unpolished, pitted metal looked like stone."

Gwen chuckled. "Those are strange-looking flower petals, but I see it. And the bright, shiny bolts crowded in the center . . . Yes, I can definitely see the flower." She turned to me. "Did you help your father with his work?"

"Only a little. He'd let me do some of the buffing. No welding, some soldering here and there. But only when he was open to having a helper." For a moment, I got a little lost in thought. "When I was fourteen, he went away for a while. A few months. Momma was sad. We missed him so much." I smiled sadly at the memory.

"Some kids make their parents cards? With crayons and paste and such? I went out to the shed and made my dad some metal art. Not as good as his, of course, but I tried." I held my hands in front of me, palms up. "The scars from the burn marks and cuts showed on my hands for years." Then my face grew warm. What I didn't say aloud was that one of my teachers was concerned about abuse and drove out to the house to meet with Momma. Afterward, I had to stop the metalwork. Momma and I didn't need any more trouble than we already had.

"Which ones?"

"Pardon?"

"Which are yours? That you made?"

"They aren't out here. They're in the side room."

"A side room? Can I see?"

Suddenly, I was fourteen again and reexperiencing the stubborn resentment I'd felt when Momma said I couldn't come out here to the shed anymore unless I promised not to touch anything. *Try drawing or painting, Lillie. I'll find a way to get you whatever supplies you need.* She'd taken my hands in hers and touched the wounds. They seemed to grieve her then, and yet she'd hardly noticed the injuries until the teacher asked about them. But I didn't want paper or pencils or brushes. If I couldn't have what I wanted, then I didn't want any of it. In time, the desire to do any creative stuff had passed. No one could make a living at it anyway, and I needed to support myself.

"Lillie? Are you okay?"

I'd wandered off mentally. "Sure. I'm fine."

"Can I see the pieces you made?"

Quickly, I fluffed her off, saying, "Maybe later."

Gwen looked sad. "I know this is hard on you. You can still change your mind if you want to. It's not too late. We can call this whole thing off."

I stayed silent.

She continued, "All I ask is to wait. One step at a time. Let's see how these look on the computer screen. At that point, if you want to continue, you'll make the call to Susan for her objective, business-savvy opinion."

Feeling tense, I asked, "Are we almost done here?"

"Yes. I'll get my laptop from the car, and we'll download the photos and see what we have."

I was sorry to have acted ungrateful. "Maybe we'll have a little snack too. I have some pound cake from Mrs. Manning. Bought it at the church fundraiser. It's the best."

"Sounds delicious."

CRÆO

We settled at the kitchen table with Gwen's laptop. My kitchen was old and faded—faded Formica, faded and stained linoleum, and a porcelain sink with the finish so thin that the dark below showed through in large patches. It was all as clean as I could make it, so if anyone objected to the appearance, they could keep their opinion to themselves. That's how I felt about it.

I poured us tea and sliced the pound cake while she downloaded the photos, and then I joined her there, but the first pictures that showed up on the laptop screen were either fuzzy or the lighting was too harsh, washing out the details.

My heart sank—which surprised me. At that moment, I could easily have said, "Never mind this crazy idea," and gotten out of the whole thing. But instead, I was disappointed.

Disappointed?

It told me a lot about what was really going on in my mind.

The photos that followed fascinated me. The metal art hanging on the wall in my father's shed looked different when showing on Gwen's laptop screen. With increasing eagerness, I watched the slideshow.

After Gwen left, I sat alone by the firepit in the backyard clearing. The clearing stretched from the house to the shed with only the pit, a couple of chairs, and a small metal table—painted light green years ago, like the two chairs, and still not too rusty—filling the space between them. All else was sky and forest—quiet except for the birds and the squirrels. Gentle sounds. Soothing sounds. A simple place.

Like my cell phone. Simple. Perhaps a little *too* basic. We'd used Gwen's phone and camera because my phone took lousy photos and my data plan was very limited. Not good for photography or emailing big attachments, maybe, but my phone did have plenty of minutes and good coverage of this area. It was reliable. Until now, I'd never felt the need for more. Without Gwen's help, I wouldn't have the digital pictures and I would not be taking this next step of calling Susan.

In my mind, Susan was the same as the day I'd met her—big blonde hair, a blue suit, and a forceful manner. The day that she'd walked into the Fuel Up Fast, I'd taken an instinctive dislike to her. When I'd realized she was meeting Gwen there and the purpose was to offer me a temporary job as a companion to an elderly man at the beach—I'd almost allowed pride and fear to keep me from taking a chance on it. Remembering that near-miss put a little more steel in my spine.

After another slow sip of iced tea, I set the glass down

on the metal table and dialed Susan's phone number.

I was expecting, maybe hoping, to leave a voice mail. I'd practiced exactly what to say. My mouth was arranged, ready to speak the message. She answered after one ring.

"Lilliane? What's up?"

"Hi, Susan. Am I interrupting anything?"

"Yes, and thank goodness, because I need a breather." There was a short silence and a noise I couldn't identify, and then she continued. "Merrick has been hinting like crazy that you were going to call me, and that when you do, I'm supposed to do anything and everything you may need me to do. I admit I'm curious. Have you started writing novels too? Seems to be the going thing these days."

"Did Merrick say why I was calling? Anything at all?"

"Nope. Totally mum, but very dramatic about *it*—the *something* you wanted to discuss. He warned me not to mention the impending call from you, to you or anyone." She gave a low, short laugh. "I think he just loves suspense . . . or thrillers, I should say. And no wonder, right? He wrote them for forty-plus years."

"This doesn't have anything to do with writing, and not with Merrick either, except that he was there when . . . the subject was being discussed."

"Okay."

"I'm probably wasting your time, anyway, but you are in the world of business and public relations and such. You know a lot of people . . ."

"As much as I'm enjoying the preamble, *I* don't enjoy suspense, so please . . . go ahead and say it."

"I don't know if you recall, but my parents died when I was eighteen."

"I do. Asphyxiation in the shed due to a blocked vent, right?"

"Wow, you *do* know."

"Hey, it's my job to know who I'm hiring as a live-in companion to Merrick. You can't be surprised that I'd be checking your background."

"You never let on that you knew."

"It was your personal business."

Well, apparently *personal* wasn't always personal. There was a certain irony in that, but I appreciated her discretion—which was also what I was counting on now.

"My father did small equipment repair for a living, but he also had a hobby. He created metal art." I let a moment pass so it could sink in.

"Metal art. That's vague. Do you mean like butterflies or ocean scenes you hang on the wall?"

"No. He put together machine parts and metal castoffs he had in the shed."

"I don't quite understand."

"I get it, truly. Gwen took some photos. I don't have a computer or internet, so she'll email them to you, if you're willing to take a look. I'd like to know if there's a market for my dad's kind of art. That's not your area of business, maybe, but you might have a feel for it, or know who does. The thing is—and this is so very important to me—I never intended to share them publicly, much less sell them. But I won't live forever. Something will happen to them eventually, one way or another, so I'm considering options now. For the time being I want them protected, including the fact that they exist and are in that shed. I just . . . I worry about leaving them here unprotected once people know about them. Folks get curious, you know? Vandals and such. Who knows what could happen?"

"Meaning you can't go back to work for Merrick if you're worried about loose lips sinking ships?"

Worried about . . . *what*? It took me a moment to realize what she was saying. Dad had an old poster hung somewhere out in the shed or workshop area with that phrase.

I answered, "Yes, that's part of it."

"No worries about discretion. Tell Gwen to send the photos. I'll look and get back to you." She gave a long, loud sigh. "But I'll be honest with you—the art market is a whole different beast—not a market that appreciates or values art because a loved one created it. There's marketability and then there's sentimentality. The two rarely work well together."

"I understand. I'm not trying to fool myself, and I need you to be very, very honest with me."

"Trust me. I will."

When we disconnected, I called Gwen.

She answered the phone, saying, "Did you call her?"

"I did."

"How did she respond?"

"She'll help if she can. She . . . I think she was trying not to get my hopes up. But truly, Gwen, I don't know *what* I'm hoping for. But this . . . scares me."

"Your father's work is remarkable. No question about it, regardless of what the rest of the world may opine. But the risk, the potential changes to your life, especially here in Cub Creek where everyone knows everyone . . . I understand that, Lillie. I do."

I said, "Go ahead and email Susan the photos."

⚭

I knew I should get up and get busy, yet I sat in my chair, gripping my phone like a lifeline.

Most likely, Susan would call me back right away to tell me not to pursue this. If it took longer for her to return my call, then she was giving it real thought, maybe reaching out to her contacts for advice.

So I sat. My palms were sweating from clutching the phone so tightly.

This was scary. Maybe the scariest thing I'd ever done.

Dad could never have done this, not with his personality or his nerves. But maybe, I told myself, he'd be proud that I was doing it for him. I hoped so.

The phone rang. Susan's number.

*Well, there it is. She's calling me back too quickly. Now I know.*

Susan said, "Lilliane, tell me what I'm looking at."

"Gwen's email?"

"Yes, but what are these photos? Tell me about this."

"My father's metal artwork?"

"Sculptures. Metal sculptures."

"Sure. Yes. Dad did equipment repair. Sometimes he'd take cast-off stuff in trade if cash was short. Or he'd see discarded stuff at the farms where he worked. Sometimes he'd shut himself in his shed for weeks, working on his projects. Sometimes he'd let Momma and me hang around." I paused. "I'm sorry, Susan. I guess I don't understand what you're asking me?"

"I see individual items, but what are they? Is that the front end of an airplane? The propellers? I see the video of the shed interior that Gwen sent. I understand your father created these metal sculptures. Did he have an art background? What was his goal in creating these?"

"No art background that I know of. He joined the army right out of high school but was assigned to work in the motor pool. He wasn't happy working in someone else's shop and chose to leave. After that, he held odd jobs here in Cub Creek and did the equipment repair I was talking about."

Her voice was all business. "So he created these sculptures until he passed about twenty years ago, and since then they've been locked up in the shed where he did his work?"

"Yes."

"I'll be honest, Lilliane. I don't know. Art is a lot about reputation. But there's also an enthusiasm component that could be at play here. There's an interesting story. But there's also a limited reach in that he stopped years ago and won't be creating more. Am I making sense to you?"

"Yes, sure. That's all true."

"So let me look further—"

"Susan, excuse me for interrupting. When you're speaking about my dad and his story being interesting . . . I don't know how to say this, but my father . . . he had some emotional problems. I loved him. Adored him, really. But he isn't your usual hero kind of guy. There's some history—"

"Lilliane." Her voice grew softer in tone. "Remember, I already know how your parents died." She coughed lightly. "Now, can you do something for me?"

"What?"

"Leave it *as is* for now. Everything has been in that shed for twenty-plus years? Leave it undisturbed for a while longer. I have some ideas. I don't know whether any of it will pan out. And don't mention this to anyone, got it? Merrick has seen it—is that right?"

"Merrick, Davis, and, of course, Gwen."

"I'll talk to them about keeping it quiet, the same as I'm advising you. Just keep it quiet for now. Give me a few days to mull this over and have a discreet conversation or two."

"I will. I'll wait to hear from you."

We disconnected. My father's story, she'd said. Simple words, but they felt like a euphemism. I'd been worried about sharing his metal art. I shuddered. In addition to that, and so much worse, Susan was now talking about exposing him— his history and his choices, perhaps even my parents and our family—to an often unkind world.

It wasn't too late to end this. I could call Susan right back and tell her to drop it. I'd say I was sorry but that I hadn't considered the full impact of this, and I wanted to end it now before it went too far.

Before I pressed her number, I stopped. I opened the shed door again, but only about a foot or so, just to let in enough daylight to manage by. The propellers overwhelmed the scene, and I slipped inside, touching the metal of the blades and resting my cheek on the fuselage. Dusty or not, it felt like home, and it was full of memories of a happy childhood. Mine.

I was alone with no husband or children to care for this—not the homeplace or my father's works—after me. Even if I did have kids, they might not understand the value of it. Maybe, in the end, I was it. The last Moore. The last of my mother's people, the Andersons, too. With no generations to come after—and if Susan couldn't help, if Gwen's hopes fell through, and in case a falling tree missed the shed and hit me instead and I could no longer be the caretaker for this—I must pursue this effort now.

☙❧

The next morning, Gwen called. "No word from Susan yet? No, you'd have told me, I know. I'm impatient and I can't get you off my mind. Guilt, I guess."

"Why guilt? You've only ever been helpful to me."

"I stirred up a hornet's nest for you during that delightful dinner with you, Merrick, and Davis by asking to see the objects in the shed, and then pushing you about taking the photos. I still think asking Susan for advice was the smart thing to do, but truly, Lillie, you need a better phone. Especially since you don't have internet at your house." She paused briefly before saying, "I don't know how you manage with the phone you have and no computer access."

"Might be that I manage better *without* than with."

"Debating the value of connectivity in our present age is a subject for another time. The reality of doing business without it is the actual problem. A more capable phone could do so much for you. Not just with connectivity and applications but also with amazing photos and videos and such. Not just here in Cub Creek but also when you travel."

"My phone works. It's affordable. I don't have any travel plans at the present, though I will go back to visit Merrick and everyone else in Emerald Isle." I paused, then said more than I might otherwise have shared because I knew her heart was in the right place. "Fact is, my money is needed for other things. My phone does its job. What it doesn't do, I'll find workarounds for. Or ask my friends for help." I grinned as I said those last words hoping it would communicate in my tone.

"But that's it precisely. I am your friend. It occurred to me this morning that I could add you to my phone plan for just a few dollars."

"Like those family plans? Gwen, I'm firm on this. While I appreciate your thoughtfulness, I don't take charity."

Gwen shook her head. "It's not charity. It . . ."

I held up my hand to signal *stop* even though she couldn't see the gesture through the phone. "No. I'm firm about that. I won't spend money I don't have, I won't lie if I can avoid it, and I don't take charity."

Gwen groaned. "Okay. I mean to be helpful. Not to give offense."

"I appreciate your help. Truly."

CRBO

Susan called in the afternoon. I was apprehensive when I saw her name on the phone screen, but I'd practiced this. It was really no different than interacting with customers at the Fuel Up Fast. I *knew* how to talk to people. The difference was that conversations between Susan and me had always been about Merrick. This was now about me and my business. I had to keep my personal feelings out of the interaction—as I'd done when it wasn't about me.

*Think like a businessperson. Like Susan.*

"I'm still assessing," she said. "But I have an opportunity for you that I think may make all the difference. We won't know until we try it."

"What's the opportunity?"

"I have a friend, a photojournalist, whom I know and trust. I can't guarantee an outcome, of course. But he has done some amazing human-interest pieces, very well reviewed. Slice-of-life articles. If he is willing to interview you—"

"Wow. Hold on. Interview me?"

"Unfortunately, your father isn't available."

"Ouch."

"Didn't mean that quite the way it sounded. It's a simple fact, though. We need a human face and a life story to attach to this. Who else *but* you?"

"I understand."

"He'll want to discuss the artwork, the artist, probably some things about your life now and then. He writes deeply touching pieces. On the other hand, he isn't gentle if he senses fakes or frauds. He hasn't done one of these lifestyle-type pieces in a while. I threw out a few crumbs, and he's curious. *If,* and this is far from certain, if he is interested in meeting with you, talking with you and seeing the metal sculptures, are you open to it?"

Susan waited, finally saying, "I can hear you breathing."

"Yes."

"Take deep breaths and let them out slowly."

I did. After a minute, I was able to say, "Thank you. I'm better. Just a little overwhelmed."

"Understandable. You aren't used to this kind of attention. Frankly, I know people who would kill—perhaps not literally—for this kind of publicity. And in the end, if the article does happen and doesn't draw interest, then we'll know there's probably no market for what you have in your shed. At least no market at this time. But if it does do well and it takes off . . . well, then, we shall see what we shall see."

While I was still breathing, she added, "And even though being my friend doesn't guarantee a positive result, especially as regards a possible article, it can't hurt either."

I heard more vulnerability in her voice this time. Somehow, that reassured me. "Okay. I'll talk to him if he's interested."

"Good. I'll be in touch when I know more. In the meantime, find Sam Markham online and get a feel for what he does."

We disconnected. Susan was as abrupt as always. But there'd been a moment in our conversation—I was sure I hadn't misheard her tone—in which I'd sensed hope and the worry of disappointment. This was no longer just about me and my dad. Now it also involved Gwen and Susan.

My first thought was to go to the library for the online research. My second thought was that I should update Gwen. And then the two thoughts merged, and I picked up my phone.

"Gwen? Susan called."

"What did she say? Any news?"

"Yes, in fact, she's suggesting an interview with a photojournalist. He does lifestyle articles. She knows him pretty well, but I've never heard of him. If you want to look him up, his name is Sam Markham."

"Why don't I come over and we can look him up together?"

"Perfect, but only if you'll let me provide supper. I'll cook something up."

"It's a deal."

"Excellent."

"And thank you, Lilliane, for letting me be involved. This is the most exciting thing to happen in my world in ages, and I'm enjoying it."

CR&O

Gwen came over with her laptop, and we looked him up together. We discussed what we discovered about Sam Markham—his articles and his photos—while we shared a meal. Until recently, I'd been solitary in my personal life, never having people over. One friend who shared a meal with me didn't qualify as an actual social calendar or as full-blown entertaining, but it was nice. Just really nice.

And then there was Sam Markham. His photo showed a sharp black-and-white image of a handsome man. I'd seen the author photos on the backs of Merrick Dahl's books, and they had that same look and tone, but the real-life Merrick was ninety. His author photo was forty or fifty years out of date, so I knew better than to place too much stock in such things. Publicity stuff seemed like just another kind of fiction. I reminded myself that while I hadn't had a career in business or public relations, my years behind the customer service counter and as a cashier had trained me to deal with difficult people—probably a lot more so than these *professional* people had ever had to work with. I just needed to keep my cool and not borrow trouble. I already had enough worries for today.

# Chapter Two

Sam Markham was gorgeous. Seriously. His thick, dark hair was combed back, but a bit unruly, and one careless lock fell across his forehead. He was dressed casually in jeans and a white button-down shirt and a loose jacket that looked super sharp, yet too naturally casual to be other than very expensive. When he saw me step out onto the porch, his smile was engaging. His handshake, as we met halfway on the stairs, was perfect in grip and warmth.

Yeah, he'd done this kind of thing a lot.

And Mr. Sam Markham was courteous. He'd arranged our interview ahead of time, and then he'd called to confirm again this morning instead of just showing up on my doorstep. He was well spoken, too, but also slightly tentative, which made his charm disarming. I wondered if Susan had pushed him into doing something that he really wasn't interested in. And for a totally out-there, mildly amusing thought—it occurred to me that if I had to pick the perfect scoundrel, it would be this man. No one could suspect him of having bad intentions. He was just that handsome and well mannered.

As for myself, I'd struggled over what to wear. I didn't know any journalists of any kind and had never been interviewed for anything. I'd been an aide for my great-aunt, Aunt Molly, and before she died she'd given me a few dresses and blouses that she no longer wanted. Ones she hadn't even worn for a couple of decades. We'd laughed at how if something was left in a closet long enough, it'd come back into style eventually, or be worn as vintage. That morning, I'd settled for a silky, blousy top and my jeans. The gray-blue color of the fabric tended to spark up the red lights in my auburn hair. But my behavior—after catching a glimpse of Mr. Markham and then being exposed to him up-close-and-personal—was embarrassing. I was hardly better than a sixteen-year-old let out of the house for the first time. I did my best to hide my silliness under a businesslike expression, but the idea of it flitted through my mind like a butterfly, tickled my fancy, and I smiled. Clearly, he thought the smile was intended for him because his fascinatingly blue eyes lit up, brightening his whole face even more. And reminding me to be careful.

"I'm Sam Markham. You know that, of course."

"Certainly. I'm Lilliane Moore. Thanks for driving all the way out here." I gestured into the living room. "Please come in." My living room was old. I'd had the outside of the house painted and a new roof put on from the money I'd earned working for Merrick last month, in June. But the interior? I'd washed the walls and cleaned the floors. Otherwise, it looked much as it had for the past one hundred and fifty years. The furniture wasn't even thrift shop viable. I refused to apologize for how it looked. It all still worked, and that was good enough.

Standing just inside, he took a long look around the room. I allowed it. What he said might make a difference in what happened next. It might end our meeting abruptly.

"This house is old."

"It is."

"Your family has lived here for a long time?"

"Yes."

He grinned, but in a friendly way. "Succinct. This interview may be short." He laughed a little. "Seriously, anytime you want to end this, say the word. I don't want to intrude or be unwelcome."

"Susan can be persuasive. I suspect that's why you agreed to come here."

"She can." He glanced around again. "But for me, it's more than that. Don't get me wrong, I like Susan and we've known each other for a long time, but that wouldn't be enough for me to make the trip. I don't want to waste anyone's time—mine or the person I'm interviewing."

I nodded. "Fair enough. How was the drive out?"

"Beautiful scenery, but lots of curves in that road." He pointed toward an old standing cupboard and a floor radio about chest high. "Do you collect antiques?"

"Me? Goodness no. I've got enough old furniture already. Those belonged to my grandparents . . . or maybe my greats." I turned away to end that line of conversation and headed to the kitchen, still speaking. "Did you fly into Richmond or drive down from New York?"

"I considered flying but decided to drive."

"You've gone to a lot of effort to get here. I appreciate that. Can I offer you a glass of iced tea?"

He followed me into the kitchen. The scars and stains and tired appliances seemed to cry out at being put on display to someone—a stranger—whose eyes might not see their beauty.

I suggested, "How about pound cake? One of my friends makes the best there is. I took some slices out of the freezer this morning, so it's nicely chilled."

"Chilled pound cake?" He smiled. "Sure. Thanks."

The back door was open to allow the breeze in. He headed there naturally. Just at that moment, a wind swept across the treetops, tossing them and making the ocean wave sounds again. He paused, seeming to listen.

As the wind passed and the air stilled, he said, "Susan mentioned some artwork. Sculptures? And a shed? Is that the building out there at the end of the clearing?"

"Yes," I said, but didn't move toward the door. Seemed like there should be more communication . . . more conversation shared before he, a stranger, barged into my past. I continued, "My father's workshop is in what used to be the old house, then a barn, that grew over the years." I waved my hand generally in that direction.

He read the tension in my voice. "It's bigger than I expected. And there's no rush. Iced tea and chilled pound cake sound perfect." He returned to the table.

When I set the plates and forks, I included paper napkins too, and I noticed he'd placed a small black device on the table. A recorder, if my guess was right. A notepad, too, with one of those teeny tiny pencils for recording Putt-Putt golf scores. Also, a piece of paper that looked a lot like an official document.

We both sat.

He reached toward the recorder, and I stopped his hand with my own.

"Mr. Markham, I appreciate your being here. Please know that. But this is about my family and my father and private things. Private as far as I'm concerned, and I'm about to risk that with the public. It's hard."

"Call me Sam, please. I don't know your story or whether talking to me will help you accomplish whatever you're hoping to achieve, but I'm willing to listen. I can't promise what the outcome will be."

"You're planning to record our conversation?"

"Just parts. I'll turn it off anytime you want me to."

"Fair enough. Though, frankly, I'm a talker once I get going, so be forewarned."

"I need you to sign a release. All it says is that I can use the photos, images, and words that come from the interview. It doesn't mean that I will, or that I'll use all of them, but if an article comes out of this, I don't want to second-guess. You need to know up front that anything can be included."

"Scary, but I expected that."

While I signed the document, he took a bite of pound cake and then glared at me.

I asked, "What?"

"You should've warned me. This is more than good."

I laughed. "That's funny. I'll have to share that with Mrs. Betty."

"Okay." He pressed the record button. "You are Lilliane Moore. You live in Cub Creek, Virginia."

"Yes."

"And I'm here to interview you for a possible article that may involve both words and pictures and may be shared in print and online and may be referenced and discussed in other venues without restriction?"

"Yes." I reminded myself that it was up to me to control what I offered up to him. Suddenly, I felt ignorant and countrified and out of my depth.

He said, "I can't promise what the article will say, Ms. Moore, or when it will be published, if at all. But if there is an article, I will do my best to ensure you see it before it's shared elsewhere. Does that help?"

"Yes, thank you."

"Ms. Moore—"

"Lilliane."

He nodded. "Lilliane, you can send me packing right now, and at any time. Remember, it's your choice."

I whispered, "I want to do this."

"Then let's finish the pound cake and get started," he said. "Tell me about yourself."

"Not much to tell. I grew up in the country. Just me and my parents. After school, I worked various jobs—mostly cashier and customer service stuff, though I also helped my great-aunt as a sort of aide in her last few years and then had a job as a companion most recently."

"You're a hard worker."

*Keep it light and simple.* I reminded myself that this could end up in print.

I threw in a smile to help lighten my discomfort. "Maybe. Mostly, I'm reliable. But even if I could afford *not* to work, I still would. I'm not good at sitting around."

He smiled in return and nodded. "What do you do for

35

fun or recreation?"

"For fun? Not much. I did go to the beach recently. First time ever. I'd like to travel more. Mostly, I enjoy telling stories."

"Pardon?"

"Telling stories? Speaking stories aloud. My mother did, and my grandmother too. Just for fun, you know. An occasional child's birthday party or a storytelling hour for kids at the library every month or so."

He smiled more broadly. "I love that. I'd like to hear you."

"Well, I'm not back on the library schedule for a few weeks. It's mostly for kids, anyway, but a parent or two will sit down to listen because they're there with their children, but I don't think you'd find it all that fascinating."

"Why?"

I shrugged. "You're worldly. You travel. You see big cities and talk to all kinds of people. My stories are from my mother and grandmother, with occasional twists that I add, but they're old and small." I could feel his attention drilling down, maybe getting personal, and I grew fidgety. I reached up and touched my key pendant hanging beneath my blouse. It was the amethyst pendant my father had crafted to hold the small key to the lock on the shed. I almost always wore the pendant on a silver chain around my neck. It helped to ground me. But then I saw Sam Markham's eyes follow my hand. I reached for my iced tea, hoping the switch in action would look natural.

He marked the hand movement with his eyes. I knew because his gaze returned to that slight bulge beneath the fabric with the chain emerging above and going around my throat. He didn't speak of it, but he would, so I preempted him.

"Why don't we take a walk out to the shed?"

Showing a little surprise, he said, "Sure. That would be great."

As I stood and moved toward the kitchen door, he asked, "Do you mind if I go out the front way? I need to get my camera gear from the car."

"Sure."

As we walked through the living room, he said, "That's a beautiful painting over your fireplace."

It was my turn to be surprised. I smiled at the oil painting of the woman dashing through the ocean waves. The movement and color soothed me, and the ocean scene was like the ultimate souvenir and had been given to me as a going-away gift by Merrick. I told Sam, "From a friend. A lovely gift." And then I continued to the door and out to the porch.

He followed me down the steps, and I waited while he retrieved a camera and a small gear bag from the car trunk.

"This way," I said, and walked around the side of the house.

This area was bare dirt. Between the hard ground and tall shady trees, grass didn't stand much of a chance. In the backyard clearing around the firepit area, the grass did better. Not a perfect lawn carpet, but not hard-packed dirt either. Sam Markham walked alongside me without a word.

We stopped a few yards away from the shed, my father's workshop.

"This was where the original log cabin stood long, long ago. When the newer house was built"—I nodded toward my home—"whichever grandfather it was at the time converted the log house into a small barn, mostly for storage. By the time my parents married and moved in with my grandparents, the house-barn-storage shed had been patched and added onto many times over. My grandparents died when I was young. My father didn't farm, but he could fix most anything, so he cleared out most of the building for a workshop." I shrugged. "You can see some of the original stone foundation of the house." I pointed along the gray stone base. "My father added the rest of this . . . additional workspace by using whatever material he could get his hands on." Again, I pointed, though he didn't need my instruction to spy the fiberglass corrugated panels mixed with sheets of plywood and metal. "Don't ask me how the entirety of it is still standing. Nature seems to work around it instead of blowing it down." I smiled to myself.

I faced Sam Markham head-on. "I don't know exactly what Susan told you, but maybe that's just as well. Ask me what you wish. I don't promise to answer, but I'll do my best."

He nodded. "Mind if I take a few outside shots before we go in?"

"Please do."

He did. And it was relatively few shots. Not like what I'd seen on TV or in the movies. His technique seemed deliberate and confident. When he stopped, he just stood there and didn't speak. Was he trying to push me to fill the silence? Or was he waiting for me to move? For a moment, I couldn't do either. In that pocket of silence, a bird called, was then answered with a warble from another bird. The breeze swirled overhead again, brushing the trees and moving the boughs. Sam Markham closed his eyes and breathed. I didn't think I was supposed to notice, but I did, and it gave me the confidence to step forward.

I said, "I wonder if you'd mind taking a shot for me? Maybe send me a copy of it later?"

"What?"

Lifting the chain from around my neck, I held the pendant in my open palm.

"My father made this for my mother. He spent a lot of time out here repairing equipment for pay or working on his own projects. He'd be out here for hours, days. Even weeks. He wanted Momma to know she was welcome to join him anytime she wanted. And she did. Lots. She'd sit in there and read or do needlework while he . . . created." I walked over to the shed door and hung the necklace chain over the lock and hasp, securing it such that the pendant would hang there, displayed there with it. The amethyst and entwined metal looked old, and yet the dappled light filtering through the branches overhead seemed to dance upon it.

I said, "You have a nicer camera than we usually see around here. Could you take this photo for me? I'd like a copy as a keepsake." I moved back.

His expression was blank. But he did take the photo and didn't seem put out by my asking. When he was done, I stepped forward again and carefully removed the chain and pendant from the hardware.

I showed him how the pendant worked. "See how the key fits into the design? It was so Momma could lock or unlock the shed at will. Not that she generally needed the key to get inside. He didn't always lock it when he was working in there. The key was mostly a sentimental gesture. Maybe a promise."

He asked, "Hold the key and pendant in your hands for me?"

I did, and he took another photo.

"If I'd known you needed a hand model, I would've gotten a manicure." I looked to see if he was laughing at my joke. He wasn't. His expression was still closed and was becoming irritating.

*Enough. Stop trying to read his mind.* Aloud, I said, "Stand back here while I open the door? Sometimes the dust of ages stirs up." I frowned at his continued lack of response and said, "It's a joke, you know. It's just dust."

"Well, I'm disappointed, then. I'd like to see the dust of ages."

"Humph. Easy to say when you aren't caught up in it." But I smiled this time and inserted the key in the lock, then flipped the hasp back. When I went to slide the door wide, I caught him taking a step forward. "Stop," I said. "I don't need help. Just hang back there till we see what we see."

More than anything, I wanted him to view the nose and

propeller blades of that plane first—for full effect. That was the best moment of all, and I didn't want him cheated of it. Deftly, I slid the right-hand door aside and then moved quickly out of the way.

His face just got more and more unreadable as he frowned and stared.

Thinking that maybe extra light was needed to show off Dad's handiwork properly, I opened the left-hand door, pushing it to the other side.

When I had both doors wide, Sam moved a few steps forward.

I stood beside him. "Well?"

His eyes were wide open and staring, but he said not a word. Not quite the reaction I'd hoped for. I said, "Careful what you touch. The sharp stuff in there is still as sharp as day one, and the dust has been mostly undisturbed for twenty years."

I paused, expecting him to go inside. When he didn't, I figured he was waiting on me, but I was wrong again because when I did move toward the open doorway, he touched my arm.

"Not yet," he said, making it sound like a request.

Must be the airplane after all, I thought. I said, "I'm happy to tell you the story about how the plane came to be here, if you're interested."

"A bomber," he said.

*Okay,* I thought. "Yes, Dad called it that. Plane. Bomber." I shrugged.

Sam gave me a questioning look. "Don't know much about airplanes, do you?"

I frowned. "No, that's true enough."

"Then allow me to introduce you to the P-51 Mustang. Also known as the *Cadillac of the Skies.*" He shook his head, his facial expression going quiet again. "And it's in your backyard."

"Well, it's in the shed, rather," I corrected him. He

didn't respond.

He fidgeted with the camera and then took photos from different angles, stepping back and even kneeling. When he stood, he brushed the dirt from his trousers.

"Okay. Will you show me the inside now?"

"Sure." I stopped a few feet into the building. "If you want the story about the plane—the Mustang—I'm happy to share it. As for the rest, my father . . . he collected metal junk. Some things were given to him in trade for equipment repair. If you can look past the regular tools and such that hang in everyone's toolshed, you'll see my father's art hanging among them." I pointed and gestured around us. "He never named them. I think of this one as—"

He interrupted me. "Your father . . . his name was?"

"James." I cleared my throat. How odd it felt to say his name aloud. "James Moore. My mother was Elizabeth. I'm named after my grandmother." Why had I said that about my grandma? I felt foolish.

"So your father, James Moore, crafted these metalworks and displayed them here in his workshop but never shared them with the public?"

"I don't imagine there's five or so folks who ever even saw them during his lifetime, and they weren't people looking for metal wall art, so if they happened in here, they paid no attention. They just wanted a mower or other equipment repaired for cheap."

"Then why now? You're thinking of selling them, right? Or of displaying them publicly? Or what?"

I crossed my arms and shrugged. "That's the catch, isn't it?"

"What do you mean?"

"I won't live forever. I've kept these safe here, from the day he died to this moment as we stand here. But I won't live forever, and then what happens to them? Or maybe one day nature won't tiptoe around the building. A pine tree could come crashing down and destroy everything he left behind."

I realized I was clutching the pendant again. I left my hand as it was. "I think these creations my father made are beautiful and . . . emotional. Maybe it's just me that reacts with my gut when I see these. Maybe not. I guess that's what I want to know. If it is just me, then I'll treasure them and enjoy them. If not, then maybe I'm doing my father and other people a disservice by keeping these creations shut up in here." I paused for a moment. "Sorry, quite a speech, I guess." I pressed the back of my hand to my lashes. Damp. Oh well. "It's time for me to figure that out."

"Why now?"

"I think I just explained that. I'm not getting any younger. I want to travel a little. Nothing big, but as it is, I must be here to take care of things. I want a choice—not necessarily to leave here, but just to be able to do something different now and again when the opportunity comes along."

He walked deeper into the shed without me. I didn't walk with him. I'd already overdosed on sociability. I wasn't accustomed to sharing so much of myself with a stranger. In fact, I hardly ever did that with lifelong friends. I was private. My people were private. We might tell stories and like to sit on a porch or around a fire and chat, but that was different. We were never pressed to tell more than what we'd offered freely. Never pushed to spill more of our inner pain for the consumption of others.

Deflated, that's how I felt. Made sense. Sharing all this personal stuff was exhausting.

"Lilliane?"

I rejoined him.

"Are you okay?"

I crossed my arms and shrugged. "Fine."

"These are amazing." He pointed toward one that was more rectangular and elongated than the others.

"*The Tin Man*. That's how I think of it."

"*The Tin Man*," he echoed.

"That convex body is actually the top of an old barbecue

cooker. Can you see the vertical line down the center? Opens in the middle. I haven't looked in there since Dad hung it, but there's smaller items inside that mimic internal organs. I think Dad was feeling whimsical when he did it. That was unusual for him. He tended toward melancholy."

There, I'd said it aloud. *Melancholy.*

"You said he sometimes stayed in here for days and even weeks."

"Yes." I pointed to an upholstered chair in the corner. "That's where Momma would sit when she kept him company out here. There or in a lawn chair. Depending on how hot or cold the weather was."

"What about you?"

"Me? Oh, well, I had school and stuff. Sometimes I was out here with them. Sometimes Dad would let me shine up parts of the metal art. He'd let me solder things. Not too much. Mostly, when he was out here, he'd get lost in what he was doing and just go his own way."

Out of nowhere, a *thangy* thud hit the metal part of the roof. We looked up in unison. A louder thrumming multiplied and traveled along the metal sheeting, filling the air around us with resonant sound until the wave hit the fiberglass sheeting. Even after it stopped, the air held the vibration for a few long seconds.

I lifted my palms and laughed. I asked him, "Do you feel that?"

"I do."

"Thor's Hammer. That's what Dad called it. It happens when the wind comes up the slope in a certain way and catches the metal just right. It happened when I was a kid, and I was scared because I thought it was thunder and lightning smack over our heads. He said I should never be scared in here. That this was a special place."

"I'd say he was right." He scanned the room again before asking, "Do you mind if we sit and talk again?"

I heard his change in tone loud and clear. He was cutting

the interview short. Might be just as well. I was exhausted.

"Sure. Personally, all this dust and talking makes me thirsty. How about another glass of tea?"

"That'd be great." We'd been walking out into the yard. He said, "Maybe we can just sit out here? I like the breeze."

I'd turned back to close the doors.

"Could you leave them open?"

My hands felt stuck. "I keep the doors closed when I'm not in there."

"Why?"

"For security. For curiosity seekers. For folks who might drop by for a good purpose but leave with what seems to them like juicy gossip." I added, "You might have noticed I don't generally call it a workshop because that word implies there's something being made, or something to be seen. It's a curiosity word. Not like *shed*."

"*Shed* isn't a curiosity word?"

"Nope. Utility all the way. Much safer."

He smiled, and with a little too much levity, he said, "If anyone comes along unexpectedly, I'll deflect their attention while you slide the doors closed." He sounded amused by my concern and pleased with his own wit.

"Perhaps my concern seems foolish to you since I'm doing this with the intent of sharing the information about this far and wide?"

"Not foolish, but I don't understand." He gestured at the trees. "There's no one here to see. You're in the middle of nowhere, removed from the world."

Sharp, hot words were flashing in my brain, words to set him straight about my middle-of-nowhere home and my concern, foolish or not. But I held those words in. He couldn't help not understanding what he had no experience with.

I said, "I'll explain after I get the drinks. I'll be back directly."

While I was pouring fresh glasses of iced tea and taking

a moment to cool off personally, I noticed him out there speaking on his phone. By the time I had the glasses in hand and was pushing wide the screen door, his phone was idle again, resting on the arm of the chair, next to the recorder. I'd forgotten he even had that device. Now I was fretting over what I might have said.

*Too late now, Lilliane.*

When I sat, I asked, "What do you think? Is there any kind of article here? I want to do what's best for my father's artwork, but if that means settling for hanging them on my own walls, I'm okay with that. I just don't want to leave them to be hauled away like the other stuff in there when the day comes that I'm not able to caretake them."

"I understand. As to the article, I'm not sure. It's certainly interesting and the metal wall sculptures are impressive. The whole shed is. I'm not sure whether it's the sculptures, the strangeness of the building, or those propellers that take this as an interesting concept into an *impressive* space, or whether it's the entirety of it speaking to time and what used to be. I need to think about it." He pulled the small notepad from his pocket. "I understand your father served briefly in the military and also that your parents' deaths were tragic. I want to be sensitive as to how that's handled. What can you tell me about his career and what happened on the night they died?"

Suddenly I was angry. *Served briefly? Tragic deaths?* Those words, though kindly meant, touched a raw spot in me. This wasn't just a *story*. This was real life. Mine. My family's history. I might be inviting Sam Markham, and the world, into it, but our lives weren't just words to be put on display like some curiosity from the past—something that needed to be *handled*.

And in that outraged moment, I almost trashed the whole effort to move forward.

I struggled mightily to tamp my emotions, but still the anger, perhaps fueled by own sensitivity and years of wearing my privacy like armor—and maybe even guilt over what I was doing—fought to bubble out in my tone of voice and word choices.

"Briefly? Yes, but he went to serve his country. He was a *crack* shot, but they assigned him to the motor pool. He told me he was disappointed, and he left because he could fix engines anywhere and not have to put up with *nonsense* from people who knew less, but who outranked him. He was a loner. Not big on social skills or fitting in. In that respect, I guess I'm like him."

I kept my hands clasped to still them, but I could feel my strong emotions flashing in my eyes. Somehow I managed to sound calm and reasonable, if slightly remote, as I answered, "My parents were sweethearts from the time they could toddle two steps toward each other. They were devoted. I can't tell you exactly what happened on the night they died except that Momma had gone out to keep Daddy company while he was working. It was a cold night, and the space heater was going. The wall vent was blocked by the cover falling over it. They were overcome by the carbon monoxide."

"And you discovered them?"

"I did. Middle of the night. I woke and knew something was wrong."

"You were young."

"Just turned eighteen."

"And you've been here ever since."

"It's home. Where else would I be?"

"But you'd like to travel?"

Some of my frostiness melted, and I smiled. I couldn't help myself. "Yes, I'd like to see some sights. I saw the ocean for the first time ever last month. I visited Biltmore in Asheville a couple of years ago. Have you been there?"

He shook his head no.

"Well, it's beautiful, and the Skyline Drive is too, but I'd like to see what's off the map."

Now he looked confused.

I laughed outright. "I've always wanted to see what the map didn't show. My parents weren't travelers, but seeing Biltmore with my great-aunt and then seeing the ocean—it woke a desire in me I'd forgotten existed."

His face had that strange look again; he was no doubt regretting the time spent here today or thinking about more interesting activities he'd had to forego to do this.

*I'll be okay. I'll figure it out and live my life, regardless.* Suddenly, the heat was gone from me. I was okay, indeed.

I said, "I apologize if I've wasted your day. There's not much excitement to my story or that of my parents. But we were happy. I wouldn't trade a day of my childhood for anything. And as for being the caretaker of my parents' memories—there are worse ways to live a life."

"What's next for you, then?"

"I'd like to go visit my friends in Emerald Isle. It's a beautiful place, did you know? But I'll always return here. This is my home. It's where my heart is." I laughed. "I've been told there are folks who have two homes, like a regular house and a vacation home? I'm not ready for that, but there's no reason I can't travel back and forth from time to time." I stood. "And what's next for you? Back to the city? New York, I think?"

"Eventually. My father lives in Nashville. I'm heading there from here."

"Oh, that's great. Sorry to have wasted your time, but I'm glad it wasn't as big a detour as it might've been."

"Not wasted by any means. It was a pleasure to meet you and to see a glimpse of your life here. I'm wondering if I need a country getaway of my own."

"Get one on a lake. I always wanted a place on a lake." I smiled to show I was half joking and being polite.

He stood, extending his hand. "Lilliane Moore, it was a pleasure to meet you."

To be polite, I accepted his hand. Then, for no good

reason, I heard myself say, "Take a short walk with me before you go?"

I released his hand, and he looked curious.

"This way." I started walking toward the shed but then veered around the right side. When I reached the forest, I looked back.

He was still following.

# Chapter Three

It was a peaceful walk up the hill to Peach Ridge, which was truly no more than a rise of land with lots of trees and a path that led up to a surprise clearing at its crest.

"Sam, I hope you don't mind, but after showing you my father's workshop and talking about him so much, it suddenly felt right to me to bring you up here before you leave."

The rough, gray stone walls of the cemetery were thick, and about thigh high, but wide and level on top. My dad had said only a master stone fitter could've constructed these walls, which were flecked with mica and now decorated with patches of light-green lichen. The stones were stacked to form a large rectangular enclosure about the size of a spacious living room. There was no gate or entryway. The headstones that were not too worn or eroded could be read from outside the wall. To get inside to weed or leave flowers, you had to climb over. An oak and a couple of sweet gums offered a little shade, and nearby something fragrant was blooming because the scent sailed on the breeze swirling around us. Beyond the crest of the hill, the view opened up and swept down to a small meadow.

"A cemetery," he said.

"Our family cemetery."

He gestured with a sweeping motion encompassing the ridge and the area around us. "Is this part of your family's property?"

"It is. This and partway across that meadow you see below."

"That's a lot of land."

"Maybe, but I'm not the first person to be land-poor."

"Land-poor?"

"Lots of land but no cash."

"Have you considered selling it? Some of it, anyway?"

"Not mine to sell. Well, technically, yes, I suppose it is mine, but it doesn't feel like it." I shook my head. "Anyway, selling would be my last choice of all choices." I touched the stone wall. "This is where my parents are buried, along with my grandparents and so on. More than metal art holds me here at Cub Creek. More than the contents of my father's workshop and an old house. As long as I can pay the taxes on it, I won't part with the land."

Sam stood beside the stone walls but stared down at the vista before us. "That's a beautiful view across the valley. Mind if I shoot a few more photos?"

"Sure. Why not?" I sat on the edge of the rock wall to wait.

"Maybe a shot of you at the rock wall with the meadow in the background?"

"You took photos of me by the shed already."

"You'll enjoy having these. I'll make copies for you."

"I'm not—"

"You look lovely."

Maybe it was being called *lovely* that snared me. I adjusted my position on the rock wall so that my back was to the meadow below.

"Be kind," I said.

He smiled. *Truly* smiled for the first time, and my heart was moved. Then the camera came up to cover his face, and he took his photos.

After a few shots, I grew impatient. "Enough," I said. "I'll walk you back. Being a city boy, you'll surely get lost."

"Not sure I'd mind being lost out here."

He was kind . . . as I'd asked him to be. I joked, "You'd be thirsty and hungry quick enough."

We walked back down the path. Since there was no longer an expectation of an article, there was no awkwardness. We were companionable now instead of interviewer and interviewee.

Sam said, "Looking at your father's metal art—his sculptures—I was seeing the ordinary bits and pieces, things we see everywhere, combined into a whole new way of seeing—from junk to fantastic. I could almost believe that I, or anyone, could do it too . . ."

"I thought the same a long time ago. Dad went away for a while when I was fourteen. Figured I'd craft some pieces of my own while he was gone. When I'd been allowed to help him, he would only let me do the easy stuff, and I thought . . . well, as you say, that I could create too. Momma put a stop to that when I burned my hands."

"Burned your hands?"

"Not third-degree burns or anything dangerous. But noticeable. A few cuts on my fingers and thumbs as well. They drew unwanted attention from outside."

"I see. In fact, I'd like to see what you created. Do you still have them?"

By now we'd almost reached the backyard clearing. We were coming around the side of the shed at just that moment. I gave him a long look, then shrugged, saying, "Why not?" Without waiting for an answer, I walked to the front of the building and stopped short. I'd left the doors open. The sight shocked and surprised me. I admonished myself. How quickly firm principles could fall by the wayside once you started relaxing them.

"Come around this way." I walked around the plane, which I now thought of as *the Mustang*, and the center worktable to the far back corner. I stopped at a door almost hidden in the darkness that led into the older, original part of the building. That door had been locked for many years, but the last I knew, the key was hidden on a shelf just above the eyeline. Time couldn't have moved it, and no one else

51

would've had the opportunity. Reaching up, I found it by touch, covered, as was the shelf, in a layer of dust. I wiped the key against the leg of my jeans, saying, "I haven't been in here since I was fourteen. I imagine it'll look different to me now being a quarter of a century older, won't it?"

"Hold for a moment," he asked.

When I stopped and looked back, he took that as permission to snap another photo. It no longer bothered me. Likely, I would enjoy having copies of the photos one day because regardless of what happened with this—this process of deciding what to do with the contents of the shed—after today this would never be the same. And that was probably a good thing.

The room's one small window was glazed with webs and the dirt of time. I found the light switch. The bulb still worked. This room had things hanging from the walls too, things I'd forgotten. A calendar from twenty-five years ago. A frame holding pressed flowers under glass, now cracked, that my grandmother had made. Some still-colorful wood-carved birds that my grandfather had enjoyed whittling were grouped on a shelf. But there were also darker things. They were crafted in metal. One of the wall sculptures was a long, narrow assortment of blades—thin blades from knives, coarser dark blades from lawn mowers, and blades from tools and household items I didn't recognize. They were all stuck fast together, almost like they'd been magnetized, to what appeared to be a screaming face. I remembered now that Dad had moved a few of the metal art pieces in here because they'd distressed Momma.

I stood there for a minute or so, blocking the doorway, remembering. It was almost like being in that cocoon again, separated somehow from the rest of the world. Apart. Yet reclaimed by it. By the past.

It would never quite let you go.

Sam was breathing behind me. I could hear the whisper of the air indrawn and then expelled. I felt the warmth of his breath as it touched my neck. But I was frozen.

He asked, softly, "Why did your father go away?"

"He was sad. Momma said so. He was gone for a few months. Six or so. I don't know exactly where to." I crossed my arms. "Oh, folks whispered. A few kids said mean things. But I didn't listen. I knew the truth of who he was. A good father. A loving husband. When he came home, he went right back to working on his repair jobs and creating things, but he didn't speak much."

"You tried to fill the void while he was gone?"

"What do you mean?"

"By creating sculptures yourself?"

"No, I don't think it was to fill a void. Mostly, I wanted him to see the proof of how much we'd missed him while he was gone and that we were thinking of him." I stared up at *The Screaming Man*, and then at his companion, a one-armed creature who had pitchfork tines emerging from an armlike metal sleeve made of a stained exhaust pipe. There were other metal wall sculptures banished to this small room.

As I moved into the room, I said, "We all have dark places in us, Sam. Do you know that?"

"Yes. Do you have a dark place, Lilliane?"

"I didn't used to think so. But all these years of keeping things locked away may testify otherwise. Regardless of what happens, I'm glad to bring light back to it." I laughed and turned to the other side of the room. "On the other hand, these are a fourteen-year-old's idea of metal art." To my mind, my metal art looked like happy flowers. Maybe one resembled a largish beetle-like insect, but he was all soft edges.

"I tended to just gather and solder and glue and see what came out. The art teacher in high school said that sculptors of rock and wood carve until they've released what's hidden in the block. For this? For me? I think I was trying to assemble the pieces to show their true natures. To give them voice, too."

"Flowers? Insects? Not sure I see that." He shook his head. "If they are speaking, I might be hearing them. An invitation. A reaching out. In appearance, I'd call them truly abstract." He snapped photos again. "Have you ever wanted to try again?"

"No. All that seems like it came from a different person, a different life. Plus, I was lucky. I never had fancy, high-paying jobs, but they were all decent employment that required some brain power. Kept me interested. I didn't have extra money for house upkeep or car repairs or trips, but I never felt deprived. My heart felt complete. Does that make sense, Sam?"

He didn't answer directly. He said, "Thank you for showing me these. For trusting me."

Feeling a bit choked up and not knowing what else to say, I patted his arm so he'd know I wasn't angry about how this whole interview had come out—or rather, that the article *wouldn't* come out—and walked away.

# Chapter Four

Sam Markham departed as politely and pleasantly as he'd arrived. He thanked me for my time, saying he'd send me copies of the best photos. We exchanged a few words of goodbye, then shook hands and he got into his car and left. His tires didn't even stir up dust in the driveway.

Deflated, I sat in a porch rocker. What should I do next? Would Sam Markham call Susan, or should I? No, I'd wait for *her* to call *me*. Meanwhile, I needed to decide what to do with Dad's metal art. It had been safe in the shed all these years, but I had a sense of time running out. Of needing to make a decision. It wasn't just that I wanted to go back to Emerald Isle for a visit. Merrick wasn't getting any younger, and being there was good for me too. But at some point, something was bound to change. I could get sick, or the shed would no longer be safe. Anything could happen.

Should I move the pieces into the house? Not the plane, of course, but the wall art . . . Most of them were very heavy. Would they be any safer stored in the house? The house was as vulnerable to theft or fire or such as the shed. Maybe more so since "shed" implied nothing of value was stored inside.

What about renting a storage unit? Joe was my ex but still my friend. He would be willing to use his truck to help me move them to Mineral or Louisa if I rented a unit there. But it would be expensive to pay those fees each month, and at best, it was a temporary solution. The sculptures would likely sit there until I died, and then some poor soul would get stuck with the task of trying to unravel and resolve my unfinished business. How was that satisfactory for anyone?

The phone rang. Not Susan. It was Gwen.

I said, "He left a few minutes ago."

"And?"

After a long indrawn breath, I told her, "I don't think there's going to be an article."

"Whyever not?"

"It was a good experience, Gwen. Went well, I think. We talked, and he looked around, and it was all very civil. But it—what he saw here—just wasn't enough for a story. At least, not for the story he wanted to write—a story that would find wide coverage."

"I see." After a long pause, she asked, "Did he actually say that?"

"Pretty much. He said he was sorry."

She sighed. "Well, then. It was a good try. There will be other opportunities."

"Gwen—"

"I mean it, Lillie."

"Maybe not the only opportunity, but it was the best we're likely to have. Feels that way. I just know that I'll have to make decisions soon."

"Don't rush. You've waited this long. Let's see what Susan has to say. I bet she has other ideas too."

"She may, but . . ."

"I have an appointment—patients waiting on me—so I need to get out of the car. I'll be thinking of you. Don't torture yourself. Just relax and wait and see what Susan has to say."

"Will do."

I locked up the shed and went about the business of dusting and washing and all the homey chores. It was easy work. As I moved laundry from the washer to the dryer, I found myself thinking about what I should take with me when I returned to Merrick's home in Emerald Isle. Could I afford another pair of sandals and maybe an actual, genuine beach cover-up instead of making do with Aunt Molly's pink robe? As if weighing in on the conversation, the washing machine gave a loud, metallic *thunk*. I took that warning seriously. I was lucky to have my own washer and dryer, but they were old. Very old.

As with all my appliances, the washer was working now, but not forever.

A little money was left from that first job with Merrick. There might be more opportunities to work for him and earn, but until those jobs happened and the cash was in my account, I couldn't count on it. Money wasn't easy to come by, and far too fast to go.

My car ran well enough for local use because there were people I could call on for help if it broke down, but on a longer trip? On my first and last visit to Emerald Isle, the motor had run hot. How many more miles did it have left in it? Needing repairs or even a tow out there on the interstate many miles from home would be an expensive proposition— more costly than the car itself was worth.

Unless I took another temporary job with Merrick . . . He'd said he wanted to discuss my thoughts about the book he was working on. How much of that had been schmoozing? Hard to tell. I'd better get in more reading time today so I could share my thoughts when the opportunity happened.

I carried the folded laundry upstairs, set it on the bed, picked up the manuscript, and carried it out to the front porch.

CRSO

Susan called. "Sorry for being out of touch. My plane landed, and I was in a hurry to get to my car. Got Sam's message when I landed, but I didn't see one from you."

"Plane? Were you traveling?"

"Traveling home. Quick trip." She paused, then asked, "How do you think the interview went?"

"Mr. Markham was very nice. Courteous. Professional.

We chatted. He took photos. He all but said that it wasn't enough for an article."

"Oh." She went silent for a long moment before saying, "You sound okay with that." She, herself, sounded puzzled.

I said, "Well, I wasn't surprised by the outcome. Maybe that's what you're hearing in my voice."

"Tell me your impression of the interview."

"Sure." I set the pages of Merrick's novel on the table beside me and put a rock on top to hold them in place against an errant breeze. I stood and stretched as I talked.

"I thought it started off well. He seemed interested. I fed him pound cake. I answered his questions as we went through Dad's workshop."

I struggled to explain. "I don't know. It was congenial and all that. I sensed more interest in the beginning, but then it seemed to sort of fade away. Began to feel more like a personal interest. He was kind and polite, but not someone composing an article in his head as he listened and snapped photos." I laughed. "Actually, he offered to send me copies of the best photos. I accepted. I'd like to have those."

"Well, Lilliane, you did what you could. I suggest we let it stew for a few days. Meanwhile, why don't you come back to Emerald Isle and give Merrick a hand? His current aide is leaving. We're going to be in between aides again, and his mood is worse than ever."

"Wow, that's a *tempting* invitation."

She ignored my sarcasm. "Let me know. I'd need you in place by Monday."

"For how long?"

"One to two weeks. Maybe three." She groaned. "I'll pay for three weeks regardless. If you can help us out, I'll arrange a car rental. Please do not make the trip in that car you drove down before."

"My car works."

"It worked, yes. But look at it this way—I need to be sure you'll make it. And you don't need the hassle or expense of the wear and tear on your personal vehicle."

This woman was getting too good at reading my mind. It threw me a little.

"I'll let you know tomorrow. Let me check my schedule, obligations, and all that. I'll call you in the morning."

"Perfect. Thanks. Say hello to Gwen for me when you see her."

"I—"

She'd disconnected. Susan didn't waste her seconds, that was for sure.

Susan could've called Gwen herself. They were old friends. In fact, it was through Gwen that I'd met Susan and been offered that first job as Merrick's companion. Maybe we were all functioning on Susan's wavelength now.

I called Gwen back.

She said, "I've been waiting on pins and needles."

"I haven't heard that expression in years."

"I'm old."

"You aren't old. Just a little older than me."

"By a decade."

"Not old."

"So what did Susan say? I presume she talked to Mr. Markham?"

"Yes. Or rather, she was flying somewhere and he left her a message."

"What did he tell her?"

"Now that I think of it, she never actually said. I told her that he implied there wasn't enough of a story to run with it and that when I suggested as much to him, he didn't contradict me. When I told Susan that, she didn't contradict me. Maybe that's how it works. Maybe when the interest isn't there, stuff just fades away."

"And that was it?"

"Yes. She'd just landed and gotten to her car."

"Oh. Well, then, she's probably thinking about next steps."

"Maybe. She wants me to go stay with Merrick again. The latest aide has given notice."

"Oh, excellent. I think you could use the diversion."

"She offered to rent a car for me to drive down."

"Even better. What's holding you back? Since there won't be an article—not right now, at least—you can go away for a while without worrying."

What she said was true. Nothing had changed. That overwhelming feeling of having exposed my twenty-year secret to the universe—of having put those cherished things at risk by doing so—made no real sense if there was no article and no publicity. A published article would be different. People—especially curious, intrusive, acquisitive strangers who might show up on a lark—posed a risk. But no article equaled no problem, right?

Gwen added, "I'm happy to swing by every day or so to check, to make sure the house and workshop are still standing. I'll even water your plant."

"Maybe . . ."

"Not *maybe*. It's *why not*. A week or two at the beach with a famous author and that very attractive Davis who's also an author? Light work and congenial companionship. And paid, to boot. I say, go for it."

附

Despite what I'd told Susan, my calendar wasn't a problem. It would be so empty that I didn't bother keeping one. The problem was I wasn't a fast reader. I couldn't possibly go back to Merrick without having first read the revised manuscript. I pushed myself to finish and decided that I was getting better at the pleasure reading thing. This was my second read of this manuscript, and I enjoyed noting the changes he'd made to the first draft. That spoke well for my reading retention and gave me a spurt of confidence. Merrick had asked me to provide feedback. Had he meant it?

I laughed.

Maybe not, but if not, then he shouldn't have used that as flattery or leverage to get me back to his house, because I had thoughts to share and he'd have to listen. He liked me better than the other aides he'd employed. I didn't know why, but almost from the day we met, we'd been friends. Almost family. Since I'd run out of family, and he had too, I liked the feeling we shared, even if he was grumpy and self-centered and demanding.

In the end, after working out the details with Susan, two rental car company employees pulled up in my driveway with a very nice, very shiny red sub-SUV. They came in two cars. The driver had me sign papers and show my license, then she hopped in the other car driven by her coworker, and they left. I didn't doubt that the rental and the delivery had cost someone, presumably Merrick, more than a few pennies.

As before, I left my houseplant with my nearest neighbor, Patsey. When I pulled up at her house driving the shiny vehicle, she walked out right past me and my dieffenbachia, asking, "What's that?" She circled the SUV. "Very nice. And red. Wow."

Oh so casually, as if shiny cars and beach trips were my usual style—*nothing new here*—I said, "It's a rental."

"Still, *wow*."

I offered her the plant.

"You're going to the same place as before?"

"I am. Only for two or three weeks."

"Lilliane, you have yourself a fine time. You've earned it, girl."

"Thank you, Patsey. I appreciate you."

She flushed pink. "Oh, go on with you." She shifted the pot in her arms, holding it almost like a baby. "Drive safely. Stick your toes in the sand for me."

"Will do."

As I drove the rental car down the winding dirt road to the paved road, I had a moment of hesitation. My foot on the brake, I felt pulled back, like a magnet was drawing me back home. I took a deep breath. I took my responsibilities seriously—I always had—but I would not be a prisoner to the past. Feeling the tug to stay was more like being motivated by guilt or superstition than reasonableness. I moved my foot to the accelerator, and when I could see the road was clear both ways, I put my foot into action.

# Chapter Five

Merrick Dahl's spacious beachfront home was in a private subdivision. He had a pool, which seemed over-the-top considering the house was right on the ocean, but then again, my idea of comfortable living was different from a lot of folks' ideas. I'd enjoyed both the beach and the pool when I'd worked for Merrick before, and I expected to enjoy them again.

It had been just over a month and a half, in fact, since I'd made the trip for the first time. Early June, it had been. By the time I'd left for home, July had barely begun. In a lot of ways, my visit there had been life changing. I remembered how worried I'd been about not having the right clothing. I owned jeans and shorts mostly, but I took my khakis, which looked more like real slacks, plus one of the Aunt Molly dresses. I'd worn my khaki slacks that first day, but I hadn't used the AC in my car because it was running hot, and so I'd sweated right through the fabric. When I'd arrived red as a beet and seriously damp, I'd horrified Ms. Susan Biggs.

It was now almost the end of July, and I was no longer worried about my wardrobe. No dress code, per se, for the job, and I couldn't think of a better place to be at the height of summer.

As I pulled into Merrick's driveway, I saw a car parked in front of the house. The garage door was open, and the garage was empty except for Merrick's car, so I drove right in. I took my tote bags from the back seat and carried them in through the side door to the kitchen. A stranger was seated at the counter there, her hands clasped, her lips pursed. She wore a print cotton top, and her hair was pulled back in a ponytail. She was maybe about my age, but there was a sharp look in her eyes that I didn't like. Nor did I like the idea that she must've heard me arrive and had sat here, with that expression on her face, waiting to greet me. Not much of a welcome.

I asked, "Are you Mr. Dahl's aide?"

"Yes. Was." She continued to sit rigidly, glaring at me. "I presume you're the sainted Lilliane?"

"Pardon?"

"Since you're here now, I'll be on my way." She added, "Oh, and the housekeeper came in earlier to make the bed and such—all but kicking me out, so she could be sure the room upstairs was ready for you."

I decided to ignore her attitude. "Where's Merrick? Any problems I should know about?"

"In his study or the adjoining bedroom. I haven't seen him since lunch. No problems that need special attention— certainly not attention from me—as far as I know." She stood, causing the stool to scrape across the tile floor. "I wish you luck."

"Wait—"

But she was already on her way out of the kitchen and striding down the hallway to the foyer. I followed, calling out again, "Wait, please."

She spun around to face me. "Why?"

"I don't know." I shrugged, confused. "Have you already said goodbye to him?"

"As much of a goodbye as he wants. And believe me, the only goodbye he wants is to see the last of me."

She opened the front door, stepped out to the porch, and closed the door behind her.

Just that quick, she was gone.

Merrick's study was directly off the foyer. On the opposite side of the open foyer was the formal dining room, and clearly he wasn't there. I went to the study door and knocked softly, saying, "Merrick?"

When he didn't answer, I opened the door. The room was empty, but the door beyond, to his bedroom, was closed. He must be in there. I'd give him a few minutes, and if he didn't come out soon, I'd go in. I looked at the study. Same as ever. There was a round table in the corner where we'd eaten our meals last time. The chair I'd always sat in at the end of his desk was already in place. Or had it never been returned to its spot at the table?

It was almost as if I'd never left. Satisfied, I sat, leaning back and crossing my legs, and waited.

The lights were off, and the room was dim thanks to the blinds and sheers, but sunlight still filtered through and touched the corner of his desk. The desk looked neat. The laptop was closed. No papers were stacked. No books were piled on the blotter.

Should I call his name through the door? No, there was no need to alarm him, since obviously he didn't know I'd arrived. I fidgeted.

Being honest with myself, I was a bit put out. I'd expected a better welcome. After all, we'd gotten along, had become friends, and he'd practically begged me to return. If the aide who'd just left had worked out, I wouldn't be here now . . . though I supposed I could've come as a guest, maybe. So there I sat, twiddling my thumbs and getting irritated. No good. Suddenly, the memory of him having fainted and fallen when he was in my care before—and how much it had scared me—returned to me, and I was scared again.

I went to the bedroom door and rapped softly with my knuckles. "Merrick?"

No answer. More loudly, I called out, "Merrick! I'm coming in."

The bed was made and clearly unoccupied. But a deep, upholstered wing chair over by the window was indeed occupied. Merrick was seated there, still and quiet. His face was turned toward the parted curtains. The light fell on his profile, and in that unguarded state every day of his ninety years was displayed. His chest was moving, thank goodness. His cane rested against the arm of the chair, and his stockinged feet were propped on the ottoman.

He'd dozed off.

Waiting for me?

Maybe, I thought. And then I recalled the words the aide had uttered as she'd greeted me—*the sainted Lilliane*, she'd said.

*Oh, Merrick. You drove her away on purpose, didn't you? To clear the place for my return* . . . My heart squeezed a little, and I touched my chest, found the key pendant beneath my shirt and clutched it.

A quick, short snore erupted, and he moved, turning his still-sleeping face toward me. And I saw the bruise.

My sharp rush of horror was quickly replaced by anger. Had she done this to him? *No,* I heard in my head. *No.* The elderly bruise easily, especially their heads. Unless his deep sleep in this chair was related to the injury . . . In this light, and from this angle, I couldn't tell how fresh the bruise was. I moved forward and leaned over him, looking for that darkest point in the discoloration that would tell me exactly where his head had been impacted.

As I hovered there examining the bruise, his eyes opened slowly. Instead of him being startled by my proximity, a smile grew on his face.

"Welcome back," he said.

"Thank you."

His hand began patting the armrest, seeking his cane.

"Here it is," I said. "But sit forward first and get up slowly. Not too fast."

"Oh, bah. Don't tell me how to stand and walk. I'm not a baby."

"No, you're not. That's why you have to be all the more careful."

He put his feet on the floor and leaned forward, pausing before pushing against the armrests to stand. He said, "What took you so long to get here?"

"Nothing, because it didn't. I had a smooth, easy drive down."

"Waiting here, it seemed like ages."

He preceded me out of the bedroom. His gait seemed steady, and he managed his cane as well as ever.

He fussed with the desk chair and got himself settled. When he looked up at me watching him, I could feel him willing me to sit down in the pulled-up chair, my old spot. I tried not to stare at the awful, deep-purple-and-green stain that started up in his hairline and came down the right side of his forehead, past his temple, and stopped somewhere south of his cheekbone. For now, I held the questions in.

"I'm going to fetch you a drink and a snack. What would you like? Speak up or you'll get what I bring you."

"Rude. Hardly here and—"

"You missed me. Remember?" I smiled. "I'll be right back."

I'd brought tea and shortbread cookies with me. We liked to call them biscuits, English-style. Mine were still packed in one of my tote bags, so I was happy to see that Ms. Bertie, the part-time housekeeper, was keeping them stocked in the same cabinet as when I was here before. She wasn't here today. Ms. B, as we tended to call her, came in on Tuesdays and Fridays.

I put the water on to heat, prepared the cups and saucers, and arranged the tea bags and cookies. Within minutes, the water was hot and steeping in the cups. I carried it all without sloshing a single drop or dropping so much as a crumb, all the way back to his study.

Seeing that bruise again—it made me wince. I tried not to let him see me cringe. I set our tea and biscuits on the desk, then moved mine closer to my end of the desk and sat down.

"So," I said. "Tell me how it's been. I met your most

recent aide. She seemed wonderful and warm. Too bad she had to leave. I imagine you'll miss her."

He grunted, but kept his attention on the light steam rising from the tea. He closed his eyes. I could swear he was doing nothing more than breathing in the steam and the mingled scents of dandelion and honey spice.

"Okay, then," I said. "Forget the polite fiction. I think you weren't very nice to her."

His eyebrows rose, causing the wrinkles in his forehead to deepen into creases.

"Did she cause that bruise on your face?"

He looked at me straight on now. "You noticed?" He grimaced. "I considered staying in the other room until it healed, but at my age, though I may be resilient, I don't heal quickly."

"Resilient?" Now I grunted. "*Stubborn* is more like it. Did she cause that bruise?"

"No, she did not. It was a simple fall. Susan insisted the aide have me carted off to the emergency room to be checked. It was a waste of time and energy. But we went and spent hours waiting on this and that, and in the end, the CT scan showed no harm done."

"Why are you so aggravated? Getting it checked by professionals was exactly the right thing to do. Head injuries are always potentially serious."

"I am aggravated because anytime an old person falls, everyone makes a federal crime of it." He stopped fussing and bit into the cookie-biscuit, carving off only a tiny corner with his teeth, then relishing it, his pleasure showing on his face. His smile made the bruise look all the more wrong.

"I fall," I said. "Not often, but I do. Everyone does. But when you fall and hit your head, it must be checked. I'm not trained for medical stuff, but even I know that. You know it too."

He took a sip of tea and then went to nibble on the cookie-biscuit again.

I said, "What did you do to that poor woman? Why did she call me *the sainted Lilliane?*"

Thankfully, Merrick didn't have tea in his mouth because if he had it would've spewed all over his desk when he laughed. I tried to look serious, but frankly, I loved his laughter. It was hearty, healthy, and honest.

He grabbed the napkin and mopped at his eyes and mouth.

"Merrick," I said with disapproval.

"I do not apologize. I did nothing wrong."

"Except make her feel unwelcome? Perhaps made tasks more difficult?" I shook my head. "Did you tell her I did things better? Because that wasn't nice at all."

"Not me. Or not much. I believe that was Susan." He broke into laughter again.

"No, don't blame Susan. She doesn't operate that way."

"Oh, she didn't *mean* it that way, I'm sure, but she kept suggesting that Stacey do things this way or that way because it worked well when Lilliane did it that way . . . and so on."

"That poor woman. Stacey, you said? 'Cause she left without even telling me her name." I didn't tell Merrick, but I was going to have a word with Susan. She and Merrick— surely without Susan realizing she was part of a plot—had made themselves into a tag team for the purpose of driving poor Stacey away. I understood Merrick's motivation, but I absolutely did not approve of his methods or manners. I couldn't believe that Susan had teamed up with him deliberately. Susan wanted to keep Merrick content and safe. She was probably trying to be helpful to Stacey in her blunt, efficient way.

I asked, "And what about the aide who replaced me when I left before?"

"She lasted a week. You know how I feel about uniforms."

"I do understand. But I also know all too well how it feels to be on the receiving end when an employer is difficult or unfair. It stinks. Truly."

He had the sense to look a tad regretful. This behavior wasn't good. I didn't know what to do about it, though.

"Have you been down to the beach yet?" he asked.

"No, I came to the house directly."

"You should go. Take a short walk. I know you enjoy it, and it might improve your mood. Perhaps we can discuss your thoughts about the manuscript over supper?"

"Definitely. Loved it, of course. Even a poor reader like me enjoys a good story." I flashed a grin his way. "Meanwhile, I'll go check and see what Ms. B left for our supper."

As I walked to the door, he called out, "Lilliane?"

"Yes?"

"It's good to have you here."

I paused. I'd been about to echo his words and say it was good to be back, but this was temporary. I had obligations in Cub Creek, and I felt compelled to remind him that this *must be* temporary.

I moved back to stand at his desk, facing him directly.

"Merrick, I have responsibilities at home. You know that. You've seen my life there. As much as I enjoy being here, I can't stay indefinitely."

His expression had gone blank and stubborn. I'd said words he didn't want to hear. I decided to say a few more.

"You can get along with some of the aides, if you'd just try, and then I'd know you were okay when I wasn't here."

He fixed me with those dark eyes. His frown was so extreme that his bushy eyebrows nearly met over his nose. "I can manage fine with Ms. B."

"No," I said.

His jaw moved, and I knew he was about to speak his mind. I preempted him.

"Please listen to me, Merrick. My parents died. My brief marriage failed. Your wife left. I know what it's like to live in a house alone for many years—a house that you used to share with loved ones. It's almost like . . . living in a museum filled with reminders of what you no longer have. I suspect it's the loneliest kind of lonely there is." I put my hands on his desk and leaned slightly forward. "But there are other people worthy of being in your life. Look at how we met and became friends. You are like family to me, Merrick. There are lots of people out there—people who aren't just trying to get close to you because you're a famous author. That aide who just left? Stacey? She might've become your friend, too, if you'd let her. If you'd given her a chance."

His expression stayed stubborn. I sighed with gusto.

"Or maybe not." I kept my eyes fixed on his face, watching for a reaction. "Her pride was hurt, so it was hard to tell. Some people are just prickly."

He glanced up. Was he wondering if the prickly remark was meant for him? He should be.

Stepping away from his desk, I said, "And now I'm going to see about our meal."

Ms. B prepped meals on Tuesday for the rest of the week; thus she'd have casseroles or other dishes marked for today, with cooking instructions attached. When I opened the fridge, I saw the dishes, but also disorder. Things had been shifted and moved around. As far as I knew, Merrick never went into the fridge. Maybe the aide hadn't been respectful of Ms. B's careful routine.

That alone would've caused tension in the household.

I slid the casserole dish out. Baked spaghetti and meatballs. Just behind it was a foil-wrapped package labeled "Garlic bread." Yum. I loved garlic and bread and meatballs, so I was looking forward to good eating. I'd never been much of a cook. Cooking for one was rarely motivating.

Per Ms. B's written instructions, I set the oven to heat, then I went to give Merrick an ETA on mealtime but paused in the doorway. He was still seated at the desk, with the laptop computer open in front of him, and he was typing, mostly hunt-and-peck style, but surprisingly fast for his obviously arthritic fingers. I was reluctant to disrupt him.

Without looking up, he said, "Well, come in. Don't stand there staring."

"We should be eating in about forty minutes. I'll set the table in twenty minutes. Otherwise, I'll leave you to your work."

"Thank you."

"It's good to see you working. I might step outside for a few minutes. Take a short walk along the crossover."

He nodded and resumed typing.

Apparently, his world had regained its normal orbit . . . almost as if I'd never gone away. I would've been annoyed at being taken for granted so easily, if not for that terrible bruise. Maybe I was his safety blanket of sorts.

It also occurred to me that a low-blood-sugar episode— same as the one that had probably caused him to faint and fall when I was here before—might well have played a part in the fall that gave him that bruise. I'd have to keep an eye out for signs of a continued problem.

In the kitchen, I put the casserole into the preheated oven, then walked back toward the foyer and turned right at the side hallway. The door at the end of the hall had a lock with a key code contraption. The code was the same as before—1120—Merrick's birthday. I let myself out. Merrick had extra security at all the entrances. Not foolproof barriers, but something to discourage the fans or aspiring authors who tracked him down. There was less of that now. Public attention had dwindled since he'd stopped actively publishing years ago.

But now that he was finishing up the new book, I wondered if he might attract more fan attention again, or even journalists. If so, he would enjoy it in a way that I never could have. Which reminded me of my own journalist.

Sam Markham. He'd been only briefly in my life for the few hours of the interview, but I'd enjoyed spending that time with him, even though it hadn't worked out for an

article. And Davis must be in town somewhere, doing
something, and he'd show up. I'd be glad to see him. I'd met
him during my first temp job here as Merrick's companion.
We hadn't been instant buddies, but there was something
special between us. No telling where that might lead, but I
was interested in finding out. Davis and Merrick had made
that long drive to see me, to bring me the manuscript and so
that Merrick could try to persuade me to return to him. And
Davis had flirted with me.

By now, I'd walked the wooden dunes crossover to the
high point, with the house behind me and the ocean moving
restlessly before me, and with an almost endless view
sweeping both east and west along the shore. It was a lovely
place to watch the sun set, and if my duties allowed, I might
try to do that this evening. The first time I'd walked out here
I'd gone barefoot and had had to hotfoot it along these
planks. I was more of a veteran beachgoer now.

The sun was hot, but the breeze was all that I
remembered and more. I lifted my face and closed my eyes,
catching the scent of greenery and sand and salt—of winds
that had traveled the world. Perhaps it was like a summary
of a map of the world. I'd had a thing for maps when I was
young, but my dad had said we were blessed—that we had
everything we needed right where we were because he and
Momma and I had each other. I'd refolded my map and not
brought it back out again, but I'd kept it tucked beneath my
mattress for thirty years.

It was about time I did some traveling. I wasn't sure
where, or how I'd fund it, but I was going to do my best to
make it happen. I'd keep my family homeplace in Cub Creek,
I'd spend time with friends like Merrick here at Emerald Isle,
but I'd go other places too. I was almost forty. I told myself
it was the prime age for traveling. A time for changes. For
appreciating what you had and wanting more. All at the same
time.

Somehow. Some way. I was going to live a whole lot

more before I gave up trying . . .

Like my dad had.

I had loved him so much. And I still loved the memory of my father. But I also understood that he'd given up trying. He'd moved his life into that shed—his workshop—and had lived his best days out there until he was done with the effort of doing even that.

CRSO

The round mahogany table in the corner of Merrick's study was where we'd eaten before. I assumed we'd do the same now. I arranged the plates and utensils, humming softly. Mealtimes were always better with two or more.

When I returned with the food, he had already left his desk and was seated at the table. I placed the food dishes in the center and then sat down with him. He ate with a good appetite, which pleased me immensely. Unfortunately, the bruised side was facing me and impossible to ignore.

"Where did you fall?"

"Does it matter?"

"I'd like to check the area, look for tripping hazards and such. You're walking fine, as far as I can see, but you've lived here a long time. There might be snares for the unwary that you're blind to because of that."

He smiled. "*Snares for the unwary.* A commentary on life."

"Sure enough. Any chance you were feeling light-headed?"

"No chance at all. I was coming inside from the pool area. I'd been sitting out there and came back inside, and somehow my feet or my slippers got tangled up. I went down. I tried to catch myself, but my noggin connected pretty hard."

"I'll check out that area. Transitions from one kind of floor to another can be tricky, especially if the light is low or

74

your mind is elsewhere."

He changed the subject. "Speaking of distractions, tell me what you think of the revisions Davis and I made to our story."

"First, I think it was very nice—an excellent idea—to include Davis as coauthor and get his help. Not because you couldn't have finished it yourself, but this book is very different from what you've written before, so I think his . . . voice is a good addition. Also, it was generous of you because having his name paired with yours is a huge boost for him."

"You're making it bigger than it was. I don't have that kind of cachet anymore."

"Nonsense. Now, to the book. I loved the changes you made. Simply loved them. I particularly enjoyed how you revised the big scene at the end. Really brought the whole story together."

"My publisher likes the manuscript too. I told them, though, that they'd have to consider any revisions you thought might be necessary."

I blushed. My face turned hot-sauce red.

He asked, "Are you well?"

"Merrick," I said, "I went from being someone who loved stories and could tell a yarn, but could hardly read a book, to someone who can tell a publisher what to keep or not? Seriously?"

"Well, in point of fact, no one can really tell a publisher what to do, but publishers are interested in what's good for selling a book. They are generally sensible. Sometimes they need someone to share the facts that will help that happen."

"Then they'll be happy to know that I am satisfied with the manuscript as is."

He grinned.

I asked, "What are you working on next?"

"Next?" He made a rude noise. "I think that was the last. I feel my brain winding down."

"Seriously?"

"Yes."

"Maybe your brain needs a break. Maybe a change of scene or activity. Are you sleeping well?"

He nodded and took his time chewing a bite of the garlic toast before he answered. "Sleeping very well. No issue there. Getting out into the world is too much effort. Davis used to come over several times during the week—we'd go for a meal or a haircut—but he's busy with edits for the book he wrote, plus he has a contract for the new one he's working on. His life is full of due dates and deadlines. And, admittedly, I move with the speed of a broken watch hand, and even then, I pay for it later with aches and pains."

"You need some sort of amusement or diversion. I'll think on it. Maybe I can come up with something." I began gathering the dirty dishes. "Ready for dessert? Or shall we have it as a snack before bedtime?"

"Suit yourself."

"Then let's have it as a snack by the pool later. Meanwhile, I'll go tidy the kitchen."

CR80

We had our snack by the pool as planned. I set it up on the table, and then while I waited for Merrick to join me, I descended the steps into the pool, but I stopped with the water hitting below my knees, enjoying the feel of the water cooling my feet. When I'd come that first time, I'd been brand new to the ocean. As for pools, my only experience had been as a kid in my cousin's soft-sided round pool. I did wade in Cub Creek from time to time, but since the wadable spots were few and the water was usually dark due to mineral content, it wasn't too tempting. Here, the water was almost warm. The little lights around the perimeter of the pool were shimmery just under the surface, and the tiles that decorated the pool below the water level looked liquid and luxurious. I still didn't know how to swim, but I'd learned how to enjoy floating (sort of) in the pool and wading out into the ocean waves. I hoped to have the opportunity to do that tomorrow after I was sure that Merrick was settled and okay alone.

In the weeks I'd been gone, he'd lost a step somehow. I couldn't pinpoint what seemed off. Just age, probably.

As he was coming up the hallway and almost at the door, I heard his low, raspy breathing.

I'd already checked the area where he claimed he'd fallen, and now I watched him cross it. There wasn't much to cause him to trip, and he seemed to navigate it fine this time, so the fall might've happened in a moment of inattention. Luckily, he'd fallen inside and not on the concrete. I was going to check on getting a rubber pad for the outside, something with good traction but that would soften a landing if he took a stumble. I'd never known Merrick to go beyond the door and table area. Surely in prior years he'd used the pool and had followed the path across the backyard to the gazebo to access the beach, but not in a few years, was my guess.

I reached the table before he did. "Tea and biscuits okay? The tea is cool by now, but it will still taste good."

A grunt was followed by, "It'll be perfect."

We both sat and sipped and nibbled. In the middle of that, I asked him what he might enjoy doing. "Now that I have that nice rental car, I could drive us somewhere. We could go somewhere that's air-conditioned. Is there a museum you'd be interested in visiting? Or shopping?"

He ignored my question, instead saying, "Davis called. I told him you were here. He said to give you his regards. He's out of town for a few days on business . . . or maybe it was family business. I don't know. Seemed to think we'd miss him. I told him we were doing fine on our own." He gave me a sidelong look. "I expect he'll show up here first thing when he returns."

Merrick had chosen not to discuss potential outings. I let

it go. I'd try again soon. I said, "He isn't in town?"

"Didn't I say that before?"

"You said he had deadlines."

"Oh. Well, okay then." He gave me a direct look. "What about your interview with that magazine writer?"

"Sam Markham. He was nice. I appreciated Susan setting it up."

"But you don't think it will fly?"

I shook my head. "No. But it was worth the effort. We tried. Nothing lost. But I need to decide what to do about the workshop and contents. It *feels* like its time."

He nodded. "I know that feeling. You can only let something ride or abide for just so long. And if you don't take the action when it's called for, sometimes you miss the opportunity forever."

Softly, I asked, "What did you miss?" I assumed he was going to tell me again about his regrets over not fighting for his marriage to Marie. But no.

"What you do and don't do. Sometimes I look back in my mind and see the years receding into the past like a stone road built of good intentions and poor choices. Among all those stone blocks of good deeds and triumphs are the ones that represent opportunities missed or the actions I took to distract myself from real intention.

"When you're young, boredom seems like a crime. Or a slow death. At my age now, I call a little boredom *good times*." He laughed softly. "So maybe you're right. Might be time for you to make whatever decision seems best. Or maybe you're just impatient after all these years of tending to the business of others instead of your own."

I agreed. "A long time, yes, but it's my business too. And I've had a good life. Like you, I can look back at the path I've left in my wake and see good and not-so-good mixed up together, but I don't see where I've made my mark. Always thought I would, even if in a small way that no one but me would notice or recollect later."

"Maybe that Markham fella will write an article after all. Might flop, you know. Might not. Be prepared either way. In the end, however it comes out, the decision will probably come down to the same basic choices."

"I expect you're right. Maybe sometimes procrastination is the way to go."

"Nah. I'm just saying don't worry about it. You have time yet to see what happens." He added, "Either way, if you do decide to break up the collection, I've got one or two of 'em stuck in my mind. I'd like to put in a bid. Keep me posted."

I laughed. "It's okay, Merrick. I'll be fine. It will work out, one way or another. You don't need to buy any."

He frowned. "I'm serious. Though as much as I admire the airplane in your shed, I think some of the other items would better fit my ability to display them here." He shook his head slowly. "But I gotta admit, if I could get that metal behemoth into my foyer in one piece, I'd be sorely tempted."

Merrick had lovely furnishings in his home, including some beautiful, very expensive paintings. The painting of that barefoot girl in the ocean that was situated on my mantel back home had been a gift from Merrick. But I hadn't really thought about his *collection* . . .

When I considered it, he had no family pictures on the surfaces of the tables, no old family portraits hanging on the walls—only objects of art and beauty here and there, tastefully displayed. So yes, maybe it did have a museum quality to it. But adding my father's strange, occasionally whimsical, and often savage-looking metal art wall sculptures into a place of peace and beauty . . . seemed incongruous.

I knew his offer was kindly meant, so I doubled down and grinned back at him. "I'll definitely keep you informed when the sale is about to commence." I winked at him. "I promise you'll get the early bid."

～♦～

Merrick tended to begin his going-to-bed process early and considered himself "in bed" soon after eight. He'd warned me in our first go-round that he often got up during the night and didn't want to be fussed over when he did that. So as he bid me good night that evening, I told him I was going to walk down the crossover to watch the sunset.

"Enjoy the show, Lilliane."

"Call me or press the alert button if you need me. I'll sprint back."

～♦～

Gwen had given me her older digital camera when I came here the first time. I'd used it then, and planned to use it again, but I didn't really know how to do more than turn it on and press the button. Plus, I didn't have anything to download it to. No computer. But I took it to the beach with me anyway. I'd keep working with it until I got better with it. Meanwhile, Gwen would help me out with the downloading, and then one day I'd have a computer of my own. Everything in its time.

As I reached the end of the crossover, I kicked off my flip-flops and walked barefoot through the dry sand down to the water's edge.

What was it about the ocean that drew me? The newness of it in my life must count for some of the attraction. Was it also the sight and sound? The rhythm of it? Electricity seemed to infuse the air around the waves rushing up onto the sand. The ocean was eternal, yet the constant shifting of atoms made it ever-changing. My flesh responded to it, tingling as chill bumps rose on my arms. But there was also frustration. Why couldn't my camera accurately capture the many shades of the water, or the gold and lavender in the sunset sky?

My lack of skill made those heavenly tones look harsh and abrasive. I did nothing more than point the camera, push a button and hope for good results. Gwen had put much more effort into photographing the inside of the shed, including bringing those shop lights, and even she freely admitted she lacked training. Maybe I could borrow a book about it . . . or sit with someone who knew how to use a camera properly and ask questions?

That seemed presumptuous. I'd better start with a book first instead of taking up someone's time.

As the darkness deepened and the moon rose, I considered that Merrick might know about cameras. I suspected no, but I could ask him. Davis might. I'd find out if he ever came back to town.

I laughed at my impatience. I'd only been back a few hours, myself. Had I expected Davis to ditch his business commitments and charter a private jet to be here to welcome me? No, of course not.

Leaning against the crossover railing, watching the night play among the tall grasses that dotted the dunes, I was amused and embarrassed by my apparent expectation that I should be catered to. By both Merrick and Davis. *Hah.*

I'd been looking forward to seeing Davis again. He'd been fun and flirty when they'd visited me at Cub Creek. Would he still be that way? Would I still enjoy it?

As the stars began to appear overhead, I reclaimed my flip-flops and returned to the house. I acknowledged that Davis had a life, as did I. Just now his life was taking him to other places, and he was focused on hitting deadlines. Was I disappointed? A little. But I'd only just arrived. We both had things, or people, who needed our attention. I was willing to bet it wouldn't keep us apart for long.

# Chapter Six

Only two days here and I was restless. Maybe a tad homesick. If I'd been home, I'd have been pining for the beach, so, apparently, there was no pleasing me. Merrick was doing computer stuff like email and napping in between tasks. It was obvious that he was content and didn't want to be bothered, so I slipped on my flip-flops and wandered out the front door and sat on the steps—a far cry from my own shabby but shady front porch.

And hot. It did seem to me, though, that the humidity was less than back home. I wondered if the salt air and breezes dried it out. I was doing my best to remember the sunscreen—something I never had to bother with back in my shady woodland.

Merrick's house faced the street and the houses on the far side, partially obscured by the privacy hedges and flowering bushes. That included Miranda's house. It was almost as big and fancy as Merrick's, but the outside, especially the yard, had a more lived-in look. For instance, you'd never see Merrick's garage door left open most of the time, even though his was tidy to a fault—which was not the case with theirs.

Miranda Wardlaw lived with her son's family, and while I never saw the son and daughter-in-law coming and going, Miranda's granddaughter was always in motion. She was still a teenager, being only eighteen, but she had a busy life. She left the garage open all the time, so all the gear and clutter of their lives was on display. I liked that. Not the disorder, but the evidence of busy lives. And busy or not, the granddaughter was helpful to her grandmother. I appreciated that.

Too bad Miranda was out of town. I would've liked to say hello. Maybe surprise her.

Miranda and I had met on the beach during my first trip here. She'd seen me at the water's edge and had summoned me to her striped canopy to help her out of her chair. She'd been reading, and the book had ended too soon. Her granddaughter wasn't due back yet, and so she needed help getting off the beach. Later, she'd tried to save me from drowning—by hitting me with her cane. Guess you could say we *hit it off* pretty much from the start. Which, it occurred to me, would make a funny but touching story to share at one of my storytelling gigs.

I missed storytelling. Words were in our blood, Momma had said. For me, it was the spoken word. Reading had always come hard for me. I'd managed to make it to the twelfth grade, but as people do when it comes to things they don't enjoy, I'd avoided reading and thus never got better at it.

From the first, Merrick had drawn my stories out of me, asking questions about my family and where I grew up and all that stuff. Speaking those words to a willing listener was as natural to me as breathing in that casual setting. And yet I was private. Private about truly personal family things. Very different from that interview setting where there was no expectation of confidentiality. So I shared stories about my life with Merrick and he had shared his stories with me. He'd brought the pages of that finished draft to me when he and Davis visited. And now, the gal who'd never enjoyed reading was hoping Merrick would start writing a new book. I was ready for more.

I hadn't heard a word from Davis. I told myself it didn't matter, but yeah, I was a little disappointed.

Missing stuff—that seemed to sum me up today.

*No more of this,* I told myself. I checked my phone for

messages or missed calls, including any from Merrick. There were none. I touched the pendant around my neck. It was there, along with the alert pendant that matched Merrick's. Talk about being connected. But in this job, being connected also gave me more freedom. I went down the steps and headed to the beach.

I was walking in the fringes of the waves, letting them run over my feet and even splashing in the water a little, when Davis found me.

CR&D

A distant shout alerted me. He was waving his hand and heading my way.

Merrick must've sent Davis down here after me. I was glad, because having Merrick watching as we said hello would've been annoying. The old man's bushy brows would've narrowed, and his dark eyes would've taken on a speculative look. Who needed all that when you just wanted to greet a friend? Not me. But I was delighted to see Davis's delight at seeing me as he crossed the sand, waving and grinning. He was wearing denim shorts and a cotton shirt, but nice, and I felt sure he'd come straight from the Norfolk airport.

I met Davis partway, and we hugged, impetuously so, and it went from a friendly squeeze to one so hard he lifted me right off my feet. Literally caught up in that hug, I didn't mind a bit. When he set me down, he didn't immediately release me, which was good because I'm pretty sure I would've fallen, laughing all the way down to the soft sand.

He said, "You look amazing."

My hair was blowing in my face. I was sandy and wearing a wrinkled shirt and shorts, and he'd said *amazing* like he meant it.

I grabbed his hand and pulled him along with me to the water's edge. "It's cooler here," I said. "Talk to me. I can't stay long, though. I need to get back to the house. Tell me where you've been and why you weren't here to greet me when I arrived." I said it with pretend arrogance, feeling pretty full of myself at that moment.

"I have lots to tell. I was in New York being wined and dined by my publisher. Can you believe it?"

"Not a doubt in my mind. Clearly, they know their stuff when it comes to recognizing brilliant writing."

He laughed, tightening his grip on my hand and swinging our hands together as if we were six years old.

"They're coming up with some kind of promotion for my books, something I'll participate in." He shook his head, and his tone softened. "When I first thought of writing a novel, I didn't take myself seriously. Didn't imagine I'd find a mentor like Merrick Dahl, famous in his own right, and that it could lead me to this . . . this time in my life." He dropped my hand and turned to me, face to face. "When a door opens, we have to be ready to step through, right? And what about you? Tell me what's going on. I'm out of date. Susan set up an interview, right? How'd that go?"

I sighed, but with a smile. "Yes, but—and it's a *big* but—it doesn't look like there'll be an article. I'm okay with that. It's probably for the best." I shrugged. "It makes things easier for me. Now I understand it's time to make my own plans and move forward."

"What are those plans? Have you actually worked out what you want to do?"

"No."

"You sound discouraged."

"Just not looking forward to it."

He took my hand back. "When you know what you need or want, tell me. I'll be there to help."

"Thank you." I stepped away. We were still holding hands, and our arms stretched between us. "I have to get back. Merrick will need his supper. Why don't you join us?"

Davis said, "I haven't been home yet. I need to check

the mail and get in packages and all that stuff."

"Then walk with me to the house. I assume you're parked at Merrick's?"

"I am."

"We'll walk together and then each get on with what we're supposed to be doing. I appreciate that you came directly here."

"To see you."

I smiled and squeezed his hand. "To see me."

⚬⚬⚬

The next day, even though Merrick had said Miranda was away visiting family, still I went and knocked on the door. Her granddaughter answered it.

"Hi, Carina. I'm Lilliane. I'm sure you remember me?"

"Oh, sure."

"Mr. Dahl told me your grandmother is out of town. I was wondering when she's returning. I'm hoping to say hello while I'm here in Emerald Isle."

"Yes, she was visiting my uncle, but she got sick. Really sick."

"Sick? Serious?"

"Serious. She's in the hospital."

"Oh, no."

"It's okay. A stomach virus, but it hit her hard. She's recovering and will probably be released tomorrow—that's what my uncle says. She'll stay there until she's able to travel home safely."

"Thank goodness she's getting better. Please tell her I said hello. Do you mind if I check back in a couple of days?"

"Course not. Knock anytime. Want my phone number? You can call me."

"Yes, please. And I'll give you mine."

We exchanged numbers, and I thanked her and left. Seemed like everywhere I went I was being reminded that time wouldn't wait—not for me or for anyone. Next I'd be seeing billboards displaying that message, maybe even blinking on and off to make sure I didn't miss it.

I made a list. Or tried. I thought I could write my options on paper, maybe positives and negatives, maybe steps to take . . . but other than a strange, lonely doodle, the page remained blank. Merrick teased me about the blank page, but then he told me not to worry over it.

He said, "It will work out. You'll know when it's time to make a move. Until then, enjoy the beach and hang out with me."

"Are you writing yet?" I asked him.

"You already know the answer to that."

"Oh."

He waved his hand around the study, flapping it like the wing of a large, annoyed bird. "There are three walls of books in here. You are welcome to any of them. Just don't turn—"

"Don't turn down the corners of the pages," I finished for him. "Someone else's book is not the same. I was hoping for a book like the one you just wrote, *The Book of Lost Loves*."

Fixing me with that stare of his—the one that he used to intimidate people and show how smart he was—he started to speak, but I flat-out laughed.

"You know that evil-eye look won't work with me."

"Seriously, Lilliane, what is wrong with these other books? There's a library in town, too, as well as a bookstore at the shopping center that's even closer. Why not find something there that's more to your liking?"

"Not the same."

"As you've said." Exasperated, he leaned back in his chair.

"Maybe you can go with me." I smiled. "It would make a nice outing. We could maybe grab something sweet at the bakery."

"We've already discussed this."

"Merrick, I respect that, but I also know you should get out of the house."

He sighed. "I'll consider it. I promise."

"You'll consider it if I drop the subject."

"Precisely."

I made a doubtful noise. "I won't give up."

He grinned. "I'll consider that too—as a promise."

# Chapter Seven

A week after I returned to Emerald Isle, Ms. B said, "You got some mail."

"Who? Me?" I'd never received any kind of mail here.

She pointed to an envelope, the kind couriers might deliver, waiting on the foyer table.

"For me?" I repeated. "Who's it from?"

She made an impatient noise and walked back to the kitchen.

I picked up the envelope. Yes, that was my name with Merrick's address. The sender was S. Markham.

The photos Sam had promised? I never doubted he'd send them, but this seemed quick. And he'd sent them here? Susan must've told him where I was. She hadn't mentioned speaking to him.

I pulled a dining room chair out from the table. It was the first time I'd sat here in this fancy room. I'd never seen Merrick in this room or the living room. Maybe the rooms had been used when Merrick and his wife were together. Likely they'd entertained back then. But not in a long time. I slipped the tip of my finger under the envelope flap to tear it open.

"What's that?" Merrick asked. He was standing in the study door. "I heard a commotion out here with you and Ms. B."

"Photos," I called over to him from where I was sitting. I held the envelope up. "Mr. Markham said he'd send me copies of the ones that turned out. This must be those. Feels pretty thick."

"Mind if I see?"

"Not at all. Please join me. Hope you don't mind that I'm using this table."

"Glad someone found a use for it," he said as he crossed the foyer.

He went straight to the adjacent chair and sat. I slid a white cardboard sleeve, like a flattish pouch and surprisingly large, out of the larger envelope. The sleeve and pouch were clearly intended to keep the photos together and offer protection. But the photos . . .

I let them spill out onto the gleaming wood of the table. The photos gleamed too. The subject of some of the photos . . . I wasn't sure who I was looking at. Was that me? The resemblance was there, but not. This woman was more than pretty. More than attractive.

Some of the photos were black-and-white. A few were color. They looked like stunning images out of a high-end, fancy magazine. Glossies? Was that the word? Not ordinary pictures.

There was me with the key pendent and another with the pendant hanging against the rough, worn wood of the shed and the old metal hasps. Me, again, with my hand reaching up to touch the propeller of the plane. The Mustang. And there were individual shots—like portraits—of the metal art sculptures. The angles, the lighting—it all worked together to pick up the textures and sheens, the blocks of shape and tone, and created almost a whole new . . . thing. I had no word for what that created thing was, but it made me breathless.

Merrick pointed a crooked finger at the one with the screaming face and knives. "I don't recall that one."

"No. It was in a small side room with the ones my mother found disturbing and wanted out of view."

"Disturbing. I suppose I can see that. But I also see the beauty. The challenge in it, though . . . I'm not sure who's challenging whom." His finger moved over the photos, continuing to hover. "And in this photo, you're holding a smaller work. I don't remember seeing that one either."

I sighed. "I made it myself when I was fourteen. I decided to give the metal art a try while Dad was away and ended up cutting and burning my hands. My mother was *not* pleased. She made me stop. And then Dad came back home, and really, there wasn't room in the shop for both of us except for when he invited me to help him."

Merrick surprised me by taking my hand. He turned it over in his, checking it.

"The scars vanished. Fourteen was a long time ago for me."

He squeezed, then released my hand, saying, "Remember what you promised."

"Pardon?"

"About giving me first dibs."

"Oh, Merrick. There won't be any dibs. Or bids either. I already told you, Markham isn't going to do the article, and since Susan isn't getting other inquiries, I do believe that was our best chance of stirring up some interest . . . and it's done. Over. Not going to happen."

He shook his head. "These photos—of the artwork, yes, but also of you—if I know anything at all, I *know* this man is writing an article. Take my word for it. The story is in the photographs. The words are only needed to provide a frame." He stood slowly, then lurched away, leaning more heavily on his cane this trip back to his study.

I stared at the photographs, mesmerized. Who was that woman? I saw myself in the mirror each morning while I brushed my teeth and tidied my hair. I wasn't ugly, but I had no style. People didn't seem to find my appearance repugnant. My ex, Joe, found me attractive. Of course, he found any number of women attractive. But *this me*, in the photos, seemed different.

In truth, I wouldn't mind being this woman. She sort of glowed and her hair wasn't styled, but it didn't need to be because it caught the light and shone—as perfectly imperfect as it was. Her curls brushed her face in a graceful way. One hardly even noticed the simple clothing.

There I sat on the cemetery wall. The scenery around me was a hodgepodge of foliage, open space, and distant meadows, but all seemed to serve the focus that was squarely on me. Me.

Suddenly, unaccountably, I was angry. I pushed at the photos. They scattered across the tabletop. I stood so abruptly that the chair nearly toppled. I walked away. *Away—yes, that's where I needed to be.* I yelled from the foyer, "I'm going for a walk. I'll be back. Call if you need me." And I ran. Literally.

I ran down the back hallway and out past the pool and to the gazebo and let myself out the back gate. All the while, I was asking myself over and over, *Why am I so upset?*

⊂⊃

Davis found me on the beach again. He said, "When I didn't see you at the pool, I knew you'd be here." He sat beside me, his bare feet in the sand near mine. "This is where you come for renewal or when you're upset. Where do you go when you're at home? I've wondered. Not the shed, obviously. So where is your safe spot, the calm place, in Cub Creek?"

My feet were dug into the sand, but I stared out at infinity. The endless ocean. Endless horizon. For reasons I didn't understand, the idea of the ocean—maybe its limitless existence—made me shake inside. Instinctively, I knew that somehow it connected with my anger at the photos, but I didn't want to think about it. I preferred to stare at the horizon.

Davis reached over and took my hand. His flesh felt warm, his grip, sure. I thought of the hug we'd shared a few days before and tightened my fingers around his. He was a good friend. And more.

Softly, I said, "I sit on the porch. Or pull weeds at the cemetery. Or just walk in the woods or along the dirt road. That's what I do at home."

He said, "Those photographs are outstanding. Of you, of the homeplace, and the metal art."

"I couldn't recognize myself in them."

He stared ahead at the horizon. "I know what you mean. The first time I saw my face in a publicity photo, I was like, 'Who's that?' It was a shock to realize I was staring at my own face and seeing myself in a way that didn't match my personal image of myself."

"Yeah. It was kind of like that."

"In this case, though, the talent, the skill, of the photographer is evident. The images are very flattering. Almost . . . ethereal. I could easily imagine you were surrounded by love . . . or maybe by angels."

My eyes were starting to burn. I wasn't going to cry. Nope. Not going to. And instead of that blowing-up feeling in my chest, it was more of a crushing sensation. Mind over matter, I told myself. No crying.

He touched our clasped hands with his free one. "You may break some bones if you don't loosen up that grip."

"Oh, I'm sorry." And I started to pull my hand away.

He kept his free hand firmly on top. "No. Don't take your hand away. Focus on relaxing."

I tried. I stared at the waves receding and returning and imagined my heart beating in rhythm with them. After a minute, I fancied I could even feel Davis's pulse communicating itself through our hands.

He resumed speaking, but in a low voice. "And so what was I saying? The photographer was skilled. I think he also saw you through very . . . friendly eyes. I can imagine that would make a difference. I give him credit for all that, and the photos are amazing, but he still fell short."

I frowned. "What?"

"Falling short? He tried, but he still couldn't capture you in that image. The beauty? Yes. The intelligence, yes. But not the essential you. He came close, though."

"I'm not that person. Never have been. Don't be cruel."

He moved that topmost hand to my face. With a light touch, a butterfly touch, he turned my face toward his.

"I'm your friend."

"Yes."

"You can believe what I say."

I wanted to.

He seemed satisfied by what he saw in my eyes. He dropped his hand away from my face.

"The photos of the metal art were pretty amazing too."

"I told you he isn't going to write that article. Probably wouldn't have drawn much attention anyway."

He smiled, his expression unreadable, but a trifle smug for my taste.

"Seriously," I insisted. "He all but said it aloud. Not enough for a story."

"I saw those photographs, Lilliane."

Hadn't Merrick said something similar? I was ready to protest, but he stopped there and didn't say more. Instead, he stood, offered me a hand up, and I accepted.

He said, "Let's take a walk."

With relief, I agreed. As I stood and walked with him, and asked him how the new book was coming along. "It's another thriller, right? Or did I assume?"

"Supposed to be. It goes well and then it doesn't. That's normal—I think. I'm sorry it's keeping me away so much."

"I was tied up with Merrick anyway. The aide took off so quickly. One minute she's in the kitchen waiting for me to arrive, and then—poof—she's out the door. I wish she'd been willing to talk to me, because Merrick isn't quite the same Merrick I last saw. I've had to watch him closely, trying to figure out what, if anything, may be wrong."

"What was wrong? She wasn't you. That simple."

I shook my head. "He has to get past that, because I can't stay but so long."

"Everyone knows that. Merrick knows it. Can't blame him for trying." He squeezed my hand. "Don't let it trouble you too much. He's a grown man, and he's not stupid. Put yourself in his shoes. If he had the choice of your company or poor Stacey—or that first one who replaced you, the uniform lady—and you were Merrick, which would you choose?"

"Judithe. That was her name. The uniform lady."

"You'd choose *her*?" He spoke with mock horror.

I play-punched his shoulder. "Don't be dismissive of her or Stacey. They deserve better than that. That could've been me. I could just as easily have found myself working for someone who refused to give me a chance."

"You are right. I stand corrected."

"You are forgiven." I moved closer, brushing my arm against his. "Why don't you join Merrick and me for supper? Ms. B always makes way too much, and Merrick is missing your company."

"And could it be that my presence might deflect some of Merrick's attention away from the photos and Markham?"

I laughed aloud, feeling light again, surprising myself out of whatever negative crap had had me in its grip. "That's true, but not the only truth." And then I felt tongue-tied. I finished the thought with, "I enjoy your company too. Join us before we lose you again to publisher stuff and deadlines."

# Chapter Eight

Over the next few days, Davis spared time for us as he could. I continued trying to budge Merrick from the house, but luring him poolside was the best I could do. I checked in with Carina. There was still no ETA on Miranda, but the report was that she was doing well. That second week sped by so fast I could hardly believe it, and I was grateful we had a third week yet to go.

It was at the end of that second week that the flowers arrived.

As I walked into the foyer, drawn by the echo of the doorbell, yet unaware, I stopped short. Ms. B was staring at me, but I could hardly see her face because of the glorious flowers she was holding in front of her. The arrangement of blossoms was in shades of purple and yellow, interspersed with red roses, in a tall red glass vase with bits of white-sprigged greenery. She extended her arms, holding the mass of flowers toward me, saying, "They're for you."

She seemed as surprised as I was.

I'd received flowers once before. Merrick had sent them to my home in Cub Creek. But prior to that? Never. I was so surprised that when Ms. B passed the vase to me, I didn't question the motive or reason, but only the *who*.

The plastic hook thingy that held the card was peeking out from between the roses, but I needed to set the vase down to detach the card from the holder.

From the study, Merrick called out, "What's up? Who was at the door?"

"Flower delivery," Ms. B said. "For Lilliane." She

looked excited and disapproving at the same time. She nodded me into action, and I opened the card. My name was, indeed, written on the card, and I thought, *Davis? Who else would send me flowers?* But no. Sam Markham. His name was written large. I read the note more slowly.

*I didn't expect the article to be published so quickly, but the editor moved it up in the schedule—which tells you how much she loved it. I hope you will too. Sorry I couldn't give you warning.*

What did that mean?

I couldn't think. My chest felt tight.

Merrick joined us in the foyer, asking, "What's wrong?"

"What does he mean?" I read the card aloud to him. "What is he saying?"

At that moment, my phone started ringing. It was Susan. I grabbed it.

"Susan? Sam Markham sent flowers. With a note of apology. What's he saying here? Has the article been published?"

"Listen, Lilliane. Carefully. Closely. Calm down and listen. *If* you get *any* calls from anyone about this, even calls from strangers, refer them to me. Don't answer questions. Tell them to call your manager and give them my name and number. That will suffice for now until we see whether we *will* get calls. Right? Do you understand?"

"I'm sorry. I'm trying to breathe."

"*Do you understand?* I'm not telling you what to do, but I'm telling you what you *must* do. We'll get some clarity pretty quickly, and then you and I will talk, and you can decide what you *want* to do."

"Yes. I understand."

"Hand the phone to Merrick, please."

He accepted and listened and then handed the phone back to me.

He said, "She's sending the link to my email."

I put the phone back to my ear, but Susan was gone.

Merrick yelled, "Are you coming or what?"

Ms. B and I hovered behind Merrick as he tip-tapped the computer keys with his gnarled fingers. It seemed to take forever for him to log into his email. At least he knew how to do all that, unlike me, but he seemed so slow. When the page for the online magazine was finally there on the screen, I stared, mesmerized. A vibration filled my chest, and I crossed my arms to hold myself together. My face felt hot. My limbs felt cold. As Merrick paged to the section where the article was, my knees gave way and I sank slowly to them, clutching the edge of the desk and trying not to throw up. The nausea passed as I listened to Merrick's gravelly voice reading the article aloud. He would pause on each photo and read the caption before continuing. My face and my father's work—and our names over and over—were displayed on the computer screen.

For one moment, I thought, *This could be worse.* This could be in some glossy magazine in the grocery store racks, right out front at the registers where the whole world would see it, instead of just being online. This was something only people with computers would see, and then, only if they happened to find it. And immediately, I knew I was surely wrong. Not having a computer—not being *online*, as everyone called it—meant *I* was the one out of step. Everyone had computers now, even on their phones. I'd seen a man walk right out into traffic with his eyes glued to his phone because he was reading something or watching a video. He was almost hit by a bus.

In a small voice, I asked, "How many people do you think will see this?"

Merrick said, "Many, many people."

"Susan said I mustn't talk to anyone about it, especially strangers, if they call and ask questions."

"Yes, very important. Let Susan field the questions for now."

My phone rang. I'd left it somewhere. I dashed to the

foyer table to grab it.

*Gwen*. Yes, I could talk to Gwen.

"Lilliane?"

"Yes, it's me. Did you—"

"I saw the article."

"How did you—"

"It's in that online magazine that Sam Markham writes for. I've been following it since he came to your house. It's pretty good—the magazine, I mean. But, Lillie, the photos are stunning, and the words that Sam used to describe you and everything else are like poetry."

By then, I was in the half bath off the kitchen, kneeling over the toilet and trying to keep my stomach contents down and about to lose the battle at any moment.

"Lillie? Are you okay, honey?" Gwen asked.

I made a noise. "No, Gwen. I'm not. Hang on." I collapsed onto the floor and closed my eyes. "If people see it and I'm not there to protect . . . to run them off . . ."

"No worries. I already called Joe. He and Willie are heading over there. One or the other will stay for however long you need them. They're taking Willie's dog and will make him comfy in your backyard."

I breathed. "Bless you, Gwen."

"Hey, I feel partly responsible, for both the good and the bad." Then she whispered, "And I'm so excited I can hardly contain it. That man did right by you. If this doesn't make a splash, then I don't know what will. Now try to calm down. Are you feeling better?"

"Yes. I'm so nervous."

"Then go out to the ocean and commune with the jellyfish and seagulls. It will help. I promise."

We disconnected. I walked slowly back to the study. Ms. B had pulled my chair up next to Merrick, and the two of them were huddled, examining the article. The blasted article. But they looked rather sweet and funny together. I stood, watching them. This was an event neither of them would forget. A rare occurrence for the lot of us.

Merrick looked up. "All worked out?"

"Gwen's sending some friends over to watch the house and the shed." I shrugged. "Not that my neighbors would cause a problem, but the property is easily accessible and absolutely private. Someone needs to be there."

"You aren't leaving, are you? We can hire guards."

"And that wouldn't attract any attention, would it?" I said, laughing, but finding no humor in it. "I think Willie's dog will do well enough. Willie is a part-time deputy, and Joe will help him watch out for things. I can't impose on them for more than a few days, though, so we'll have to figure something out." I ran my hands through my hair. "I guess I never really thought this would happen. And now . . . but it could still fizzle out to nothing, right? I mean, it makes sense that I'm halfway to crazy over it because it's about me and mine. And you all know me, so it's exciting for us, right? But who else is going to care, really?"

My phone rang. Davis's number.

"Lilliane, have you seen the article?"

When I didn't answer right away, he asked, "Where's Merrick? There with you?"

"Yes." If only he could see Ms. B and Merrick, pulled up practically cheek to cheek, and now watching me on the phone. It was hard to stay lost in anxiety and upheaval seeing the two of them, but I was managing it. And Davis was trying to help steady the ship. Gwen was handling things on the home front. Lots of old military movie allusions were suddenly playing through my head. Did I feel like I was preparing for battle? Maybe so.

I said to them, "It's Davis." To Davis, I said, "Yes, I've seen it."

"Wow," he said. "Have you actually read it?"

"Parts of it. I found it hard to focus."

"Are you excited or worried?"

"Yes. Both." I waved my hand as if to dismiss my

confusion. Of course, he couldn't hear my hand signal. "Gwen called. She has friends watching out for things at the house and shed."

"Excellent. I know Markham didn't give an exact address, but anyone could ask, for instance, at a nearby convenience store. They'd know where the Moores live along Cub Creek. Am I right?"

"Exactly. Yes." I was grateful he understood.

"Your friends have eyes on the place, so it's all going to be fine. Have you eaten?"

"Breakfast." I decided not to mention the bathroom trip.

"Make sure you eat lunch. I'll be over later today."

Merrick said, "Lilliane, take my laptop." He unplugged the power cord. "Take it where you can read it in peace." He held up his finger to make his point. "Stay close enough that we'll hear you in case you need us."

"Hold on," I said to Davis, trying to think. Yes, I wanted to read it, but not in front of others, not with them watching my face. Not only for the reason he might be assuming. My ease with reading and my comprehension had definitely improved, but trying to read the computer screen while hanging over his shoulder was awkward, and I could hardly see the words clearly enough to make them out.

Ms. B said, "I'm going to get lunch together while you read it, Lilliane."

Though I knew Davis must've heard at least parts of what Merrick and Ms. B were saying, I explained to him, "Merrick's going to let me use his laptop to read the full article alone."

Davis said, "Good idea. It's a great write-up, in my opinion. Based on my own experiences, I strongly suggest that you don't take your initial reactions to heart. Keep an open mind and read all the way through to the end before you make judgments."

"I'll try. See you later? I'm sure I'll be here."

"Lilliane, no worries about that. I always know where to

find you." He finished, "Remember to reserve judgment."

We disconnected. Merrick followed me into the dining room, made sure I plugged the cord into the wall outlet, and then, pointing at the laptop screen, he said, "Move your finger here to move the page up and down. When you're done with the first page, use this finger to swipe left and the next page will be there. I am nearby if you get stuck." He gave me a pat on the shoulder and left me.

# Chapter Nine

The article's title shouted in big, bold letters, WHERE PAST AND FUTURE COLLIDE, and below that, in smaller, lighter letters the subtitle read, *A story of life, of death, of wood and metal—my visit to Cub Creek.*

*Tell me about it,* I thought. And apparently Sam intended to do exactly that, because he started *with* me, mentioning how much I loved where I'd grown up but had a yen to travel. He wrote that emotional ties, sometimes physical ties, kept us grounded, but the grounding could also mean we didn't take off on our own in the natural course of things and failed to follow that which called to us. There was a phrase that shook me: *lost amid the generations . . .*

I pressed a hand to my eyes. They stung just a bit. I refused to cry. You couldn't read if you were crying. I did as Davis had recommended and removed myself from the story. I ignored my emotional reactions and tried to read the words objectively.

There was a photograph of the house and the front porch with the heavy branches of ancient trees hanging low, almost framing the photo. Near that image was the photograph of the massive, mismatched shed/workshop, and then a close-up of me holding the pendant in front of the lock hasp.

Sam wrote about my parents, not saying too much about my mother, but writing mostly about my father. There were lots of words to read, and they were interspersed with pictures. I sensed the photographs were truly the reason for the story happening, much as Merrick and Davis had suggested. Was that why the editor had decided not only to publish it but to move it up in the schedule?

The photographs were hypnotic. For me, that might have been a given, but even trying to view them objectively, I could see that *certain something*. The house photo made me think of Faulkner, for some strange reason. Maybe it looked like it belonged to Southern Gothic fiction? I'd have to check that out later. But the exterior view of the shed reminded me of the grittiness of those Wyeth paintings where everything looked angsty and vaguely threatening. My eyes felt glued to it, in an effort to understand what I was seeing.

I tensed, then forced a breath in and out, blinked, and continued.

*James Moore was a troubled man. Also, I suspect, a brilliant man not in step with the world at large. Adored by his wife and daughter, good with machinery but unable to function under those in authority, he took to his shed, his workspace. It was cobbled together with panels of fiberglass and wood and whatever worked as the space grew, and his work, within it, likewise grew. Like ancient workers of metal and forges, solitary figures who stoked the flames and wielded tools to beat and create, James Moore transformed the forgotten castoffs of life into new creatures. I walked into that workshop with the last surviving member of many generations and was, unsuspecting, struck dumb by the sight of the propellers and nose of a P-51 Mustang, renowned as the Cadillac of the Skies in World War II. The interior of the building—no matter how much light was directed inside— was like a shadow world of madness. Electrical light could never be enough. These were creations forged of ancient dark and light but by the hand of a man using simple tools, and my mind stretched to cover the distance between disparate instances of time, past and present, and to secure the connection.*

There were photographs of *The Rosette Stone* and *Warrior Shield*, and they were labeled as such, just as I'd told him. The photographs were in color and showed the aged wood behind them and the various tools and things sharing the wall with them.

Sam wrote, *I would like to have met the man who forged these works. Works of art? Yes. Works of a troubled soul? I think that must be true. But mostly, these are authentic works, crafted and created by a man who didn't fit into the world we claim to want. In reality, while part of me was alarmed by these works, a large part of me also wished to stay, to stare, to ponder, as if by looking long enough, or perhaps at just the right moment, I might glimpse the basic truth that exists within each of us. We aspire to better—yet we cannot achieve that without confessing the dark. And perhaps, just perhaps, that is what James Moore was communicating and attempting to do himself. Trying to confess and share what he could not express in words, either to his daughter or the world, and perhaps even to himself.*

The next photos included the metal wall sculpture with the knives, along with *The Tin Man* and others.

There were more words written as he ended the article, but the last image caught and held me. Sam and I were in that small room with the dusty, begrimed window behind me, allowing in only a low light. I was turned toward the workbench and holding one of the small sculptures I'd made, but the larger, harsher ones created by my father showed on either side of me. The soft amber light from the window backlit my profile—not an exact profile, but a three-quarter view. The camera caught motes in the stream of light near my eyelashes, and in the light cutting through my hair and softening the dark around me like a crown, and it caught my eyes focused on the small metal sculpture that I was holding and the smile on my face.

Seeing it stole my breath again. It was almost like being back in the workshop with Sam, with the filtered light and dust. And with Dad there. As if all at the same time. Even now, maybe in sympathy or remembrance, I could feel a sneeze building. I closed my eyes and held my breath until the sensation stopped.

The article ended with *In a world that is so often filled with chaos . . . it was a time out of time . . . surrounded by the forest . . . a sojourn in the nexus of time itself . . . a pocket of . . .*

I sat for a long moment in silence, still facing the computer screen but not seeing it. Instead, seeking a moment of peace, of breathing, to calm myself. To allow the thoughts to arrange themselves in my brain in a coherent, actionable way. I couldn't pick out exactly what it was—which components were the ones that were jelling together and creating this . . . this new urgency I felt.

*This is something*—that's what I heard in my head, like an actual voice was talking soft and low near my ear, insistently. *Something, something, something . . .*

Something, yes. But what did *that mean*?

In my mind's eye, I saw that map—the one I'd had as a child and kept under my mattress—and it was as if someone had taped it to a virtual wall in my head and was sticking a pin into a specific location and pointing: *This is* something. *Pay attention.*

My fingers dug into my hair. I felt the pain as strands tangled around them. Crazy. Was I crazy? Like hearing the strike of that mythic hammer again ringing in my ears. Of feeling the burns on my hands and not caring. Slicing into my thumb when a sharp tool slipped, but hardly noticing because I was forcing the metal to assume a shape—the shape it needed to take to become . . .

I began to shake. Freeing my fingers from my hair, I hugged myself, my shoulders hunched against the overwhelming feelings.

Merrick was there. I hadn't heard him approach. He sat next to me.

"What's wrong, Lilliane?"

I was staring at my hands as if they'd talk to me. Palms up, fingers splayed, staring at them like I could read the lines.

"I don't know, Merrick. Something—something I don't understand came over me. Like . . . as if . . . this is more than . . . more than about whether art collectors will be interested . . ." I shook my head. "Something important. But I can't quite grasp it." I flexed my hands despite myself and stared again at my palms. I remembered where the scars—long gone—had been.

"Or maybe you can. Maybe you want to, but you are afraid."

He took one of my hands from where it was suspended in front of me. He held it and patted it, then gave it a squeeze. In that instant, he was my anchor.

"Don't run away from this, Lilliane. Don't run. This is big. You live your life in countless important ways, but you are not impetuous. You don't do big things suddenly. Am I right?"

He gave my hand another gentle squeeze. "It feels shattering, but you don't have to allow this into your heart and mind all at once. It's frightening—big changes are, big opportunities are—but don't turn away from it. When creation—illumination—strikes, if you reject it, it may move on and not come back."

I blinked at him through tear-filled eyes. "You've felt this before?"

"Yes, back when that first book of mine sold to the publisher. It was so long ago, but watching you sitting here feeling this, I'm remembering. I was so young when my first book was published, in my twenties. I can hardly remember being that young, but I recall how sure I was of everything, and how surprised I was that a publisher wanted to take on that first book—the one I'd written in secret during the college and grad school years. Believe it or not, I regretted submitting it to him and almost declined the offer."

He took a breath and continued. "I had an identity, or so I thought, and it revolved around working toward becoming a partner in a prestigious law firm, not around a lifetime of making up stories. And not even literary tomes, but commercial thrillers. In fact, I'd been working at writing and publishing for more than a decade when I realized that, for me, there was no going back. I'd become, perhaps despite myself, successful at writing books." He gasped, drawing in a small breath as if feeling the shock of it again. "I'll never forget that rush of…practically every emotion that can be experienced by a human being. I'd become famous under the author identity and now must own it, and continue to live up to it. And be exposed to the potential for failure, too, before my friends and the world, with each new book or a bad business or social decision."

"It was frightful, but it was also a gift, Lilliane, to fully understand that I could never go back to the life I'd planned. I also remember the jolt of life, of feeling as if I'd never truly lived before. It was visceral, Lilliane. Almost like being born into who I was supposed to be."

"And stunning to consider how I might not have chased it—the books that were yet to be written. That I might have missed the proverbial boat."

# Chapter Ten

Still seated beside me at the dining room table and holding my hand, Merrick said, "Don't do anything right now. No rash moves. No running away." His voice was calm and even. "Let this seep in. Tell your brain to ignore it for a few hours, maybe longer if you can manage it. Let the sensation of it work its way into your consciousness. When it doesn't feel so shocking but still feels exciting and scary, that's when you can begin to plan. Understand what this may mean to you and what to do about it. Let Susan work her magic. Talk to her tomorrow when you're sane again."

I blubbered a bit when I tried to laugh. *Sane?* Maybe he was right. Maybe I was teetering on that edge right now.

He continued, "Because you and I know it's about more than marketing works of art. It's about much more."

Having no words at the moment, I settled for nodding. It had to be enough.

"May I give more advice?" He looked concerned. "I'm not accustomed to you being such a good listener, so I'll take the opportunity while I have it." After a brief pause, he grunted, apparently assuming consent. He said, "Go out. Either to the pool or down to the ocean. Wherever sanity and peace in its purest form exists for you, just go there, sit, and don't think. No thinking yet."

He was still gripping my hand, and now he touched my thumb, the soft flesh of it where twenty-five years ago the worst scar had been. Did a ghost of it remain?

I offered him a smile. He released my hand. I nodded again, and then I stood and walked away.

❧❦

I had a good life. A respectable, relatively ordinary life. Some people might consider it dead-end or unfulfilled—and I read that truth in the eyes of certain customers when I worked the counter at the Fuel Up Fast. It looked a lot like pity or maybe a snap judgment of me as someone unimportant or unambitious. But I ignored them. Their opinions about my life didn't matter because they were seeing me through their *own* filters, which probably prevented them from seeing their personal shortcomings. I knew enough to dismiss that sort of thing. Within my small world, I'd been content enough and had had some fun and even a few small triumphs from time to time, but always with a sense that there was more to be had. Yet I also had my duty. I'd thought I was protecting the shed and my father's workshop for his sake—in his memory—and, of course, cherishing the past and my precious memories.

But.

Maybe I'd had it backward.

Saving it, protecting it for me to look back on? Or *for* me. For when I was ready . . .

I'd gone down to the beach and now I lay there in the sand. The waves had been rolling up and washing over my toes and then my ankles. This wave, the forerunner of the incoming tide, reached the hem of my shorts. But still I lay there, staring up at the blue sky. A few puffy clouds scudded by overhead. Maybe when the ocean reached the back of my shirt, I'd feel enough energy to move. My hair would already be full of sand. But really, it made sense. After all, what did wet, sandy clothing mean to anything or anyone at the beach? It was to be expected, right?

"What's wrong with you?" Miranda asked, exasperation strong in her voice. "Do I need to intervene? Don't you know most people put on a swimsuit when they go swimming? Though some don't, of course. They wear their birthday suits. I went to one of those beaches long, long ago. It was a sight, I'm telling you. But I don't peg you for a suitless swimmer."

I turned my head toward her and saw her feet and the end of her cane.

"I'm not swimming."

"You will be soon." She chuckled. "What's it they say? Time and tide change for everyone."

I frowned. "Not quite what they say." I groaned. "Still true." I pushed up to a seated position and grinned the biggest grin I owned. "It's good to see you, Miranda. I'm glad you're back." I took in her standing there, dressed in her usual beach attire that started with a wide-brimmed hat on top, moved down to a long-sleeved shirt and slacks, and bare feet. The slacks were rolled up to display part of her shins. She was standing steady. Her color was pretty good. Maybe a trifle too rosy. "How are you feeling?"

"I'd feel better if I was sitting. Help this old woman back to her seat."

Truth be told—or admitted to—I felt resentment at having my funk, my dark state, disturbed. Even by someone I would otherwise have been happy to see.

"Where's your granddaughter?"

"She brought me down and set up the canopy, but she had to run off to school. I could've waited in my chair for you to get yourself up and come over there to chat, but . . . but you have that . . . I don't know. Like an aura. Like you wanted the ocean to drag you out and carry you away. You must be half mermaid, always tempting Poseidon this way. You needed interruption. I was sure of that."

Embarrassed, I rose to my feet and brushed at the sand sticking to my skin and clothing. My wet denim shorts were heavy with salt water. I looked at Miranda, really looked, and saw how the flush on her face was deepening. Beads of perspiration were forming along her hairline and even under her eyes. I took her arm. "Let's get back to the canopy, and then I'll give you a proper hug."

We slogged through the dry sand, arm in arm.

I asked her, "You were sick?"

"My granddaughter told me you came by the house."

"Merrick said you were away. I was worried. I hope she didn't think I was being nosy."

"Not a bit. I was visiting my younger son in Tennessee and took ill. Not badly, but we old folks live on the edge of dehydration, which tends to upset all the other internal workings, so it doesn't take much to sideline us. I'm fine now."

"I'm glad to hear it."

She sat in her chair and motioned toward the small ice chest. I flipped open the lid and grabbed a bottle of water for her.

"Take one for yourself too," she said. "You look parched."

"I should get back to the house."

"Spare me a few minutes. Merrick won't mind."

I took a bottle of water for me too.

"Have a seat. Having to look up at you strains my neck."

And yes, there was a second chair. For the first time. I suspected she'd come out here because she'd somehow become aware I might be on the beach. Maybe after a call from Merrick? It wouldn't be the first time they'd teamed up for a cause.

I sat, then unscrewed the bottle cap and took a long drink. I closed my eyes, relishing the feel of the cold water going down, cooling my body from the inside out. I pressed the cold bottle to my forehead, and a speck of ice dropped down inside my blouse. I left it there to melt. It felt good. I'd been parched and hadn't even realized. When I finally opened my eyes, I saw Miranda was staring. Was that sadness in her eyes?

"I'm fine," I said.

She harrumphed.

"Truly." I moved the bottle to my cheek. It felt so good. "What about you? Are you recovered now?"

"As recovered as I'm going to be." She grimaced. "One hundred percent—rather, my *new* one hundred percent. That goalpost seems to shift far too often." She said, "So, when I heard you were back with Merrick, I was hoping to see you. You, however, aren't yourself. I see that written all over your face. What's up?"

I looked away and slowly shook my head.

Miranda sighed. I felt guilty.

"It's not you, or about not wanting to tell you about it," I said. "I just don't know where to start." I pressed the bottle back to my forehead.

"Best get yourself a fresh bottle. That one's gotta be warm by now."

I did. New bottle. Still icy. It felt good to my poor, whirring brain.

"Don't start at the beginning. Tell me about today."

Groaning, I asked, "Do you use a computer?"

"Of course."

I groaned again, more loudly. "Am I the only person in the world who doesn't?"

"Nah. Lots of young folks use their phones for computer stuff that old folks like me still want that big computer screen for."

"I have a phone, but it's a simple, cheap one. It doesn't do all that stuff. And the online things it tries to do, it doesn't do well." I shrugged. "I was perfectly happy with it."

"Ah. You look like you're rethinking that."

"I don't know. Not really rethinking it, but thinking I may no longer have a choice."

"You like being cut off. The ability to be cut off from the world is getting harder to achieve. I remember how that was once upon a time. Long, long ago. When the only phone was on the kitchen wall, and unless you hid in the closet with it and whispered, everyone heard your conversation. And

113

probably listened in and made comments all the while. When a person really could disappear and there were no heat-seeking surveillance tools or satellite imaging or Bluetooth in our cars and phones. I do remember that. That time had its comforts—but it did also have limitations."

"That's how it is in Cub Creek. At my family home in the middle of the woods. I had to leave that world for jobs, but otherwise, I could mostly stay in . . . my own world. I might think about doing other things, travel and such, but . . ."

"Wanted to have your cake and eat it too?"

"Maybe."

"Cause that's what it's about, you know. Balance. The universe will always try to balance itself. For everything you add to your life, you give up something."

I stared straight ahead.

She said, "It's your life, and you're the only one who can choose what to keep, add to it, or let go."

Still staring ahead, I asked, "Did Merrick talk to you today?"

"No. He's friendlier now, but we aren't exactly close friends. We haven't spoken since I've been home."

Now I stared at her. "Are you sure?"

"Quite sure. And since you've showered me with suspicion, you should tell me what's going on."

"An article was published in an online magazine. It's about the metal art sculptures my dad created twenty-plus years ago."

"And?"

"I thought it was a good idea when I agreed to the interview." I shrugged, still holding the bottle, still capped. "I thought maybe it was time to see if anyone was interested in buying any of them."

"Seriously?"

"Well, where's the value in me dying and leaving his creations to be seen as curiosities or trash and hauled away for scrap metal? Or that shed . . . one day it's going to fall in on itself. It's way past its expiration date."

"What shed?"

"The shed that was a house, then a barn, and that my father enlarged and ended up using as his workshop."

"You never mentioned your father was an artisan."

I looked at her again. "Artisan."

"Great word, isn't it? So your father created art, and you're ready to sell it off?"

I gaped. "No. That sounds awful."

"Your reasons are sound."

"Nevertheless . . ."

She said, "It feels wrong?"

"No, not so much wrong as . . . misguided. Like the right question but the wrong answer." I felt like I was on the verge of spilling the whole thing out all over, but as I opened my mouth to keep speaking, she interrupted.

"So where's this article? Online? You mean on the internet? How do I find it?"

All the pent-up angst spilled out of me, pushed out by annoyance. "I don't know. Merrick showed me. Susan sent him a link in an email."

"I'll get Carina to find it for me. What's the site called?"

"The magazine?" I gave her the name. "The journalist who wrote it is Sam Markham. That might help her find it."

Miranda laughed. "Hah. Seems like I know yet another celebrity. All my friends are getting too hoity-toity for me. I'm thinking I'd better get autographs while I can."

I made a rude noise, then said, "Did I see some cookies in that cooler?"

"Yes, ma'am. Why don't you fish 'em out and we'll share."

And we did. For a little while, though nothing was resolved, it all felt a little less dire.

Before long, Davis came looking for me. He spotted me under the canopy with Miranda and walked our way.

I turned to Miranda. "I'd better go. Thanks for being concerned."

"You'll be fine. You'll always land on your feet, Lilliane. You're the most stable person I know. Not invincible, though, so be kind to yourself."

"I will."

"And who's this man coming over here? I believe I've seen him around."

I stood. "Davis McMahon. Also a writer and a friend of Merrick's. I'm sure you two have met before. Maybe at Merrick's just before I left last time?"

"Ah, yes. I believe that may be true. A brief encounter. Happy to meet you officially."

He smiled, sharing his charm with her as he took her hand and shook it gently. "Pleased to see you again."

I said, "Why don't we walk you home? Davis can bring some of your things. You look flushed."

"No . . ." She broke off, seeming to think better of it. "If you don't mind, I think yes, that would be good."

I put her tote over my shoulder. Davis emptied the melted ice water from the cooler and put it in her cart. On top of that, he put the chairs. He even dropped the canopy and fastened it on top of the load with a bungee cord. *Wow,* I thought. By the time Miranda and I had hobbled our way across the beach and reached the path, Davis was on the move. He caught up to us before the path opened at the end of the road. Merrick's house was a short distance to the left. Miranda's house was to the right. She was moving slowly and leaning on me for stability, but bearing her own weight, and I thought she was walking well. Even so, I was glad we reached the house when we did.

Carina answered the door. "Grams, I thought you were going to call me when you were ready to come back."

"No worries. Had my friends here to walk with."

Carina smiled and stepped back just enough to let her grandmother enter, then she was right there on Miranda's other side and between us she reached her chair and settled in it.

"I'll get you something to drink, Grams. Not sure you should stay out there like that anymore. I know you used to . . ." Her voice faded away.

Miranda gave me a half smile and heaved a sigh that sounded an awful lot like regret. She gripped my hand. "Do it now," she said. "Don't wait, 'cause time and opportunity are fleeting things."

I patted her hand. My hand placed on hers reminded me of Merrick's gesture earlier when we were seated in the dining room.

"I'll remember," I said. And then felt odd for having said it that way.

Davis said, "I left the wagon in the garage."

"I guess we'd better go. I kind of abandoned Merrick."

"Go, dear. I'm going to have a drink, put my feet up, and settle back in the AC and take a nap." She grinned. "There's even a right time for a snooze, and I'm about to seize the opportunity."

Carina was back, and we all said, "So long" and "See you later," and then Davis and I left, heading back to Merrick's.

# Chapter Eleven

We walked across the street and up Merrick's driveway and then around the side of the house. I punched in the gate code, and we passed into the backyard area and the pool.

Davis said, "A penny for your thoughts."

"You can have them free of charge. I'm feeling better now. It was so overwhelming to see my . . . life? Not quite that, but things precious to me . . . on a computer screen. Just goes to show how quiet my life has been." I added, "It's still overwhelming, but I think I'm over the worst shock." I laughed but not with joy—only in disbelief. "A shock? How can I even claim it was a shock? I agreed to this. I participated in it. I didn't understand the enormity of it—" I stopped abruptly, hearing my nerves revving up again.

"Maybe you're giving it more angst than you should? It was a fantastic article. No objective person can say otherwise. It's personal to you, and you're the one who'll have to deal with any ramifications, so it's totally reasonable that you're concerned. But you also have friends, and you have help. You'll be able to deal with whatever comes."

"True. But . . ."

"But?"

"I'm not sure. I'm still sorting it out in my head . . . and in my heart. Maybe it's about more than I understood when I agreed to start this . . . endeavor."

"Do you think Sam Markham might have been less than honest?"

"Not at all. When I say *more*, I mean inside myself. What I want for myself."

"Want to talk about it?"

"No, not yet." I touched his arm. "Thanks, though. It's just too new."

"At least you sound calmer."

"I am. I'm dealing with the *what-ifs* better. For the moment, anyway. Merrick said I would if I gave it time to work through my head without interfering. I guess this is what he meant."

"You haven't heard from Susan yet, have you?"

"No. Not a peep. She'll tell me when there's something to share. I'm fine with waiting because I'm rethinking the whole thing. Selling, not selling . . . I don't know. Maybe doing something altogether different. But it's time to decide, not to procrastinate."

He waited, and when I didn't say more, he said, "Let me know if you want to chat, whether to vent or to brainstorm. I'm your guy."

"Thank you. I may need your help with something, but I'm not sure how far I'm ready to dive into it. There are practical concerns too."

"Like what?"

"I was going to ask if you had any experience or knowledge about how to use cameras, but that's been preempted, I think, by the need to be better connected. I've heard people talk about cell plans and coverage areas and data limits and all sorts of words that sound like gibberish. Now, I need to learn to speak this particular gibberish."

"I can help with that."

I smiled. "I knew you could. I don't want to be pulled into getting more than I need or can afford. I don't have the kind of income that can absorb new monthly bills without having to give up something like eating or electricity. But if you would educate me about it, I'd be better able to figure out what will work best for me. For now, this is just about upgrading my phone to make it slightly more useful."

CRED

That evening, after supper, I sat out by the pool. Merrick was getting ready for bed, and it was fortunate that his drapes were light-blocking because sunsets were late this time of year. The sun was still shining brightly. Thanks to the shade under the table umbrella and with the breeze picking up the moisture from the pool, there was enough coolness to it to make it pleasant. Beaches could be hot, true, but living near one all but guaranteed an ocean breeze pretty much 24-7. Between the ocean breeze and the salt air drying out some of the humidity, it was surprisingly pleasant. And I enjoyed it, despite the magazine article and everything else on my mind.

"Lilliane."

It was Merrick. He was dressed in his pajamas and robe with the belt pulled tight, but his bony feet were bare. I got a kick out of that. He'd started ditching his slippers when I was here before. He'd joined me poolside one evening, and when I'd mentioned the missing slippers, he'd said something to the effect that I was almost always barefoot, and he'd wanted to try it for himself. Apparently, he'd kept it up. This evening, he was holding a folder. Papers were tucked inside. I sat forward, interested, thinking maybe he'd started another book after all. I was pleased about that. Would he ask me to read his early pages again?

He said, "Before Davis came over this afternoon, I asked him to perform a task for me, else he would've been here sooner, I can promise you that. My printer is good enough for most things, but I wanted you to have the best printout I could give you. I know you prefer to read paper instead of on a screen. Plus, these are handy. No wireless or electronic equipment needed." He offered me the folder. "I swore Davis to secrecy and debated with myself as to whether I should hold these until tomorrow and let you get a good night's sleep or give them to you today. You seem much calmer this evening. I thought . . . I hope that if you do want to reread the article on paper, then you might find it relaxing to do so out here. I know you like it out by the pool."

I accepted the folder from him. "Thank you." That was easy enough to say. "And you're right, paper is easier for me." I stood, holding the folder, but I didn't open it. "Would you like a snack before bed?"

He sighed. "Not tonight. It's been a very full day. I'd like to go to bed. Maybe watch some TV while I fall asleep."

"I'll put water and a snack on your nightstand, in case you want it."

I made sure that he had his alert pendant handy, and his phone was charged and within easy reach on the nightstand, then I left him, closing his door behind me. Or mostly closed. I left it open a crack, so I could more easily check on him later. I picked up the folder where I'd left it on the foyer table and returned to the pool area.

The printouts were beautiful. This was more than a simple copy machine job. Before joining me on the beach, Davis must've found a genuine print shop with some high-tech equipment to be able to get these sharp, glossy pages from a digital file. I did feel calmer this time as I read through the article, but the parts that had caused me concern about the safety of the property still worried me. I called Joe.

"Lilliane. Hey. That thing the magazine guy wrote was really cool. Nice photos too. How did I not know what was in that shed?"

"I was never much for talking about it. I guess that changed after so many years, at least a little. Plus, we weren't married very long. You moved out almost as fast as you moved in."

"Not quite, Lilliane. We lasted a little longer than that. Plus, me leaving was your idea."

"You didn't fight me too hard over it." It was all good-natured talk. Joe and I had been friends over the years since we broke up. He was always willing to lend a hand when my car needed work or something about the house needed attention. "I wanted to tell you how much I appreciate you keeping an eye on things at the house and the shed."

"Happy to help. I'm staying here tonight, and Willie's coming back in the morning, and Gwen later in the day."

"Any problems?"

"Not yet. But we'll keep an eye out. I'll never forget how fast the old Gresham house was stripped after word got out that he'd died. No family in the area. No one to watch out. Those fabulous carved mantels, the stained-glass windows . . . gone. Just gone. What was left was wrecked. I've asked myself, Why? Did people go out to see it, being curious, and then just decided to help themselves? Or was it more? There's a secondhand market, maybe, but I see all those antique and junk shops filled to the rafters, and I can't imagine . . . Never mind. All I know is that no one messed with Mr. Gresham's house until someone posted on social media about it being vacant. It was like a signal to the hounds to hunt." There was a pause while he sipped something or other. "Sheriff is sending a cruiser out here from time to time too. We'll watch the place for you, Lil. No worries. You do what you need to do. Your friends are here."

Tears were threatening again. I bit my lip to hold them back.

"You okay, Lil? You got awful quiet."

I nodded, but he couldn't see that. "I'm fine. Sorry to sound choked up. It's your fault. The fault of all y'all for being so kind. Thank you. Please let the others know how much I appreciate their help."

"Will do. Any idea when you'll be back?"

"Not yet. A few days. I need to come home again. I have things to think about."

"Well, you owe me, you know."

"What?"

"When you get home, I expect to see inside that shed before it gets all disrupted. I got a look at those photographs. That guy sure knows his way around a camera. With words, too. But I would like to see your dad's work in person."

"I promise, Joe. No one disturbs it until I give you a tour of my daddy's workshop."

"I'll hold you to that, Lilliane. And don't you worry about anything here. Just take care of business and have some fun at the beach while you can."

After we disconnected, I continued sitting at the table, feeling the tears building behind my eyes, pushing to spill out. I set my phone on top of the folder in case the breeze picked up, and then I walked into the pool, clothes and all. I went straight down the steps and out to the middle, where the water came midway up my chest. The heavier fabric of my shorts took on weight, but the rest was fine. I held my breath, flexed my knees to jump up a few inches, and then folded my legs under and sank beneath the water, almost in slow motion.

I didn't stay under long because I needed to breathe. When I rose above the surface, the water streamed from my hair over my face. I shook the wet off, brushing the drops away. I pushed my feet against the pool bottom and leaned backward with a vague idea of moving gracefully into a floating position on my back, but I didn't have that skill yet and had to laugh at myself when I sank under again and struggled to find new footing.

By now, the sun was low and the sky was painted in gaudy tones—celebratory yellows, gold, and orange, streaked throughout with violet. I stayed in the water, staring up at the sky and watching the show. And after a while of half floating there, I realized I'd totally forgotten about needing to cry.

I spread my arms wide and leaned back one more time, feeling the water cover my shoulders and soak the back of my head. Maybe this time, I thought.

And I tried again.

# Chapter Twelve

Susan called as Merrick and I were finishing breakfast. I excused myself to Merrick, saying, "I'll be back," and I walked away from the study, not seeking privacy but wanting to be free of distraction while we spoke.

As I crossed the foyer, she was saying, "The article generated interest, perhaps more to the benefit of Sam Markham than for our purpose, but I've had a couple of contacts that I'm checking out, and I'll let you know more when I know more. Also, some of the interest Sam's getting related to the article may yet translate into other things. I'll repeat what I said before—please don't change or remove anything from the workshop yet. My instinct is that the overall mystique of the works' environment will play into their marketability."

"Okay."

"Don't be disappointed, Lilliane. We weren't expecting to get eager buyers right off the bat. This is different in that we don't have a producing artist, nor do we have posthumous works of an already established artist, so for collectors or others who might be interested, it may take a little time to get sorted out. Or not." She paused for a breath. "Are you doing okay?"

"Yes, I'm fine. Merrick and my friends are very supportive."

"He told me you have friends back in Cub Creek who are watching things. I considered suggesting hiring a caretaker to stay on the property while you were gone, but sometimes a stranger in the area will attract curiosity. People may start thinking there's something valuable that's easy to steal and resell. Much better if you have friends doing it, so long as they're reliable."

"They are."

"Lilliane." Her tone sounded softer. She repeated, "Lilliane, you aren't saying much, and I can't read your tone of voice. How are you feeling? I don't want you to be discouraged. My instincts tell me this is leading somewhere. We must tend it and keep it going. Also, you aren't tied to working with me on this. I find it intriguing, and if I think of a more appropriate person who'd be willing to shepherd this, I'll recommend them to you. Meanwhile, how are you?"

Her business persona had gentled into one more personal. I suspected I was hearing the real Susan. The one who inspired such trust and loyalty from Merrick.

"I was overwhelmed at first. When I saw Sam's article yesterday, it threw me. But I've calmed down now. And frankly, I'm okay with this effort taking more time. I need to think through the best possible options."

"Excellent. Exactly the right attitude. Which leads me to another question. In the article, Sam wrote about how you helped your father with his work."

I said quickly, "In a very small way."

She continued, "Be that as it may, it's an interesting fact and a sweet image. And those smaller pieces—the ones you did when you were a kid?"

"They aren't anything special."

She didn't respond to my remark but continued speaking. "Sam was exactly right about the article concept of crossing timelines and generations. Themes of continuity across the ups and downs of life. Perhaps that's why my instincts are insisting it's important to keep things intact. I need to mull over that aspect more."

She stopped talking. Was that it? I was waiting for the next sentence. Hadn't she been building to something? Or maybe the building feeling was in my head alone.

"Actually, Susan . . . call me crazy . . . I can't even imagine that I would do this, but I was thinking I might try my hand at it again. Maybe just for old time's sake. Perhaps in memory of my parents before breaking up the collection. Is that totally off-the-wall thinking?" When she didn't respond, I said, "I'm not a kid, but then again, I hope I've got a few good decades ahead of me. But I don't feel prepared to engage with it. My dad knew how to do those things properly. I think I'd just make a fool of myself."

Susan whispered, and I struggled to hear her.

"What?" I asked. "I didn't catch that?"

She cleared her throat and spoke again, saying, "I'll be in touch."

I pressed the back of my hand to my wet lashes. All this emotional crap was getting ridiculous.

"Sure. Whatever you say, Susan. I've said it before, and I'll say it again. Thanks for your help."

She disconnected, and I stood there for a long minute, feeling that I'd lost the thread of something, of some idea, some thought, that should've had more airtime. But it was done, and I had a new motto—don't rush it. Let it grow and see what kind of crop you have before you try to harvest it. I returned to the study to collect the dishes and breakfast debris.

Merrick was finishing his toast and last sips of tea. He gave me a sharp look but didn't say anything. I thought he must be waiting for an update from the phone call. I said, "No news from Susan. And that's probably good news. She asked me to keep the works all together in the shed, to keep them as they are, and that's good with me for now. And to keep watchful eyes on the property, which is being done."

"Do you want to hire professionals to provide security?"

"No." I shook my head. "Susan and I agree about that. Bringing in strangers, whether as security or a caretaker, might actually attract more attention."

He nodded. "Let me know if you change your mind

about that."

Plates and debris loaded in my arms, I smiled. "I'm so fortunate, Merrick. So many people are trying to help me. I'm blessed in many ways." I sniffled. "Need anything else? No? Then I'll get on with the cleanup." I went to the kitchen. As I rinsed the dishes and loaded the dishwasher, thinking of all the helpful friends and goodwill I was being gifted, it occurred to me that I could do something for myself. I'd never been dependent on others for figuring things out. Tomorrow, when Ms. B was back for the day, I'd do exactly that. Take a sort of field trip. A fact-hunting expedition. About cell phones and such. Not to buy, but to find out.

"Lilliane?"

Merrick was in the doorway.

"Yes? You okay?"

"Right as rain. In fact, I feel like getting out today. You offered to drive. Still willing?"

He sounded good, but I read deception in the shifting of his eyes and the tap of his cane, which made me curious.

"Of course. Would you like to go anywhere in particular?"

"Yes. Just local. I'd like to leave in an hour."

He wasn't telling me anything more? Did it matter? Apparently not. This was Merrick's adventure, and I was the chauffeur. Okay by me. I was tired of thinking.

"I'll be ready."

"It's a date," he said.

ଔଏ

There were too many front steps, and it was hot outside, so we exited through the kitchen hallway into the garage.

I'd never actually driven anywhere with Merrick, much less with me behind the wheel. Davis had driven the two of them to my home in Cub Creek. He'd said Merrick had slept most of the trip. He wasn't sleeping today. He was in a good mood, *a rare fine humor*, as my great-aunt might've said. And I was the only member of the audience, so I got the full blast.

"Watch that curve up there, Lilliane. Slow down." He worked his imaginary passenger brake by stabbing at the floorboard with his cane.

"I've got it. Calm down. Tell me where we're going."

He all but barked, "It's a surprise. Turn left at the light and head toward the bridge. We're crossing over to Swansboro and heading a short way out into the country."

"The country?" I asked, glancing over at him.

"Keep your eyes on the road. Watch out for that car ahead. It's turning."

"I'm watching, and I know how to drive." Distracted by his warnings, I had to stop short at the light and threw my arm across his chest.

He laughed.

As we crossed the bridge with the sound glittering below us and views of the shores and marshes and docks, I tried to look and also to pay attention to the driving. Merrick had sense enough to stay quiet for at least that part.

We passed some businesses and homes, and I was wondering whether Merrick had lost his way, when he motioned for me to take a left at the next intersection, which I did. We were truly out in the country now. Homes were widely spaced. No subdivisions or businesses.

He said, "At the next crossroads, turn north, then go on for about a mile and we'll be there."

"Be where?"

He grinned, looking smug, and yet I caught in his look uncertainty. Maybe a tiny hint of worry. Second thoughts?

I asked, "Are you sure you want to do this . . . whatever it is?"

"Oh, absolutely," he said. "Even called in a last-minute favor yesterday afternoon to make it happen. Turn left at the next curve."

It was a dirt road. A driveway. Neater and better maintained than the dirt track that led to my home in Cub Creek, and the trees were fewer. There was a lot more grass, and it was neatly cut. A trim house was set well back from the road, probably built about 1910 or 1920, judging by the style. It likely looked even better now than when it was built—back when smallish farmhouses were more utilitarian than trendy. And it *had* been a farm many years ago, I was sure of that, because crops must surely have grown in those wide-open areas that were now only grass. Beyond the house, the corrugated metal roof of another building was visible.

Merrick said, "Yesterday while you were at the beach, I called a friend of a friend. He helped me with a surprise for you."

I frowned as I pulled up alongside the house and got a better view of the outbuilding. The doors were open. It was clear to see that this was a metalworking shop.

"Merrick," I said. "You didn't."

"I did." He gave me a hard look. "Just go along, please. It will cost you an hour of your life. You can decide later whether to say thank you." He was already fussing with the door handle and pushing it wide. The heat rushed in.

The man who came out to greet us was darkly tanned and muscled, and when he pulled the safety mask off his face, he looked more ordinary. And it was hot, naturally so, as was the inside of the building, but large, industrial-size fans were working overhead. They kept the air moving, which helped, but it was hot. I hadn't been in there for more than a minute when I felt the prickling of sweat forming and dripping down my spine.

Some of the smells took me back to when Dad was working metal in his shed, but the interior was totally different. Neat. Clean. Dad had been a stickler for keeping the floor—whether dirt, concrete, or wood—clear, but his table and shelf surfaces were always cluttered.

Certainly, this man's workshop was less chaotic than where my dad had done his work.

Merrick said, "Mr. Forbes? Thanks for letting us drop in last minute, so to speak."

"You're welcome. I understand you wanted to see how to work metal?"

Merrick gestured toward me. "This is Lilliane Moore. She's from Virginia. Her father worked with metal. Been gone many years. Now she's thinking of picking up where he left off. Since her father isn't around to show her the ropes, and I know nothing about it, I thought it might be helpful for her to get a look at an actual metalworking concern and to see some tools in action."

As Merrick was speaking, I'd gasped. Merrick had made a lot of assumptions based on things I hadn't even said. Had barely even had those first inklings of in my own head.

Mr. Forbes fixed me with a look of doubt and concern. My instinct was to disavow Merrick's words, but I stopped short. I *was* curious, and it was interesting to see a workshop as nice as this.

With courtesy and what I hoped was an appropriately apologetic attitude, I said, "Mr. Forbes, this visit is a surprise to me. I hope we aren't wasting your time too badly. My dad didn't do the kind of metalwork that you seem to do." I pointed toward the fabricated metal shapes and the smaller, more intricate metal items—all utilitarian and made for actual purposes. "He collected cast-off metal items and put them together to make them like art. Like metal sculptures."

Mr. Forbes nodded. Some of the concern was clearing from his face. "Sure. I know of folks who create art with metal, both inside art or bigger garden pieces. One even did a big commission, a modern metal sculpture for a nearby college."

I shrugged. "Dad's metal art sculptures have been hanging in his workshop for the past twenty years. I tried my hand at it when I was a kid." I nodded toward Merrick. "As he said, I'm thinking I might give it a try again." Mr. Forbes didn't need to know it had been a sudden thought—out of almost nowhere and barely half formed—or he'd know we really were wasting his time. I said, "When I tried it as a kid, I made a mess of it. I don't know what I need to make it work, or to do it safely."

"Don't want to be losing digits or damaging eyes."

"Exactly." I touched the worktable and the tools. Dad had some like these. Old and worn. These were not new, but certainly *newer*, and they looked more impressive. "I'm not sure how far I'll take this idea, anyway. Maybe seeing this will help me make up my mind." I smiled. "It's hot work, I can see. In fact, if you don't mind, it's really too hot in here for Mr. Dahl. He needs to be in a cooler location."

Mr. Forbes was staring at me. He squinted and seemed to be thinking on whatever was in his head, then he said, "Was that article I saw on my computer about you and your father?" He walked toward me, stripping off his gloves and holding out his hand for a shake. "I thought you looked familiar. No wonder. I was looking at it just this morning. Amazing photos." He slowed for a quick shake and then walked past me to Merrick. "Mr. Dahl, let's get you on the porch."

Merrick's face was flushed, and he was leaning heavily on his cane. He *wasn't* perspiring, which worried me. My initial thought was that the porch wasn't good enough and maybe he should wait in the car. I'd have to leave it running for the AC to work, but we weren't going to be staying too long anyway. Not with Merrick here. Not with me being so unprepared for it. But as Mr. Forbes ushered Merrick the two steps up to the porch, I realized it was an old screened porch, enclosed now with crank glass windows. They were all cranked shut, and he had an AC unit running in there.

He held Merrick's arm until he was safely seated in a rocking chair.

"I'll be right back. I'll fetch us something cold to drink."

Merrick leaned his head back and closed his eyes. He said, eyes still closed, "I'm fine. No need to make a fuss."

Mr. Forbes was back just that quick. He pressed a glass of iced tea into Merrick's hands and put another on the table near me. He returned again with plates of chocolate cake with ornate silver forks on the side. He said, "The wife broke out her secret recipe triple-chocolate cake. No sugar issues, I hope? It's a treat, for sure." He winked. "She says it's restorative." He left and returned yet again, this time with his own drink and cake.

"This is very kind of you, Mr. Forbes."

"Kirk Forbes. Please call me Kirk."

"Well, then, please call me Lilliane. Again, thanks so much for allowing us to barge in. I take it that Merrick worked this visit out somehow and we weren't a total surprise? But it was a surprise to me. Otherwise, I would've had questions prepared."

Merrick made one of his rude noises and grumbled a few slurred words under his breath. Unbelievably, I knew what he was saying. I ignored it. Maybe I would've come along or maybe I would've refused, but still, he should've warned me in advance.

Frustrated, totally forgetting our host, I said to Merrick, "How did you even know I was thinking of trying the metal art? I didn't myself until yesterday."

Between bites of cake, he said, "I knew. Saw it in your eyes right away. At my age, there's no time for delay."

"But it was *my* business, Merrick. *Mine*."

"I never mentioned you. I let them think it was me."

"You? Oh, never mind."

Mr. Forbes—Kirk—was looking back and forth between us.

"I apologize for the two of us, Kirk. We sound like squabbling children. Merrick is my friend. He means well."

He waved his fork at me. "I *am* your friend."

Kirk's cake was still on his plate, untouched. He asked,

"Tell me about your father, what he made and what you're thinking you might want to do." He smiled. "And then we'll talk about what I can do for you."

Merrick set his fork on the plate. "I'm going to put my head back and take a nap. Feel free to take your conversation back out to the workshop when you're done eating. And, Lilliane, mind you go fill up your head with information. You have to fuel your brain, get it started thinking, so you can make well-grounded decisions."

⊂⊰⊱⊃

Kirk and I walked through his workshop. He told me about the jobs he was working on, which were very much about crafting metal items from scratch, so we spent more time talking about safety measures and modern tools and such. At first, I felt like an imposter, but Kirk broke out the patience, just as his wife had broken out the to-die-for chocolate cake, and he made me feel welcome. He asked about my father and his artwork, but his patience was accompanied by good manners and he didn't stray into personal matters.

"I should get Merrick home. Even though your porch is air-cooled, it's still stressful for him. He doesn't get out as much now."

"You work for him?"

"I do, yes, but we were friends almost from the day we met."

"I thought you were his daughter or granddaughter."

"No relation."

"How old is he?"

"Ninety."

"Wow. Don't think I'll make it that long. At least not in that good a condition."

I smiled. "I feel the same. I guess it comes down to genetics and luck."

"Maybe. Feel free to come back anytime. I'll give you a go at the machines and the tools."

"Thank you so much."

As we exited the workshop, he said, "It was my friend Tom who asked me to do a favor for a friend of his. He didn't say much else and never mentioned the article or Mr. Dahl or any of that. Pure chance that I happened to see the write-up this morning. I was checking email and a few professional metal sites I track. I get their newsletters, and one of them mentioned a man, a recluse who lived in the woods, who'd left some outstanding metalworks behind for his beautiful daughter to inherit and gave the link to the article." He waved his hand. "Not my words. Not intending to be brash. Just stating what the newsletter said. That's part of why I was confused. I mean, there you came, walking into my workshop almost straight off the internet. I saw your resemblance to the woman in the article right off the bat." He shook his head. "My wife calls such coincidences serendipity."

I knew I was blushing, but I also knew he couldn't tell my blush from the overheated flush. "Thank you, Kirk. Excuse me while I get the car started. I'll get the AC running to cool the car off, and then I'll join you on the porch and collect Merrick."

Merrick was contentedly sipping tea and chatting with a woman who was porch-sitting with him. I assumed she was Kirk's wife. I thanked her for the tea and cake, and together we escorted Merrick out to our car. With waves shared all round, we drove away.

"Well?" Merrick asked.

"Well what?"

"You know. Don't be stubborn. Was it a good idea or not? Did it help you think about future options instead of focusing on present worries?"

"It has made me realize that you enjoy playing fairy godmother. I'm going to get you a sparkly wand for your birthday."

He grunted. I expected a rude remark, but he said, "Glitter. I want feathers and glitter on it."

I looked over and saw the wide grin on his wrinkled face.

He said, wagging a finger at me, "Hey, keep your eyes on the road."

# Chapter Thirteen

At home, I settled Merrick into his chair in the study and left him to nap while I washed up and then fixed our supper. For tonight, Ms. B had left a dish of pasta, a container of marinara sauce, and her special-recipe meatballs. I found a head of romaine lettuce in the fridge and made us a fresh salad to go along with the entrée. I was cooking when Davis called.

"Hello!" I said.

"You're back from your field trip?"

"We are. Did you know what he was up to?"

Davis said, "Only sort of."

"Humph. I could've used some warning."

"I'm on my way over. You can get even in person."

"Oh, so you're hoping to mooch some supper off us, are you?" I laughed. "It's Ms. B's meatballs. If you haven't had them before, you're in for a treat." I added, "Use your key and come in quietly. Merrick is napping—or he'd better be."

"I'll come straight around back. See you in five."

CR80

Over supper, Davis talked about the book tour plans.

"Lilliane, they're checking with me about cities I'd like to visit. The publisher's marketing group. Can you believe it?"

"It sounds fabulous."

Merrick said, "Book tours aren't as common as they used to be. This must be a big deal to them."

"They're billing the tour as 'the thriller trio.' Not those

exact words. That's all still being worked up. There'll be the three of us. It's an honor to be included. It'll be timed around the release of my book and, of course, the releases of the other authors. *And*," he added with emphasis, "promoting the future release of Merrick Dahl's newest novel and '*his journey from thriller to heart*' in *The Book of Lost Loves*."

"Wow," I said, excited. I stood and clapped. Merrick and Davis were grinning and congratulating each other.

Davis had mentioned the names of the other authors. One was a genuine best-seller with a solid track record and movies to his credit. Both authors were known to me because I'd seen their names at the library and in ads. Apparently, the publisher was rushing Davis's book to press to ensure it was available during the tour. Per both of them, this was almost unheard of. It truly was a huge opportunity for Davis. I was excited for him, but along with that came lesser feelings. Less worthy stirrings. Maybe even a little jealousy. I pushed those low feelings away. I tried to think of fun things to say, even though I knew nothing about book tours and European cities.

One day I *would* know, I told myself. In fact, a blogger out there in the online metalworking world had called me beautiful, right? Had noted my father's amazing works of art. If that could happen, then almost anything was possible. And then my spirits truly did lift. I laughed along with my friends and made all the right noises, because for Merrick, this was an excitement long delayed. The delight on his face as he and Davis bounced ideas around was undeniable.

Merrick might not be able to travel with the others in person, but he'd certainly be there in spirit. And while we'd miss Davis, Merrick and I could, and would, share the fun from a distance.

CS&SO

After we'd cleared away the supper dishes, Davis and I

walked outside. We went down along the crossover as far as the high point and leaned side by side against the railing, enjoying the sweet salt breeze, the soft evening light, and each other's company.

"Lilliane," he said, taking my fingers. "I'm sorry I'm so focused on all this writing stuff, with book tours and deadlines and commitments to keep. It's what I've wanted, have worked for and hoped for, but I wish it wasn't taking away from the time we could be spending together."

"I understand. I'd like to see more of you, but truly, I have obligations and distractions too. I get it."

"I have to fly back up to New York for a few days."

"New York? Publisher meeting again?"

"Yes, though this one has to do with Merrick's book."

My smile was heart-filled this time. "The one you wrote together?"

He shook his head. "The one the three of us wrote together."

"My part was only to offer advice, but I appreciate being included."

"Susan asked me to meet with the editor. Susan gets the credit for cooking up this joint book tour combining the newest releases and upcoming releases with Merrick's publisher." He had a moment in which his face lit up as he added, "My publisher too."

"Are you good with sharing the tour?"

"Absolutely. I'm lucky to be part of it. I don't have the kind of author chops that can drive a tour like this. Maybe one day, but not yet. As for Merrick, he can't be there in person, but having his name connected to mine in that way can only be helpful." He grinned. "You'll miss me, I hope. And I'll miss you more than I can say."

He put his arms around me. I leaned against him, and then my head was resting on his shoulder. His position shifted. He was going to kiss me. The moonlight drove out practical concerns and worries about the future, and the nearby waves danced to a timeless rhythm. Davis drew me close and pressed his lips to mine, and I was glad.

And yet, the kiss, his arms, the moon peeking at us along the horizon . . . felt right but also wrong at the same time. I understood Davis was exhilarated and that this, for him, was a celebration. I returned his embrace and his kiss, but for me, it felt bittersweet. New York. European book tours. The world was pulling him away, and I felt pulled in a whole different direction. It was as if I'd asked too much of fate, had found my happiness basket nearly full and grabbed for it too greedily, heedlessly, and now fate was about to start taking some of the good stuff back.

But why? Why must I feel that way? That feeling of . . . loss when I'd lost nothing?

Perhaps Davis sensed that sadness in me, because he lifted his head. Only inches separated our faces. I saw a question in his eyes. I put my hand to his cheek and guided his lips back to mine. Regardless of whatever else was on my mind—obligations, responsibilities, economic realities, and even fear of stepping out too far beyond the world I knew— I wasn't ready to say goodbye to him or to any of the craziness in my life just now. I would hang on to the good for as long as I could.

# Chapter Fourteen

That evening, with Davis gone and Merrick in bed, I sat at the table near the pool. I was tired. Merrick had been tired too. In fact, he'd seemed so weary that I'd stayed in his study, waiting just outside his bedroom while he donned his pajamas and rinsed his teeth and such. He didn't want my help with that, and I tried to respect his privacy and his vanity as much as I could, but if he fell or just ran into difficulties, I wanted to be within earshot. When he stuck his head out the door, barking, "I'm almost done. You don't need to loiter out there like impending doom is about to strike me down at any moment."

"Sleep well, Merrick," I said, rising from my chair. "I'll be out by the pool for a while before going up to bed myself. Call if you need me."

I stopped in the kitchen along the way to grab a tall glass of iced tea. I took two of the chairs from the poolside table and moved them out from under the overhang so that I could sit in one and prop my feet up in the other. I rested my head against the back of the seat and watched the stars appear overhead.

Discouragement seemed to overlay everything.

Nothing had gone as I'd expected—not with the idea of finding galleries or art collectors interested in my father's work, and not with the article. Despite that article causing me extreme angst, it seemed to be yielding no results, and now my thoughts were going rogue. My brain was trying to take me in a whole new direction. The originally desired results seemed to be morphing into something very different.

Metalworking, indeed. As Merrick sometimes said, *Bah*.

I looked at my hands. My nails were nice, though not professionally manicured. For someone approaching forty, these hands with their deceptively long, slim fingers were surprisingly capable. But could these hands work metal? Was I strong enough to force my will upon such tough objects?

Listening to Davis talk about his book tour was stirring up my lifelong dream of traveling. The idea of buying an actual, genuine suitcase and a ticket to somewhere fun was tempting me away from what I should be thinking about.

I couldn't afford to travel. I couldn't afford much, and certainly not that. Again, discouragement. I didn't get this way often—maudlin, as Aunt Molly would have said. Or maybe *dissatisfied* was a better word. I'd learned long ago that when reality and possibilities conflicted, it was best to focus on the present and the tasks at hand.

When my phone rang, I grabbed for it.

Joe said, "Lilliane, everything's fine."

Which meant that everything *wasn't* fine.

"What happened?"

"Well . . . nothing happened, exactly. I figured you'd want to know that two different cars pulled up in your driveway today. I went out to the porch, but they took off before I could ask what they wanted."

I was almost too spent to care. "Maybe the GPS satellites have gone crazy and are routing the folks driving to Lake Anna through my yard." I offered a weak laugh.

"You sound tired."

"I am, Joe. Bone weary."

"I been there myself, but not tonight. Keeping a sharp eye out here. Maybe you don't want to hear the rest. We can save it for tomorrow or the next day."

"Hear what, Joe?"

"So you *do* want to know . . ."

141

He was stretching it out to get even with me for making light of the news he'd already delivered. "Just say it."

"Bobby Harrin showed up."

"Bobby Harrin?" That *was* bad news. He'd never come to my house before. At least, not that I knew of. Couldn't necessarily know for sure when it came to the Harrins, since they rarely announced themselves. "And?"

"Behaved himself. Could see he was curious, though. Tried to joke me into letting him see inside the shed. I didn't, of course, but I could see him thinking—his brain gears churning. Almost like they got calculators working in their heads, the Harrins. Never a good thing. He hung out for a while and then left. Raised my hackles. No worries for you because we're keeping a close eye on things, but those Harrins . . . no one wants to be on their radar."

"Thank you, Joe. Must be time for me to come home."

"Not necessarily. I mean, what are you gonna do with Bobby that I can't? Even Gwen intimidates him more than you do. She was here checking on things when Bobby arrived. I admit that seeing his reaction to her being there gave me a laugh later. Anyway, Willie has given the sheriff's office a heads-up. We've got it handled here."

"Thank you, again. But it's not fair to any of you. Not fair at all. I was planning to leave here at the end of the week, but I can move that up."

"Don't, Lilliane. Let us do this for you."

After a long pause, I said, "I'll be home by the end of the week. Do please call me if anything, however small, triggers that Spidey sense of yours. I trust you, Joe."

As I disconnected, I sighed, feeling torn between here and home. The geography and the memories of it all, but also missing my friends. Either way I went, I'd miss friends.

Merrick cleared his throat. I looked up. He was standing in the doorway.

"Did you hear?" I asked, feeling resigned to the inevitability of leaving . . . but it bothered me when

Merrick's decline was so worrisome.

He stepped forward carefully, relying more than ever on his cane. I dropped my feet from the chair and gestured to him to sit. The fatigue in his face eased as he sank into the cushions.

"Who is Bobby Harrin?"

"Local guy, local family. If something walks away, folks tend to think of them first. I've never had a problem with them. But—and I'll admit it freely—I find them, and Bobby's interest, somewhat alarming. When you talk to them, there's a look in their eyes, as if they are always sizing up opportunities."

"Susan would be willing to hire security for the workshop."

"She would. But I still don't think it's the thing to do. She and I agree that strangers coming and going and hanging around my property would spark curiosity, and even some . . . hard feelings . . . over me, a local gal, feeling the need to bring in paid security and, again, strangers. Outsiders."

He nodded. "I don't want to see you leave, but I do understand. You could go home to Cub Creek for a few days to check on things."

"Might need to be more than a few days, Merrick. I can't continue to impose on my friends this way. They have their own full lives."

"They don't mind helping. Allowing people to help . . . they get a lot out of it too. You should remember that."

I smiled. "I'm generally very independent."

"Yes," he said. "But why? It's very selfish, you know. Not letting others in."

"Says you."

"Takes one to know one, right?"

"Amen to that."

"So." He said the word loudly and with emphasis. "Therefore, I'll be adult about letting you go, but you must agree to do something for me first."

"What? You know you don't need to bargain for my help with anything."

"Davis is going to take you to one of those phone stores. He's going to get you a new phone—a fancy one that will do everything and do it fast."

"I can't afford that."

"You can. It will be on my phone plan. I have lines available on my plan that aren't being used. You won't be able to tell the difference, nor will I. It'll be like having your own account, except it won't cost you anything. I won't have access to your conversations or anything. It's like a family plan. I'll feel good to be getting better use of what I'm already paying for."

I stared at him, thinking. "It would be good to have a better phone plan for communicating."

"And photos. It'll be almost as good as a nice camera. You can send me photos and texts. No data limits." He paused, perhaps in case I'd respond. When I didn't, he added, "The phone is my gift to you. That's the favor you're giving me. The cost of the service is nil. The phone will be my gift. Davis will take you so that you won't try to get by with a lesser product. He wants to go tomorrow before he leaves town again."

"Okay." I agreed mostly because I didn't know what else to say. I told myself I was committing only to shopping for a phone with Davis. Like that fact-finding mission I'd already planned. As to whether we'd purchase it? That would be a whole other question. I didn't want to argue with Merrick. Not about this. Not about his generous, thoughtful gesture.

"Excellent." He grunted. "Better for me to keep in touch with you."

I smiled. "Not about me? It's for your convenience?"

"Of course," he said with more energy than before. "Also for Susan. If she gets new interest from someone about the metal art sculptures, she needs to be able to reach you reliably."

"About that . . . ," I said. "I may be reassessing things."

"Of course. You are thinking of doing some of that metal art yourself, but one doesn't preclude the other."

"Actually, I'm thinking that the sudden yen I had to pick up where Dad left off is foolishness."

"You think our little field trip yesterday was a mistake?"

"No." I shook my head. "On the contrary—seeing Mr. Forbes's workshop opened my eyes. Made me think. I'm almost forty. If I'd really wanted to craft metal or anything else, I've had two decades to get around to it. And I haven't even thought of it until now. I think that what I'm experiencing is basic, bare-bones procrastination. My brain is telling me to think about this shiny object over here because I'm stalled on the shiny object I should be resolving now. Before I go off on tangents, I need to either empty the shed and hang the metal art elsewhere—in my house or wherever—or give it up altogether and burn the shed down."

He frowned. His bushy eyebrows met in the middle and stayed there. "What?"

"You were so quiet while I talked on and on that I wondered if you were dozing off. And no, I'm not going to burn down anything. But it's time to act or to walk away. Going home . . . it will give my friends a break from watching the place, and it will also give me a chance to reassess now that a little time has passed."

"Makes sense." His expression eased, and he laughed softly. "A reminder to you: I was almost forty when my real life began. Everything that came before—*everything*—whether it was chasing women or getting what I thought was the perfect job or lucking into a publisher who wanted to take on that first novel, and even all the experiences and the novels that came while I was living for the next big thing, was no more than preparation for, the realization and acceptance of the life I was meant to live." He shook his head. "It wasn't all perfect. I made missteps. You already know some of them, like my regret over not fighting harder for my marriage, but if you must deal with heartaches and other troubles, then it's much better to deal with it as your true self—not as someone trying to live out other people's ideas of what makes a successful life."

I looked aside. There was truth in what he said. But did it apply to me? My brain hurt. Too many questions. Too many doubts.

"I need a snack. What about you?"

He nodded. "You are right, Lilliane, as you so often are. Heady, philosophical discussions always drain the calories— as does being chased by worries or other wild animals. A snack would be welcome, and then I must get my beauty sleep."

# Chapter Fifteen

The next day, after Ms. B arrived, Davis took me to the store. I tried to put aside my discomfort about the phone and the cost of it. I told myself that it took humility to accept a gift, especially an expensive one, and that I needed this and Merrick wanted to be able to reach me more easily. He wanted photos and texts and all the stuff I wouldn't or couldn't do with my current phone and plan, he said.

As with the reliable rental car, this phone made it possible for me to be more accessible to Merrick.

Also, I ended up with a new number, so I spent a fair amount of time calling my friends to give them the number and to update the ones who needed to know about my plans.

Susan said, "I have someone lined up to come in the day after tomorrow to stay with Merrick. I'm sorry I don't have anything firm as far as the metal sculptures. I do hope you'll keep the collection intact in the shed. I believe the right collector will come along. The article is still circulating, and I heard Markham has been approached for another opportunity related to it. I'll ask him about that when he calls. My point is that the word is still getting out there."

"It's okay, Susan. I truly appreciate your efforts on this."

"Seriously, Lilliane, big things don't happen quickly. There's always a lot more going on behind the scenes, sometimes for years, than anyone can guess. Overnight success is rarely overnight. And if it is, then it's most likely a flash in the pan and will die out as quickly as it occurred."

"I understand."

"You mentioned you might have additional plans for the metalworking?"

I sighed. "I was thinking about it, yes, but I don't really see it happening. The idea came to me in one lunatic moment born out of overexcitement about the article and the fear of next steps."

"Go home and clear your head. Sometimes a person needs to be in place—in that place that most concerns the problem—to think realistically. It's easy to indulge in abstract terms when you're removed from the situation. Being home can orient you." She added, "And when you're ready to come back to the beach, just come. You don't have to come as an employee or a contractor or a temporary worker. You can come as a friend. Merrick will always be happy to see you. I think you know that, but I wanted to make sure there was no doubt."

❦

*No place like home*—it was a truism that had always been true for me.

Three weeks gone since I'd left Cub Creek for Emerald Isle, and less than a week since the article was published, not to mention that Davis and I had moved our friendship forward with a kiss under the moon, yet the homeplace looked exactly like the homeplace had looked forever. For the generations I'd known it, anyway. A few changes had happened along the way, like how Dad had enlarged the barn/shed/workshop. But nothing big. Nothing that altered the essential fabric of this place that had been and was still home to me. Even the people, including loved ones, came and went. But I always returned.

This time the small difference was Joe sitting on my front porch and I glimpsed Willie's dog secured to a big shade tree in the backyard. Both seemed content and unbothered. The dog howled once as I drove up to park next to Joe's truck. Joe saw me, waved, and left the porch rocker to join me at my car and help carry my belongings in. Not that I'd taken all that much. More than the first time I'd gone to Emerald Isle, for sure. My baggage was expanding, along with the rest of my life.

Joe surprised me by not even mentioning the rental car I was driving. He'd known about it, of course, because my own car was parked in its usual spot, and it had a few leaves stuck to the roof and hood, testifying that it had been here, parked, for the whole time I was gone. The rental car company was coming to pick up the vehicle late today or tomorrow, but Joe didn't know that. Joe was a car guy. Yet he said not a word about it, so I wondered what was on his mind.

"Hey, Lil. Good to see you." He offered a friendly hug and took the bags from my hands. "All's well here."

"No trouble?"

"None. So you think you'll be selling the . . . the what do you call them? Sculptures? What?"

We went into the house, and Joe set my bags down at the foot of the stairs.

"I always called them metal art. I guess they are like sculptures because they aren't flat like paintings, but they hang on the wall instead of standing on the floor like a statue."

"Got it."

I knew he wanted to see in the shed, and he'd earned it. I'd never allowed him in there during the brief time we were married. I'd told him it was full of my parents' and grandparents' stuff and had no room for anything else. Maybe it had been that way with my heart too.

"Want to take a look inside?"

"I do."

"Then let's go."

He went into the shed—into Dad's workshop—and looked around. I waited at the door. Every so often he'd spot something, a common item, perhaps, that he knew from working on cars and other things, and he'd point and exclaim and maybe even laugh a little—but he was quick to point out that he was laughing in amazement that someone could take such random objects and turn them into art. "Oh yeah, it's art, for sure. Never mind the other words like *metal* and *sculpture* and such. It's art." He joined me back at the doorway and stared at the propellers in front of us. "What are you going to do with all this?"

I shrugged. "I'm not sure. I thought that if there was a reputable collector who was interested, I might work something out with him. So far—nothing. We might not find anyone like that, and if we do, I might get cold feet. So I don't know. But I *do* know that it's good to be back home."

"You want to keep the dog with you?"

In the end, I said no to the dog. I had no experience caring for animals, much less a big, burly, hairy mess like Bear. Though I did wonder if I was making the right choice.

Nope, I told myself, I'd never needed a guard dog before. This was still my home. Still Cub Creek.

"I fixed your floodlight in the back."

"I have the kitchen door light."

"Not good enough. I shimmied up that light pole and fixed what was broke and ran a new line out too. Better coverage, in case you truly do need to see out here at night."

"Was anyone messing around here after dark?"

"No, though the dog did get agitated a few times. Could've been raccoons or coyotes. I looked around and couldn't see anything."

I locked the shed door, and Joe loaded Bear and his house and supplies into his truck. I was almost sorry to see Joe leave. I'd never minded a solitary life, but more and more I just felt alone. And he was good company. He wasn't Davis, of course. But Joe was less worrisome romance-wise, and he was handy too.

He watched me through the rolled-down truck window, with Bear panting in the passenger seat beside him. "What are you smiling about, Lilliane?"

"Nothing. Just thinking that you're a good friend."

"Always, Lil."

I stepped back from the truck and waved. He returned my wave and drove off.

I sat in the chair by the firepit and called Merrick. I reported I'd made it home without any trouble.

"Thanks again for the phone," I said. "It's very nice."

"My pleasure. I appreciate you accepting the gift so gracefully."

"It's your turn to do the same. Which of the metal art sculptures would you like? I'll give you a few days to decide, but when I come back to visit you, I'm bringing it with me." I added, "As a gift. And I'll expect you to accept that gracefully too."

I wasn't doing anything drastic quite yet, but the shed's unbroken timeline was about to be disturbed. In addition to the one I was giving Merrick, I was going to hang one of Dad's works in my own house. Maybe more than one. No more waiting.

We chatted a little longer and then disconnected.

Alone, with only the breeze ruffling the leaves and birdsong in the air, I returned to the workshop and unlocked it. Inside, pushing the phone buttons just as Davis had showed me, I recorded my own video, like those *before* and *after* ads you see in commercials. This was only *before*, of course. I wasn't sure what *after* would look like, so it was all the more important to capture the before *now*—before I moved on to *next*.

I walked around the main room, taking video of the walls and tabletops, then I circled the center work area and the P-51 in the front. Lastly, I videoed the small room, focusing in on the metal that had been relegated here by Momma. I sat in Momma's chair in the main workshop area, and as the day's light dimmed, I watched the videos and even shed a tear or two. I could never have done anything like this with my old phone.

I'd come back tomorrow and talk while I recorded the videos, telling about them and throwing in some memories.

These were just for me. I was documenting my memories to be able to view them again in years to come . . . after things had changed.

After full dark, I tested Joe's floodlight. It lit up the backyard in stark relief like a circus ring where the opening performance was about to commence.

Heck, the neighbors from a mile away would see it through the trees and come to investigate. I switched it off, leaving only the lesser light burning by the kitchen door.

The night was warm but not too humid, so I left my bedroom windows open and enjoyed the familiar scents. I stood with the old lace curtains pushed aside and looked out at the shed bathed in moonlight. In the night, with the details altered by shadow and the colors drained, I could almost make out how the old log house must've looked on its stone foundation, how my forbears had turned it into a barn and my grandfather had kept it patched up over the years, how my father had added to it for his own purposes. So much history. But in all honesty, I was the only one who cared about what had gone before.

When I was gone, it would matter to no one. Folks would say, *"Remember that woman? The one with the crazy parents? Nice enough people, really, and their daughter was a smart gal but could never bring herself to leave home."* They'd shake their heads and add, *"Such a pity."*

Enough. I would hear no more imagined voices tonight.

I allowed the curtains to fall back into place and turned to go to bed. I was a little on edge but truly didn't expect any trouble, but with the window open, I'd be able to hear noises. I'd never worried about sleeping here alone before, and I wasn't precisely worried about it now, but I was wondering if maybe I should've kept that dog.

# Chapter Sixteen

The next morning, my front door was open as it often was in the morning before the day's heat built up. My screened door kept out the flies and such—and gave a false sense of security, since that was *all* it could keep out. Even an excited puppy could push through that screening without a problem. A raccoon, if he wanted to come inside, wouldn't be deterred in the least, so maybe that's why I was listening in the background. When I heard a car driving up, I assumed it was Gwen dropping by for a chat, but when I reached the screened door, I didn't recognize the vehicle.

The small pickup truck stopped short of driving right up to the house and sat parked there on the dirt drive for a long minute. I couldn't see who it was through the windshield, but it looked like a couple of somebodies were in there, and what movement I *could* see indicated a conversation was happening.

I kept my hand on the door but held off opening it. I was imagining this, of course, but I could guess that conversation was going one of two ways. Maybe a wife was telling her hubby that he should've looked at the map 'cause he'd taken a wrong turn somewhere, in which case they'd either turn around in front of the house and drive away, or they might knock on the obviously open door and ask for directions. The alternative was that they were curiosity seekers. They'd driven to the end of my dirt road, seen the car, realized someone was home, and paused to discuss it. If their purpose was innocent, they'd likely see the open door and a person standing behind the screen watching them. They'd come up to the house and explain politely what they wanted or needed. If their purpose was less than honorable . . . then they'd do exactly what this car did. It backed away. Didn't come closer to the house lest I get a better look at them. Nope, they backed down that narrow, rutted road and around the curve, and they were gone.

I could've hopped in my car and chased after them, but there was no value in that. They hadn't technically done anything wrong. In fact, I could've imagined more drama in what occurred than the actual act deserved. Maybe it had been nothing more than two people who took a wrong turn while driving through the country.

Reluctantly, I closed the front door and locked it. At the kitchen door, I looked out. No one was in the yard, of course. I was a little edgy. This was a good reminder, though, not to take peace for granted.

I picked up my cell phone and called Joe.

He answered, asking, "Everything okay?"

"Everything's fine. I was thinking, though, that maybe I could borrow Willie's dog again. Do you think he'd mind?"

"What *aren't* you telling me?"

"Nothing. Well, except someone must've got lost because they drove partway up to the house then stopped and backed out. Gave me pause."

"Probably nothing. I'll talk to Willie. One or the other of us'll bring Bear out this afternoon, if that works?"

"Thank you."

"One thing I should tell you. I didn't leave it on purpose, but maybe it's a good thing. I left my shotgun on top of the cabinet in the kitchen. It's not loaded. The shells are in a box on top of the fridge."

"You can come get it when you bring the dog."

"Think on it, Lilliane. You're a good shot. Don't use it if you don't need to, but it's good to have options."

"No, Joe. I know what you're saying, but that's not my way."

"Well, that's that, then. I'll see you later."

CR80

When Joe arrived, he had Bear in the front seat with him. The dog had his nose stuck out of the half-down window. He was so huge, his black furry self filled the opening. Joe drove on around to the backyard, but carefully, because the trees and bushes in the side yard made vehicle access tricky. I met him out there. When he opened the door, Bear jumped down without hesitation. He sniffed at my feet and then trotted around the yard, smelling everything as if he thought he was a bloodhound paid to pick up a scent. Hoping to, maybe. Meanwhile, Joe dropped the truck gate and lifted the doghouse out. He carried it over to the same huge, shady tree that Bear had camped under before.

"His dishes and food are in the blue plastic tub," he said, and carried it over to the back porch.

He introduced Bear to me again, and then the two of them took a quick walk around the shed, even in the back where the brush was thick and prickly. Joe pronounced it all good, secured Bear's line around the trunk of the tree, and left. Bear lifted his head to watch Joe go, but otherwise he didn't seem interested.

His line was long but not too long. I wanted to scare away trespassers but not injure them. Biting would get Bear in trouble and cause me headaches too.

I pulled one of the chairs by the firepit over within Bear's reach, and I sat there. He eyed me, almost interested. I called Gwen while I was sitting there so Bear would get used to my scent and to the sound of my voice.

"Hey, I'm back, and I wanted you to know I still have Willie's dog in the yard, just in case you decide to stroll around back. I don't think he'd hurt you, but he might give you a scare."

"He's fierce looking, but mostly a sweetheart." Gwen

laughed. "Like a teddy bear. *Bear*. Get it?"

"I get it, but I have to correct you. Willie didn't train him for cute and cuddly."

"I'll remember that and stay on his good side." She changed the subject. "So you're back. I got your text and your change of phone number. How is Merrick?"

"He's well. Showing his age, I guess."

"And your Davis?"

"*My* Davis?" I laughed this time. "He's good. As thoughtful as ever." I would *not* be mentioning the kiss.

"Oh."

"Oh, what?"

"I expected more romantic words."

I let that pass. "I have more pressing concerns right now."

"Offers?"

"No. Nothing has materialized. It's okay, though. At least we tried, right? Now, I need to make some decisions."

"You know I'm a willing listener if you want to chew things over."

"I do know that. Thank you, Gwen."

"Thank *you*, Lillie, for letting me have a small part in it. I've loved being involved. If you need anything, you know where to find me."

We disconnected soon after. Bear seemed utterly content. I shifted his food and water dishes to move them a little more out of the way of the leash, and then I went back into the house.

I wasn't used to having a dog to care for. I could see how a guard dog—or even a loud dog—could be handy, but I didn't know what my future looked like. How could I adopt a dog? For that matter, how could I commit to anyone? Man or dog?

With Bear on the job, I decided I could leave for a quick run to the grocery store. It was a few miles to Mineral—the closest town with a grocery store—so *quick* was relative, but

I went straight there and back, and all was well when I returned.

*Relax, Lilliane,* I told myself. *Don't read* bad *into every odd moment. Don't let your worries about what's next make you see portents of disaster.* And that thought gave me a chuckle. I'd forgotten that was Granny's word. *Portents.* I loved the drama that word came packaged with, especially if you said it right, drawing it out, raising your hands and opening your eyes wide as you did.

In fact, that reminded me I hadn't done a storytelling hour at the library in forever. I'd called a few people with my new phone number and texted others, but I'd missed telling Debra at the library about my new number or that I was back. I would take care of that right away. In the end, I had to leave a message. But that was fine. I'd be running over there in the next day or so anyway for other purposes.

⚮

In the night, I woke. I lay there, listening to the night, to the sound of leaves rustling. Distant thunder. And then a metal rumbly sound and Bear barking. A few short barks and then a low growl—likely with raised and bristling hackles. The sound certainly *raised me* straight out of bed. I was down the stairs and in the kitchen almost before I knew I was moving. I remembered Joe's shotgun in that moment, but I didn't stop to climb up for it. Instead, I found the broom handle with one hand as I hit the floodlight switch with the other.

# Chapter Seventeen

Barefoot in the dirt, artificial light bright around me, and with Bear dancing as if ready to give chase, I yelled as loud and mean as I could, "I'm gonna unleash this animal, and you're about to be chased through the woods. This is your head start. Run now and don't come back. Next time, I'll be holding a shotgun instead of a broom."

The anger and adrenaline—and fear—made my voice fierce. I'd given it full rein, and to make good my threat, I walked carefully over to Bear after making sure he knew I was one of the good guys and grabbed his leash, taut despite the length, and moved my hand toward the catch on his collar. His growl was still low and directed toward an area beyond the shed, which made me fairly certain that no one was sneaking up behind me. But despite the threat, I didn't turn him loose. How could I? It might not even be a human. A real bear might've brushed against the metal on the side and made that thunder sound. Not wild dogs, though, because I'd hear them making those whiny, squeaky noises. Someone's pet could've gotten out for the night, of course, but I didn't put much stock in that because Bear likely wouldn't have gotten so het up over a cat or a terrier.

I heard nothing. No one running away through the woods. Nothing that sounded like anything, except for an angry woman and an excited dog out here breaking the peace of the night.

Bear had stopped growling. I knelt beside him and gave him a pat on his back, called him *good boy* and *brave dog* as I thanked him for watching out for me and my home. When

I stood, he went over to his water dish and all but emptied it quenching the thirst he'd worked up. That was good. It told me that whatever threat there'd been had most certainly passed.

I refilled Bear's water dish and decided to leave the floodlight on for the rest of the night. That light poured in through my open window and annoyed me. Probably bothered Bear too, but it couldn't be helped. Not for tonight, anyway.

Lying there in the spoiled darkness, I was thinking that if not for Bear's bark, I wouldn't have thought twice about those noises. Noises like that? I'd heard them countless times through the years. Noises that, in the past, I would've caught with half an ear, rolled over, and gone on sleeping.

Almost forty years on this earth—I'd had overwhelming loss when my parents died, and I'd had heartbreak and guilt when I realized I'd made a huge mistake in marrying Joe out of loneliness and we'd divorced. For the first time, though, I felt the loss of innocence. Of a simple, taken-for-granted good night's rest. Because now, because of my actions, I'd invited in the outside world. Whether any evildoers had been out there tonight or not, I'd introduced that possibility into my life.

I raised my hand into the stream of light and examined how the shadows fell around the bones and muscles of it. So much like my mother's hand that I'd held when we walked through the hills or in town. Like my father's hand, as he'd repaired equipment and created his art. And I heard my father's voice from long ago as I was deciphering the mysteries of an old map, asking him what those lines and marks actually looked like in person. I'd asked him if we might go and see. He'd told me we'd stay right here at home where we already had the best of all worlds with each other, together at Cub Creek.

*The best of all worlds together*, he'd said. And maybe he was right. But then again, he'd left. Left our home. Left me. He and Momma had both left. Together. And they'd gone without notice and without me.

I dropped my hand back to the coverlet and clutched the folds.

Mistake or not, and even if I'd never exposed my personal family business out there for the curiosity of others, stuff would change. Time drove change. No one could hold on to one good moment and expect it to last a lifetime.

I couldn't go backward.

And wouldn't, even if I could.

Whatever was going to come next . . . I needed to own that.

.

# Chapter Eighteen

The next morning, with Bear fed and watered and happily sprawled in the shade of the tree, I was back in the workshop, recording videos. This time, I talked as I walked along, recalling my childhood, my parents, and memories of my father crafting the metal art. I was trying to be thorough because this was my first step in preparing to take down the metal sculptures from the walls. At a minimum, I'd be choosing one for Merrick and one for the house.

Why not? Right?

I was circling the P-51 Mustang, the *Cadillac of the Skies*—thank you for the education, Sam Markham—and telling the story of how Dad came to have it and of him trying to collect other parts to expand it, when Bear began making soft chuffing noises. Low sounds. I paused the video when he barked. But it was only one bark.

From the doorway, I saw that very same man, Sam Markham, squatting in front of my borrowed guard dog with his hand extended and Bear sniffing his fingers. The dog backed up a step and gave another bark, a rather friendly one.

"Seriously?" I asked. "You're corrupting my protector?"

Sam looked up and flashed me a smile. He gave Bear a pat on the head and stood. He faced me directly, but didn't move forward. Instead, with his arms mostly still at his sides, he turned his palms outward as if asking permission, or forgiveness. He said, with a straight face, "Don't blame him or me. My charm is hard to resist."

*Exactly what I thought the first time I saw Sam.*

I smiled back, asking, "How long has it been?"

"Since the interview? A month." He countered, "You received the photographs?"

I nodded. "The flowers, too, along with the note."

"Sorry about that."

"Not your fault. Or was it?"

"No, though I could've put my foot down and insisted they pull the article as they were hitting *publish* . . . and thereby given up any hope of goodwill toward myself or for your cause for maybe forever."

I sighed. "I appreciate what you wrote. It was truly a lovely piece. The photographs were amazing. I met a man, a metalworker, who said he saw the article shared on several metalworking websites." I smiled. "He treated me like a celebrity. It was pretty cool."

"Mind if we chat?"

"Not at all. Excuse me for a minute while I close the door." I pulled the shed door back into place but didn't lock it. I wasn't going far. I said, "Shall I fetch us some tea? We can sit out here, or if you prefer the air-conditioning, we can talk inside."

"Out here is fine. Beautiful morning."

"I'll be right back."

And I was. As we settled in our seats with iced tea and a plate of the shortbread cookies, Sam asked, "Protector, you said? Protection from what? You didn't own a dog when I was here before."

"Still don't. He's a loaner." I sipped my tea. "The concern about curiosity seekers is real, but I haven't had any trouble yet. Just nerves."

"Are you back here for good, then?"

"No. I mean, yes. I live here. But I do plan to go places, especially back to visit my friends at the beach." I paused, then added, "I presume it was Susan who told you I was here."

"Yes, but only because I asked her if it would be okay

for me to visit you in Emerald Isle. I didn't know how Mr. Dahl would react to that, or you either, if I arrived uninvited."

"Good thinking." I shrugged. "Why didn't you ask me about Merrick when you came for the interview? He would've been a better subject for your article. Much more high profile, right? I kept expecting you to ask about him. Like when you mentioned the painting on the mantel, or my job in Emerald Isle, or even about my relationship with Susan. You never did. Which, the absence of asking, seemed strange." I left it there and punted the conversation back to him.

He smiled. "He *was* on my mind. I was hoping there'd be an opportunity for an interview with him, too, at some point in the near future, but the interview with you was totally separate from that. Susan brought you to my attention. I already had plans to travel down this way to visit my father, and so when Susan called . . . it felt . . . oddly convenient. Not quite *destined*, but maybe a little of that too. To be honest, I didn't know what to make of what I was seeing with the works of art, and even the barn/shed/workshop, which is pretty bizarre all on its own."

"You seemed interested at first . . . but then I could tell you were disappointed."

He leaned on the arm of his chair, toward me. "No, never disappointed. Just seeking direction. Trying to seek out the story that underlay, and tied together, all the elements."

I waited.

He said, "All the parts kept dancing around in my mind after I left here, until, in the middle of a touchy conversation with my father, I attempted to change the subject by mentioning the P-51. My granddad flew one in the war, and my father is an aficionado of old planes. He made me give him all the details. Somehow—and I refuse to say we bonded over a bomber—but the rest of the visit came together like . . . like it was destined, after all."

"Destined," I said.

"It's a good word."

"Unless the destiny is unfortunate."

He laughed. "You win."

"Maybe I *will* win, once I sort out next steps." I smiled. "I'm glad about your visit with your father."

"Thank you," he said. "And speaking of next steps . . . I have something else to tell you. And for the record, I tried calling before dropping in like this, but your number is no longer your number."

"Susan could've given you my new number."

"I didn't know to ask. At any rate, I have an offer from a magazine—a traditional, genuine, in-print magazine with glossy photos. They want to include the article about you and the sculptures in a special edition that they're putting together about people and unusual inheritances."

"There's a show on TV about that."

"This will have that kind of vibe, I'm told."

"Are you asking my opinion?"

"No. Trust me. You've come this far, and the article is one of the best I've written in a while—in my opinion. This can only be a good thing. I've already agreed to the terms, but I wanted to tell you myself, and to ask if there was anything in the article that made you uncomfortable. I can't promise to get it edited out, but I'll try."

"Thank you. The article was fine. More than fine."

He nodded. "I'm glad." He shrugged. "So, I was also thinking I'd like to offer a brief follow-up to the article. If the magazine doesn't want the additional material, I can use it for online promotion after the magazine is published."

"I don't know what that would be. A follow-up?"

"Your next steps, for instance."

I groaned so loudly that Bear chuffed again, and Sam's eyes widened.

He asked, "A sore spot? Or a quandary?"

That tickled me. I couldn't help laughing. "Some people have quandaries. I have problems. Might be nice to have quandaries instead. Sounds better."

"What's your quandary?"

I glanced over at the shed. It was inanimate. It wasn't listening to our conversation. And yet it had occupied such an important place in my life for so long . . . I wasn't sure if maybe it might be just a little aware.

"I've spent too much of my life watching over . . ." I waved my hand toward the building. "Over all that. I don't want to give up any more of my life and breath and energy to it, if it means I can't live my life as I choose. I want to have it—or the contents—to appreciate and enjoy. But this *watching* thing must end. Simply must."

I sort of drifted away, thinking it *must* end. At least, it must change. And then I thought of that idea of me picking up the craft and making it my own . . . That same thought that had come to me at Merrick's house, while I was sitting at his dining room table in front of his laptop, swamped me again. *Had I been saving it for more than history? Perhaps also for my own self. My unfinished . . .*

Sam said, "Pardon? I didn't catch that."

Had I spoken aloud?

I shook my head. "Maybe I wanted to be heard." This time I *had* spoken aloud.

"Heard?" He looked confused but interested.

"Okay, so here's the thing. A few days ago, I had a moment . . ." I breathed. "More than a moment. It shook me. I thought that maybe I'd been saving the workshop for me . . . for my actual unfinished business."

"Doing the metal art yourself?"

"Merrick saw it in my face practically the moment the thought flashed into my brain." I regretted mentioning Merrick in connection with any of this. I would never want anyone to think I was using my relationship with him to further my own interests. "If you do write a follow-up, please don't bring Merrick into it."

"He would add an interesting flavor to it, for sure."

"Don't. Promise me."

"I promise. I'll keep it out of your article. But tell me more."

"Merrick surprised me with a visit to a metalworking shop. That's where I met the metalworker I mentioned."

"And?"

"It was interesting, but especially helpful in reestablishing reality. I'm not a kid. I don't have the muscles or skills or experience that Mr. Forbes has. Or that my father had. If I'd truly wanted to create metal art, I wouldn't have waited two decades to think of it."

Sam surprised me by reaching across and taking my hand. He held it lightly, gently, and only long enough to say, "Things come in their time. Don't dismiss something because of the nays. The negatives. Only give it a pass if the positives aren't strong enough. And—this is something I feel strongly about—there's never any harm in trying."

❦

Sam left soon after. Bear watched him go and looked a little sad. I felt the same.

I waved as he drove away and then returned to where we'd been sitting. A little tea was left in my glass. I drained it.

Sam had asked permission to contact me again in a few days. He thought the follow-up to the article would be interesting to readers, regardless of which direction I chose. I had agreed to be in touch. But I had no idea what I'd be telling him.

The sound of a vehicle came to me. Not Sam returning. More like a truck. Within a minute, Joe came walking around back.

"There you are," he said. "How's it going?"

I watched him move toward me, as lanky as he'd been when we were kids in school, but he'd grown into his build long, long ago. There was still a soft spot in my heart for Joe, and I hoped there always would be. He was a part of my life—perhaps as much as the others. But he was one of the few who'd known me back when—and had never failed to give help when I needed it.

"It's good, Joe. All good. No matter what."

"You've been thinking again."

I laughed. "I have."

He sat in the chair where Sam had been a short time before. Both Merrick and Davis had sat there too. I'd have to take better care of it. Maybe enshrine it or something.

Joe asked, "What are you smiling like that for? I'm almost scared."

"Just thinking some more." I leaned forward. "Call me crazy, Joe, but I'm thinking I might try crafting some metal myself." I waited, then, for his reaction.

Bear had come over, and Joe was scratching the dog's head. He was thinking too. He shrugged. "Why not?" he said. "Except you'd better let me go over the wiring first. Not at all sure it can handle the electrical load of newer tools. I expect that your dad did a lot with hand tools, and the electric tools probably drew less power back then."

He made it sound unremarkable. The whole idea of it. Just down to the practical mechanics of how to make it happen.

"Shouldn't be too hard to upgrade, but don't use any power tools until I check it out. Might spark a fire and burn the whole place down."

Horrified, I said, "I hadn't thought of that."

"Well, then, that's why you told me, I reckon."

"I reckon so, Joe."

He grinned.

"I'll take a quick look before I go." He looked at me for agreement. "The reason I came by was to see how last night went."

"Bear barked in the middle of the night. I got out and

looked around. Didn't see anything amiss. Likely a raccoon or such."

"Likely," he said.

I saw his concern.

"Lil, I was thinking you might put up some cameras. Security ones. Maybe one to cover the backyard and one to cover the front. A lot of 'em work by internet, which you don't have, but I can look around at what might work for your situation and recommend something."

"Cameras?" I shook my head. "I don't like the idea of that."

"What else is new? You never did like change. But give it some thought." He stood. "Meanwhile, lemme go check out the wiring. I've got some equipment in my truck. I'll be right back."

છ৪૪৩

I kept him company in the workshop while I was sorting it out in my mind. Ditching the "shed" image altogether and imagining it fully as a workshop. There was no harm in that. The secret was out and about all over.

Joe checked the wiring from source to end. He was down and under and twisting and using a meter to measure something or other. Some of the time I watched him. Some I spent picking up tools—old ones still lying as dad had left them. It was bittersweet, but I blamed the dust for my itchy eyes—not the memories.

As if reading my mind, Joe said, "You need to leave the doors wide open. Best way to get the worst of this dust cleared. You could maybe put a room fan in the opening to get it stirred up and moving out without disturbing everything else in here." He came to stand next to me. "But don't use the fan yet. The wire casing is showing serious wear. I'm gonna replace the whole line. I'd better check the fuse box first. Might need to replace that too." He muttered

168

a few words under his breath.

"What's that, Joe?"

"Oh," he looked a little embarrassed. "I was just saying there's no way any of these old light bulbs in here should even be working. Not with the lines like this. And that bulb." He pointed over our heads. That bulb's gotta be twenty years old at the very least. When's the last time you changed it?"

"Can't say I recall." Had I ever? Didn't think so.

"My point exactly." He shook his head. "Well, be that as it may, I'll get the wiring fixed up."

I put my hand on his arm. "Joe, I dislike putting you to all this effort for something I might not even do."

Joe laughed, but kindly. "You'll do it. No question. You always say no first. But once you get to thinking about something, you *will* do it. And you *are* thinking about it, aren't you?"

"I am."

"Well, there you go. You can thank me later when you figure out I'm right."

CRRSED

I walked through the house, trying to imagine one of Dad's metal art sculptures on my wall. No one in my family had been big about making holes in the walls. I remembered a few framed pictures on the walls when I was very young, but after my grandparents passed, they'd sort of disappeared. After my parents died, I found the smaller pictures stored in a box in a half-ceiling storage closet. The larger photographs were stacked against the wall. I'd taken them out back then. Had lined the portraits along the wall and wondered who the people were. It would've been nice if someone had introduced me to the images of my forebears—someone who knew their names. Grim men with twinkly eyes, women who looked equally grim and less twinkly. But there was a kindness I could see in their faces, and in some of them, I saw the features of my mother's face.

I'd moved them, one by one, back into the closet. From the box, I'd chosen a few to display, like one of my mother when she was young and one of my parents around the time they'd married. My mother's parents too. But I hadn't hung those photographs. That felt a little too much like commitment. Instead, I'd set them on the furniture, leaning them against the walls rather than hammering nails into my walls.

And now here I was, thinking about hanging one of Dad's sculptures on those same walls. I'd need to consult someone—maybe Joe—as to how best to hang them without bringing the plaster and lathe down.

I'd left the workshop doors wide open. Joe couldn't work in there with all this dust, and he was coming back after work to start the wiring. Hopefully, some of the dust would be cleared out by then—old dust that was more like a blanket, such that when you tried running a cloth over it, it just sort of pushed around. I'd tried a small shop vac, but it had clogged the filter up in no time. So maybe sunlight and a breeze would help clear some of the dust that machines couldn't.

I was tempted to take the *Rosette* sculpture down to display in the house. Momma had liked that one. But I was more strongly drawn to the *Warrior Shield*. I remembered helping Dad with that one while Momma sat in her chair crocheting and singing softly, and the smell of new-fallen autumn leaves and a hint of smoke and heat as Dad had hammered, soldered, and welded, working his skills and talent upon the hubcap and bolts and chain—it all kind of married into the one big memory.

Carrying the stepladder over, I set it in front of the *Warrior Shield* and tried to open it, but it resisted. In no mood to be obstructed, I applied pressure with my foot against the lower rungs and forced it open. I climbed the steps until I could rest one foot on the worktable. Lightly bracing myself, balancing between the ladder and the table, I stretched my arms, my fingers, to reach for the sculpture.

Dad had hung most of these sculptures with a big hook and a couple of nails strategically placed in the two-by-fours to keep them from swaying. I assumed a similar arrangement was hiding behind this work.

The shield looked much bigger close up. I checked my balance against the ladder and worktable, then leaned toward the wall a little more, my arms outstretched, my fingers reaching toward the metal where the sharpest edges framed it. In my head, I heard, *Careful, careful, careful,* and just then Bear barked several times. Frozen midreach, I looked, and there in the doorway stood Bobby Harrin.

"Don't move," he said.

I stared, frozen. I'd known him—mostly known *of* him—most of my life. He came from a long line of dubious people. We traveled in different circles and had never interacted much. He was tall and wide, dressed in jeans and a T-shirt, with a ball cap on his head. Not exactly a handsome man, but he looked a lot like my idea of a pirate, especially when he grinned. Unlike Sam, this man could never cheat me because he'd never get close enough. Except for today. And as I was thinking uncharitable thoughts, he spoke.

"Just stop where you are." His voice was as rough as his manners. "That ladder's about to topple." He crossed over and put a hand on the A-frame to steady it.

I told myself to save my annoyance for later—after I was safely down on my feet again. And yet, I hesitated.

Bobby was maybe five years or so older than me, and so tall and broad-shouldered that him bracing the ladder for me was a nothing thing. If he'd wanted, he could've just reached up and lifted me down one-armed without effort.

Felt like I needed to establish a pecking order here.

"All right," he said. "You can come down now."

Staring at him, I said, "I can handle this fine on my own."

"Said every person who couldn't and then came to a bad ending."

I almost laughed at the irony. *Bad ending. Harrins. Hah.* Still not moving, but trying to sound more neighborly, I asked, "How are you doing these days, Bobby?"

"Staying out of jail as best I can."

"I heard you came around here checking things out while I was gone."

"Did. Curious was all."

"Okay."

He offered his hand, and I took it until I reached the ground.

"Look," he said, pointing at the folding hinge where it joined to the back upright of the ladder. The hinge had all but twisted out of place.

Had I done that when I'd forced it? Maybe, but more likely it was already damaged, and I'd finished it off. Maybe the ladder would've failed, maybe not, but I wouldn't have wanted to find out while on top of it, balancing a heavy metal sculpture with sharp edges.

I should be wearing heavy gloves, anyway. I should've thought of that.

"Guess I need a new ladder. And I owe you my thanks, as well." I stepped back. "Can I offer you a glass of tea?"

He shook his head and gave a shrug. "Heard you were back. Was hoping to take a look inside here."

Since he'd already been in the shed helping me and the doors were wide open, I could hardly say no.

"Don't touch," I said. "It's all sharp and dusty. But you're welcome to look. I'll fetch us both some tea."

"You sure?"

"I'm sure."

He nodded and wandered deeper into the workshop, while I made a quick trip to the kitchen. I stood at the kitchen window for a long minute, watching him. Couldn't see much because it was darker in the shed, but what I could see was reassuring. His hands were in his pockets, and they stayed there, as he stood in mostly one spot and looked by turning his head. I figured he was doing it that way for my benefit. It seemed to me that maybe this was a good thing. He would see these weren't items easily sold, and he might decide it was better to gain goodwill. Like a good character reference. If anyone asked, I might say, *Bobby Harrin? Oh goodness, no. Bobby didn't bother a thing. Was just curious. Did, in fact, prevent me from having a serious fall . . .*

Who knew for sure? But I knew him well enough to know that he had some angle or other—whether to profit or schmooze or impress. And what about Bear? I hadn't heard a peep out of him. He was watching, but in a lazy way from a shady spot under the tree.

I used the good glasses. They weren't fancy, but it was to let him know that regardless of whatever else, I was being level with him. I wasn't offering him a drink in a plastic cup that suggested he could take his drink and run on along. An actual drinking glass implied one was expected to stay and finish the tea.

Back outside and by the chairs, I offered him the tea. We both continued standing as he accepted the glass and gave it a long look, then lifted it and drained it. He continued holding it after it was empty, with almost a puzzled expression on his face.

I suggested, "Shall I get you a refill?"

"Thanks."

I returned with his drink. This time he downed it more slowly, then shook his head, saying, "Not sure what you put in it, aside from tea, but it reminds me of the tea my momma made."

"Must be the touch of lime in it." I put the tips of my thumb and forefinger together. "Just a smidge. It's a secret, you know."

He grinned, and this time maybe he didn't look quite so much like a pirate. In fact, I was seeing a whole different aspect to his face.

I set my glass on the small table between the chairs, and he did the same.

He gestured back toward the shed, and asked, "Your dad made all those metal things?"

"He did. Feel free to have a look."

"I will, and thank you."

As he strolled along looking at them, I followed trying not to hover.

He asked, "Why'd he kill himself and your mother too?"

I felt jolted. Shocked. How could he speak those words? Say them at all...much less in the middle of my father's workshop and his tools and creations? The very place where he and Momma had....

He said, apparently oblivious and not looking my way, "Was it on purpose? People said . . . you know." He stopped. There was silence, and he looked at me. "Sorry, Lilliane. It's been so long, I didn't think you'd mind me asking. I remember him, you know. I was a kid when it happened, but he always treated me okay when we crossed paths. Always seemed odd to me he'd choose to go that way."

He gave no sign that he could see the earthquake happening inside me. He seemed . . . dispassionate. Simply expressing thoughts he must've had noodling in the back of his brain for two decades. To me, it felt . . . appalling.

"You okay, Lilliane? You look pale." He grabbed my arm.

I struck at his hand, his arm. "What the . . . What are you thinking?" I shouted, sounding hysterical. I closed my eyes and tried to breathe slowly.

"Hold on, Lilliane. Sit down." He kept his hand near my arm. "I thought it was so long ago . . . I didn't mean to upset you."

I'd pressed my hands over my face, over my stinging eyes, but now I smiled between my fingers. I dropped my hands and drew in another ragged breath. "No, Bobby. I apologize to you for my . . . extreme reaction. I was . . . not expecting that question." I added, "If you don't mind, I need to step back outside into the fresh air and sunshine."

Together, we stopped by the chairs again, but still I didn't sit. I was done with this conversation and not inclined to invite him to linger—which sitting would've done.

Bobby spoke softly. "I remember him. He was kind to me."

"Yes."

"You ever want to talk about it, I'd like to know."

"I've never really known the answers myself."

He rocked back and forth on his feet, clearly uncomfortable and likely regretting he'd dropped by or had brought up the subject.

I asked, "Why'd you come by when I was out of town?"

I'd surprised him. I saw it in his eyes.

He said, "For that reason, mostly. You were gone. I heard about the article in town, and I remembered him, so I looked it up. Cool pictures. Kind of took me back to my childhood—back to when I was just a kid who got into trouble from time to time. Kid stuff. I came by, hoping to take a look. I knew you were out of town that first time. Figured dropping by then would inconvenience you less."

"I made Joe promise me not to show it to anyone."

"He kept that promise. No hard feelings."

"I was worried, you know, about people getting curious, maybe breaking in and doing who knows what."

He frowned. "Like who?"

"Like what happened with John Gresham's house."

"Ah." He looked away, then back at me. "All the folks here are proud of you. Proud that one of our own . . . I don't know the right words. Clumsy with them. But proud that one of our own made it into the press"—he laughed—"and in a good way."

I made a face, feeling embarrassed, and decided to sit, after all. "Not quite in print. You mean online."

"No. Local paper." He sat in the other chair, lowering himself into it with a soft sigh. "They reprinted something or other. I don't know how they got it done, but they did, and it was right after it came out on the internet. Saw the page tacked onto the bulletin board in the municipal building in Mineral. It didn't have as many pictures as the online spread did, but it was still pretty cool."

He shook his head in a way intended to be reassuring. "No one around here will mess with your things. Outsiders driving in? Now that's another thing. As for local curiosity seekers . . . your car being parked out front with a house light left on or Bear's bark at the ready should be enough to discourage them." His expression turned serious. "If you have a problem with someone from around here, you let me know."

It was a tempting offer. His attention to potential problems might be more effective than the sheriff's office, and in a quieter way—but it might not be as nicely done. Plus, the favor might come with strings. Certainly, it would come with obligations.

"Thanks, Bobby." I cast a glance Bear's way. "Speaking of Bear and barking . . . I would've expected him to announce you. I heard nothing from him."

Bobby smiled. "Who, Bear? He and I are old friends."

"Apparently so." I stood. "Do you want to see any more of the workshop, or do you have any questions?"

Bobby eased himself up from the chair, coming to a stand with a hand to his back. "No, that was enough. One other thing I'll mention. Get some help with taking that thing down from the wall, even with a good ladder. There's enough metal in it to weigh a . . . well, more than one person should try to handle."

"Thank you. I believe you're right. I'll take my near accident as a warning to ask for help. And I'll also get myself a new ladder." I smiled. "Thanks for the save, Bobby."

"My pleasure, Lilliane."

"Mr. Harrin? What brings you here?"

We both turned, startled. It was Gwen. I'd never heard her speak in such a harsh tone. I opened my mouth to defend Bobby—an odd impulse on its own—but noticed a slow smile growing on his face. A smile that said he was glad to see her.

"Helping a neighbor, Miss Foster. What I do best."

"That so, Mr. Harrin? I wasn't aware you were into doing good deeds."

"As often as I may. As often as I'm allowed."

There was subtext happening here that I couldn't grasp. The more Bobby grinned, the darker the frown grew on Gwen's face. She shifted her gaze to me.

"Lilliane. Any problem here?"

She'd called me Lilliane. Not Lillie. Seeing them here together, I was thinking they were probably closer in age than I'd thought. In fact, it seemed to me that he looked more presentable than how I remembered him. Maybe a tad more civilized. Haircut, new T-shirt . . .

When Joe had called me that evening in Emerald Isle and said Bobby Harrin had come to visit, I told him that I'd come right home. He'd said no need in that because Bobby was more intimidated even by Gwen than by me. Perhaps Joe had misread that. Maybe what Joe had read as intimidation on Bobby's part had represented a different kind of subtext altogether.

"He saved me from a bad fall, Gwen. I'm most grateful."

Her frown eased. "Well, that's good, then." But instead of directing the words to me, I was quite sure she was speaking straight to Bobby.

And somewhere in the midst of all this strange conversation, Bobby's cap had moved from atop his head to being in his hands. Politely so.

Gwen nodded, her frown disappearing, though her manner stayed cool. I now noticed that Gwen was holding a white envelope. She saw me looking and flashed me a quick smile.

"It's why I came. I had some of the photos printed from those we took in the shed. I thought you'd enjoy them." She held the envelope out toward me.

I accepted it with a thank-you. "Too sweet, so kind of you." On impulse, I said to Bobby, "Gwen has been instrumental in helping me do all this with the article and everything. Don't know what I would've done without her."

"Oh, yes, ma'am. I don't doubt it." He reached up and smoothed his hair back just as he glanced at her.

All the more remarkably, Gwen looked away, but she also reached up to tuck strands of hair behind her ear.

"I need tea," I said. "Can I offer you a glass, Gwen? Another for you, Bobby?"

They both declined.

Gwen said, "I must rush off." She turned to walk away, but stopped after a few steps. The quick look back was aimed at him, not at me. "Behave yourself, Mr. Harrin."

"Yes, ma'am."

Bemused and bewildered, I waved goodbye to Gwen.

Bobby said, "I'd best be getting on too. Anything you need before I go?"

"No. Thank you. I'm all set."

He nodded.

I said as boldly and seriously as I ever had, "She's my friend, Bobby Harrin. You should understand that. I don't want anyone hurting her or . . . disappointing her."

He nodded, saying, "She's keeping an eye on me. On purpose. We're going out for supper tonight. Out of the area. A waste of gasoline, I say, but she's worried over what people will think." He laughed as he put the cap back on his head. "I expect reform may be in my future." He walked away with a light step. Might even have had a bit of swagger happening there.

No way in the world was I going to mention that he'd

blushed when she'd spoken to him.

I watched him go in wonder. It had been Joe's mention of Bobby Harrin's curiosity that had prompted me to dash back here to Cub Creek. Imagine that. And all the while I was worrying, Gwen had had it all handled.

# Chapter Nineteen

Joe was due to finish up the wiring and the new electrical panel. Bear was napping under the shade tree, and I was hanging out in the shed. The decades-old dust was slowly clearing from the interior, and I was feeling more comfortable in that space where my past had . . . was even now . . . colliding with my present. The difference was that the coming together was beginning to feel more like a warm family reunion than a red-hot family feud.

I could figure this out.

As I picked up tools that were last discarded by my father, I held one in my hands, then set it down and moved on to another. I was also picking up other things he'd left behind, like a hubcap that was already old twenty years ago. Its once-shiny surface was dented and scraped, yet I could still see my reflection in the metal, distorted and showing my own flaws. But the resulting image was beautiful too, as a part of the whole. Also, I found an old plastic food container full of bolts and nuts. It clunked as I picked it up. It came to me that I was sorting and separating the tools from the material that could be used to create something.

A short, rusted chain was wrapped around an ax handle that was missing its ax-head. I dropped the chain on the hubcap. The chain slid over the curved surface and caught in the edging. Here were a couple of curved flanges from who knows what. I set them aside and noticed an old outdoor barbecue fork with rusted tines. I held it up and stared at it. *Dad, what were you planning to do with this?* I shook my head. When I set them down beside the hubcap and caught the interplay of the hubcap rim, the chain, and the shape of the flanges . . . I decided to find out for myself what Dad might have had in mind for these items.

But using the actual tools to weld and join and such? I wasn't ready for that. I did need training.

Joe was more optimistic. He brought me a pair of heavy-duty gloves, size extra-small, and a helmet with a face shield—used—when he came to finish up the wiring. Bear greeted him, and I came to the door of the workshop and waved.

"Had a friend who didn't need the safety shield anymore. He was happy to have it gone. Might need to wash it up a little. The gloves . . . well, you're gonna need those if you want to save your hands."

"I'm not actually doing anything yet, just pushing stuff around and thinking."

"You'll be ready when you're ready."

My phone rang. I grabbed it from the workbench. "Hang on, Merrick. Just a sec." I said to Joe, "My friend Merrick. I'll be in the yard talking to him if you need me."

Joe nodded, and as I walked away, Merrick said, "*I* need you."

"I was talking to Joe."

"Doesn't matter."

"How's the new aide?"

"Not likely to kill me. Unless it's death by boredom." He cackled, which told me he was amused by his wit.

"Merrick, you are good at creating excitement. You don't need anyone to do that for you."

He sighed loudly and with gusto. "It's not that. She won't talk to me. Oh, she'll say *yes* and *no* and *what do you want* and all that stuff, but she won't *talk*."

"I'll come visit soon. I promise. Meanwhile, did you get my texts with the photos? Do you like the metal sculpture I chose for you? If not, speak up now, 'cause these things are heavy and sharp. Not really good for manhandling needlessly."

He ignored my question. "Any news from Susan?"

"No, but Sam Markham himself came by. He's got some big opportunity that came from the article." My word choice implied I didn't know specifics, since the specifics weren't mine to tell. Merrick would push for the details if he thought I had them. "He wanted to know if I was okay with the article as written. Told him I was. So that's that for now."

"But nothing from Susan?"

"No, but that's okay too. I'm rethinking the selling idea. You knew that already. The original plan with Susan of perhaps finding an interested art collector or gallery would've resolved some issues, like getting them out of the shed and on to better things. And the idea felt all good before when we came up with it, but not so much now. Dad's artwork has been here so long. Maybe this is where the pieces belong. Maybe the risk doesn't even matter."

"There, do you see?"

"See what?"

"You *talk* to me." He stopped, and I heard him sipping something. "Davis is out of town. Miranda came over. Moving very slowly, I must say, but moving."

"She was very sick."

"Not since she came back, right?"

I said, "Not that I know of."

"Well, glad she recovered, but she didn't linger long. That granddaughter of hers brought her over for tea but got tired of waiting for her, I think."

I heard the *lonely* in his voice. I heard it so loudly that I could almost tell what color it was. Red, I thought. The color of a beating heart seeking connection.

I understood his need. I peeked in on Joe. Clearly *he* didn't need my help. As I walked back out of the shed, heading for the chairs, I said, "Did I ever tell you about the time my daddy taught me how to swim?" And I waited.

After a short but definite pause, Merrick said, "You

don't know how to swim."

"Exactly," I said.

He grunted. "What happened?"

And for me, those were the magic words. What happened and then what happened next . . .

"Well, my dad liked to fish, and one of the farmers he'd done repair work for had a stocked pond. He offered my dad the opportunity to fish as partial payment for the job. One Saturday in June, Daddy said, 'Lillie, grab a hat and come fishing with me.' I'd never been fishing and had begged him nearly to death to take me, so this was a dream come true. Not only did I grab my straw hat, but . . ." As I continued speaking, I was pretty sure I heard Merrick's desk chair squeak, and I knew he was settling back to listen as my heart spoke to his in the language we both knew best.

CR8O

That afternoon, I drove to the library. It was a few miles, but not far, being just on the north side of Mineral proper. I hadn't been there since . . . well, it had been the day that I was preparing for my first trip to Emerald Isle and had dropped by to tell them that I'd be out of town and not able to take my storytelling slot.

I was way overdue. But not to return borrowed books. I laughed a little at my wit. Nope, I was overdue for borrowing some.

As I entered, I felt awkward about my purpose—books I wanted to borrow—and I slipped quietly into the nonfiction section. The photography how-to books were easy to find, but metal-crafting books? None of them seemed to be quite what I needed. Finally, I found one that had clear illustrations of tools and information about different metals. It was probably too basic for most, but I needed simple reading and basic information, so I selected it as a good starting point.

Debra was at the checkout desk. I saw her just as she

saw me. Her face brightened in a wide smile. She was a bubbly person. Always enthusiastic, she would have something positive to say about anyone and anything. If she couldn't think of something or some person in a positive light, then she didn't speak of it or them at all.

"I heard you were back from the beach."

"How'd you know?"

"Oh, my goodness, Lilliane, you are the talk of the town. We're all eager to keep up with you these days."

She reached for the books I was holding, but I tightened my arms around them. Suddenly I was shy about giving them to her. Everyone within earshot would hear what I was checking out. It might take a little longer for the news to filter outside the library building, but soon everyone, including the ones not in earshot just now, would know.

"Hand 'em over, honey."

I did.

"Oh, nice." She looked at them as she checked them out into my custody. "I can see what *you're* up to." She returned the books to me and quickly came around to my side of the desk. She touched my arm. "Come with me."

She led me to the announcements board near the front door. I'd missed seeing it when I'd tried to sneak in.

Someone had printed off copies of the online article. The copies were clearly just that, and the contrast was off such that the pictures were too dark. I couldn't help thinking of the copies that Merrick had had Davis obtain for me. These weren't as clear, even so they went straight to my heart.

Debra was saying, "Everyone has been so excited since this came out. I hope that you'll come back soon and do your usual storytelling, but I think it would be so amazingly fabulous if you'd do a talk for the adults too. I can see it now. Not just about your father and his work—but also about your experience with being interviewed and being suddenly famous and all that."

I smiled politely. It felt forced, but aside from feeling flattered and touched, I didn't know what to think. I'd never be able to stand in front of grown people and talk as if I was someone . . . famous. Never.

Debra said, "Well, don't say no. Give it some thought." As if she'd read my mind by observing my face, she added, "Never say never, Lilliane." She patted my arm and gave a bubbly little laugh. "I'd better get back to the desk. I see a line forming!" And she was gone.

I held myself together until I got in my car; I put the books on the passenger seat, fastened my seat belt, and then it rolled over me—laughter. I thought of Merrick and Davis, and now me. Merrick had grown tired of the attention, but he still enjoyed the idea of it. Davis wanted the attention and chased the opportunity to catch it. But me?

I laughed again. The very idea of me being famous was bizarre.

Backing out of my parking space, I pulled out onto Route 522 and headed home to Cub Creek.

I avoided that kind of attention, but I was flattered, certainly. Mostly, I just needed to figure out what I wanted and how I should pursue it—to make up my own mind—before these temptations and other shiny baubles succeeded in derailing me.

❧

Susan called. "I received some calls expressing interest, but nothing has come of them yet."

I said, "At this point, I think that we should only be talking about the sculptures and not trying to keep the shed exactly as my father had it. I feel it's time to start moving at least some of the sculptures out. If something were to happen, I'd rather not have all of them in one location."

"I understand, and what you say makes sense."

"There's also the consideration that I want to come back

and visit Merrick. Maybe visit for a week or so and then come home for a week. I can't do that indefinitely . . . and I think . . . he misses me. *But* I don't want to disrupt the current aide situation, so I didn't say anything to Merrick. It's important that he have consistency. Or is that constancy?"

"Both, I think. And I agree. He does miss you. You two make a great team."

"He's sounding fragile."

"Hopefully not so very fragile. I think his health is good, considering his age, but he's too solitary now."

"Give it some thought, Susan. Meanwhile, I'm sorting through my father's things in the shed. I promised Merrick one of the metal art sculptures. And while I'm in Emerald Isle, I'm going to visit that Mr. Forbes that Merrick introduced me to, for practical advice about equipment and safety measures. Still not sure where I'm going with that idea, but I'm keeping my options open."

"Aren't you worried about security at Cub Creek?"

"Of course, but I can't allow the desire to protect my past—protecting *things*—to interfere with what's important to me now and in the future."

"Be sure, Lilliane."

I was annoyed. I thought she'd be pleased. "If you don't think it's a good idea . . ."

"Lilliane, whatever you decide has to be for you—not for your parents and not for anyone else. For *you*."

CRSO

When Joe brought the new electrical panel, he came with a broad-shouldered, dark-haired man who carried it. Joe, himself, was toting something else—some odd gifts.

"Morning, Lilliane. This is my friend Nick. He's a bona fide electrician. He's going to make sure I set all this new wiring up right."

"Pleased to meet you, Nick."

"Yes, ma'am. Happy to help."

Joe said, "I told him you wouldn't mind him seeing those metal art sculptures your dad made."

Having no choice, I was gracious. "Of course not." I gave him a serious look. "But no touching. And no photos, please. Not yet."

"Oh, no, ma'am," he said.

I softened it by adding, "There are lots of sharp things in there, and it's dusty too. But looking is okay."

He nodded. Joe handed him the panel and said, "I'll be right in after a word with Lil."

Nick left us.

"Joe? I wasn't expecting a stranger."

"He's a good guy. Owes me a favor, and I got to thinking that this wiring job had to be especially sound, considering."

"Considering." I smiled at him. "And what are those things you brought?"

He'd set a small stack of items next to one of the backyard chairs.

I looked more closely. "A hubcap? Some old tin-punched pieces?"

"My mother sent them, with her regards. Said you might use them in your new projects."

I gaped at him. "Honestly?"

He shrugged.

Should I laugh or cry? Was I going to be finding "gifts" like this being left? Instead of people hauling their junk to the dump? It was coming to my house? Maybe that was how my mother had felt when Dad had started bringing home more junk than he'd left with . . .

Actually, these were pretty sheets of tin. The punched patterns were intricate and might add an interesting touch to something that would otherwise look hard and cold. I set them back down beside the hubcap.

"Joe, would you care for an iced tea? Maybe sit a minute

and chat?"

"Chat?" He looked a little worried. "You aren't going to tell me you're dying or anything, are you?"

Aghast, I said, "Why on earth would you ask such a thing?"

"You seem different, somehow. Like you're considering a big change . . . or something. If it's the metal thing . . ."

"It's not. I'm not. Or maybe I am. But have a seat. I'll be right back. Want any cake or cookies?"

"Cake. I'm always good for cake."

I grinned and shook my head.

He said, "I've got some news too. Maybe today is the day to share it."

"Sure." And then I felt that same blip of worry that Joe had expressed. Usually, Joe and I just spoke our minds. I hurried inside to pour our drinks and put slices of cake on plates. I was back in a jiffy. "Here we are."

We stared at each other for a minute. I don't know what was in Joe's mind, but for me, I saw our past . . . our school days . . . dating and marriage . . . divorce practically right on top of it. But we'd always gotten along. Been friends. How could anyone not be friends with Joe?

"I need your help. More help, I should say."

He grinned. "That's what I'm here for."

"You mentioned security cameras and such a couple of days ago." I shook my head. "I can't keep out someone who's really determined to get inside the house or the shed, but what can I do to deter them?"

Joe sipped his tea. A slight frown creased his forehead as he thought. I waited.

Finally, he said, "Dogs are good for security, but judging by the way you're asking, I'm guessing you aren't planning to be here."

"On and off. I want freedom to come and go."

He nodded. "Most of those systems run through wireless

internet connections, as far as I know." He squinched up his face, thinking, then said, "I'm going to connect you with a friend of mine who manages that kind of business. You know I'm always happy to chew over stuff, but for this, and since I'm hearing a time limitation in your voice, I think it's best to go direct to the expert. He'll take a look at the layout and what you have to work with."

"Soon, right?"

"Is this about your friend back in Emerald Isle? Is that your concern?"

"A big part of it, yes."

"Are you two serious?"

I hit a blank. My brain did a quick review of what he'd said. I shook my head. "Merrick is much older than me. We are friends, yes, but . . ."

Joe laughed. "I meant the other guy, but since his name didn't jump to the front of your brain, I'm guessing you aren't as sold on him as we all thought."

"You all thought? Who's *all*?"

"Now don't get offended about your friends wanting good for you."

I breathed out an angry sigh. People will talk. Always talk. That was true.

Joe asked, "So you're thinking of going back and forth between the beach and here?"

"I'll confirm that as a *yes* so you can report back to *all* the others."

He said, "If you don't want me to, I won't breathe a single word of it to anyone."

I closed my eyes and shook my head. When I looked at Joe, I said, "It's good to have friends."

"It is indeed, Lilliane."

"You'll put me in touch with your friend?"

"Right now." He went to his contact list and selected a number.

I waited while Joe and the man chatted. Joe gave a brief

explanation, my location, and then there seemed to be some issue as to when he could come. Joe said, "Ms. Moore needs to be able to travel because she's got an uncle who's elderly and ailing." He added, "Very elderly."

More words were exchanged, and Joe turned to me, "Is tomorrow morning okay? It'll be early. Maybe eight a.m.? He'll swing by before his first appointment."

"I'll be here."

They finished up just that quick.

"Thank you, Joe. Merrick's not my actual uncle, but he might as well be family. I worry enough about him. Now, what's your news?"

"I'm getting married."

After all these years? I was stunned. "Congratulations."

"I should say that I'm getting married if she says yes when I propose."

"What? You haven't proposed? If you truly want to marry her, then don't delay. You might lose the opportunity."

"I didn't do so well as a husband the first go-round."

"Joe, you did fine. It was both of us. We weren't ready. And when we smartened up, we understood we were better as friends. I have treasured our friendship. Do you think she'll mind that we're friends? Many women wouldn't want their husbands spending time with female friends, especially ex-wives."

He laughed a little. "You aren't far off the mark. At first, she wasn't all that happy with me spending so much time over here. But when you became a celebrity, she didn't mind so much. She might be one of the *all* group, but I promise I don't repeat anything personal. Just what I'm doing over here. I hope you don't mind me asking, but she'd like a look in that shed. I thought maybe I could arrange that. Maybe it would soften her up for the proposal?"

"Joe, she'd be a fool not to accept your proposal, however you offer it. I hope she's good enough for you."

"I'd like to introduce her to you. Would you mind?"

"I'd be honored." I touched his sleeve. "One more thing, Joe. Before I lose you altogether to the woman you love . . . I have a ladder problem. Do I need to replace it, or can I . . . can *you* fix it?"

☙❧

Joe and Nick left after finishing up the wiring and examining my ladder. Joe told me I was good to go as far as the electricity went, and as for the ladder, he took it with him and left me with one he kept in his truck bed.

And before he left, both men put on heavy-duty work gloves and lifted down two of the metal art sculptures and carried them into the house. Joe said, "When you know where you want to hang them, you let me know. Don't do it yourself. You'll damage these walls."

"Thanks, Joe."

He was that kind of guy. I hoped the woman he was planning to propose to understood how special he was.

That afternoon, I fiddled with odds and ends in the shed and continued my battle against the dust. When I needed a drink and to cool down, I carried the welder's helmet into the house with me and set it beside the sink. I'd wash it out good while I hydrated with iced tea.

On impulse, I used my new phone to record a quick video of the safety helmet by the sink as I started the water running and squirted a dollop of dish detergent into the sink. I said, "Getting ready to wash the helmet, Merrick. What do you think?" I hit the recording button to stop it and then sent the video to him via text. He'd get a chuckle out of it.

And then I noticed a text that Davis had sent me that I hadn't responded to. And I'd missed his phone call.

When Joe had asked who I was worried about getting back to the beach for, I'd assumed he'd meant Merrick. It made sense. For one thing, I didn't think he knew about Davis, and so why would he be referring to him? Yet, my reply was instinctive. My first thought hadn't been about Davis . . .

But that was because Davis was healthy and mobile. Not someone who needed me . . . Or he sort of needed me, maybe. I knew he missed me . . . when he wasn't busy.

I felt that sinking, almost sad feeling I'd experienced when he'd kissed me. I'd spent my life committed. To loved ones. To things. Even to memories. I felt confused. I had feelings for Davis, and he had feelings for me too. But we were both busy with totally different pursuits. Resentment stirred. If I continued along my own, new path, I couldn't fit with the things he was involved in. Plus, Merrick needed me. I could only stretch myself just so far.

But avoiding Davis didn't resolve anything. He deserved better.

I texted him, *Sorry I missed your call. Be safe and well until we can talk. I'll be back soon.*

Not great, but it would do.

I looked at the soapy water now in the sink, dipped a clean rag in, and squeezed out the excess. Holding the helmet in one hand, I went to work with the other. As Joe had said—when I was ready, I'd be ready.

When Merrick responded to my text, he wrote, *LOL. When are you coming back?*

I replied, *Soon.*

⊂⊰℘⊃

The next morning, I was up bright and early and met Kerry Brooks as he drove up in his SUV, clearly marked as *Brooks Home & Business Security*. He came straight up the steps and introduced himself, and we discussed my concerns, and he checked out the property. He had some advice but agreed that the location would make it easy pickings if no one was here. "But," he said, "we have options that will help give you peace of mind. Joe mentioned you don't have Wi-

Fi, and we should talk about that, but even so, we can probably get you what you need."

"This would need to be for the house, but also for the large shed in the back."

"Yes, ma'am. I've heard about that shed. Would love to see inside. Would help as far as determining security needs as well."

We took the tour.

"One thing you might consider is to let folks know that they're welcome to drop by. Most won't, but the curious ones, the ones most likely to trouble you, can get it out of their systems."

"What? Like by posting a card in the grocery store window?"

He laughed politely. "I can see you think I'm joking, but I'm not. Remove the mystery and enlarge your group of supporters—people who feel personally invested in helping."

"It's an interesting idea."

"As for getting the word out? Just tell Joe. He knows all the people. But I suspect you already know that." He grinned.

CR80

Susan called and left a message. It said, "I'm leasing a car for you. Merrick insisted. He wants you to have safe transportation back and forth to visit him. It's my fault. I mentioned your thought to him that you might spend a week or two with him and then go back home again, and he ran with it as if all parties were agreed. I should've expected that." She paused, and then her voice sounded softer. "I thought about what you said, your assessment of his state, and I . . . I guess I agree." She disconnected.

She followed up with a text. *Sorry for omitting. Car will be delivered tomorrow afternoon. Use it for your own purposes. There are no restrictions on mileage, and it's covered by our insurance for any misadventures.*

Then I saw Merrick had texted. It was a string of emojis showing laughing faces and tools. I replied back, *Ha ha.*

Given the money that it would cost me to get the security system in place so that I could have some peace of mind about my home and everything else here while I was with Merrick again—and it would cost me most of what I'd saved from working for him before—I replied to Susan's text, *Thank you.*

CRSO

Joe put the word out, and a few people actually came by. *Demystifying* is what Kerry had called it. Joe agreed. Most of those who came were already friends, or were now friends. I let them look, but not touch. That seemed to be enough. They strolled through, exclaiming over the metal art, or over the old tools, or about the dust. And I had to admit it worked out well. Meanwhile, I was sorting things out in the house and in the workshop, preparing to drive back down to Emerald Isle.

I stopped under the shade tree and knelt while giving Bear a scratch. "You've been a big help to me, Bear. Good boy." He was panting and looked a lot like he was smiling. "Somebody will be coming to pick you up any minute now. I bet you'll be glad to be back home." And I swear his ears perked up and his eyes opened wider.

*Home.* It was kind of a magic word. Not just for people like me. But for dogs, too, apparently. For good or ill, home was home.

"I've done what I can, Bear. I hope all will be well here without me."

CRSO

I grabbed the phone. "Hey."

Davis said, "I was worried."

"I texted."

"Exactly."

"I'm not exactly good at it, you know. I tried."

"What's wrong?"

"Nothing. It's going well. I'm getting ready to head back to Emerald Isle. Where are you? Still in New York?"

"For a few days more. Lilliane . . ." He made an impatient noise. "You say nothing's wrong, but it feels like there's a million miles between us, not just a few states."

"It's true. We're being pulled in different directions. I'm trying to do right by home and by Merrick, but it's tricky straddling six hours between the geographic locations, with both needing me and having claims on me. If I don't get done what needs doing, or don't make the right decisions—what happens, or fails to happen, will be my fault."

"Lilliane, that's no good. No one needs that kind of pressure."

*Sigh.* "But," I said, "the time is now. I feel it, Davis. In my bones."

"When do you plan to go back to Emerald Isle?"

"Very soon. I had some security measures installed here. My friends will continue to keep an eye out, but more of a passing glance instead of having to camp out here."

"There's still risk."

"Yes, there always is. But I want something more now. I want to talk to you, get your thoughts on it, but it's still jumbled. I want to talk in person."

"I understand. Seems like we're both ping-ponging back and forth for a while."

"Plus your writing deadlines," I added.

Davis made a noise. It sounded more like a groan. He gave a sad laugh. "I'll tell you what I'm telling myself. Try not to get too lost in the trees—meant metaphorically, as in getting lost in the details. Not referencing Cub Creek."

I laughed. "Whether it's trees or sand dunes, sometimes

it's fun getting a little lost."

He said softly, "I understand the appeal. If you decide to do that, I hope you'll take me with you."

I said, "You have an amazing opportunity. If I didn't understand how amazing, then I would from what Merrick has said. And he's so excited, basically being on tour with you, even if not in person."

Davis laughed. "He'll be the fourth guy on the tour, though in name only. We'll be promoting that novel as an upcoming release with a lot of hyperbole about Merrick's storied—literally many-storied—career."

I smiled, though no one was there to see. "I love that."

The warmth, tinged with sadness, in his voice was unmistakable as he said, "Yeah, I do too."

Davis was thinking too far ahead—of a time when Merrick would be a memory instead of his gruff, ornery self. We'd both miss him, but I'd had a lot of loss in my early life, and I'd learned a little about enjoying your people while you had them and not rushing into the future. No one could control that, anyway.

"I might work with the metal myself. You know about that, right?"

"You mentioned Mr. Forbes and going to a metalworking shop. Are you really thinking of doing it yourself?"

"You don't think I should?"

"No, that's not it. If you told me you were going to craft wings from bedsheets and launch yourself from the shed roof, I might offer advice . . . but metalworking? I used soldering tools in my high school shop class about a thousand years ago, but that's as close as I've ever come to working with anything like that."

"Hmm. But you've come close to launching off a roof with a sheet?"

I heard little noises through the receiver before he finally said, "Actually, one of these days, I'll tell you that story . . ."

"No. I don't believe it."

He laughed. "See how much you still don't know about me?"

"In actual fact, I know very little about you. Maybe you can tell me more when we meet up in Emerald Isle."

"I have an idea. Call me when you're heading back to Merrick's. I'll make sure I'm there for at least part of the time."

"Seriously?"

"And—we owe this to ourselves—for a few hours we'll get lost. We'll run away together."

I laughed. "What on earth are you talking about?"

"A date. We'll go out to dinner, at the very least."

"I can't leave him alone in the evening."

"We'll do it on a Tuesday or Friday when Ms. B is there. You and I can go out for lunch. A nice one."

"I suppose we could." I gave a little groan. "Merrick will be speculating."

"So will I," he said without explanation. "It's a date? And I mean that literally. A date. Our first official going-out meal together without chaperones."

I laughed. "True." A thought occurred to me—an annoying one. "Are you inviting me out on a lunch date because you think I need a distraction from everything?"

For a long moment, there was silence, but then he said, "Yes. Not because you need another distraction, but because I'd like to be that distraction."

❧

When I'd worked jobs for the past twenty years, they'd been mostly cashier and customer service, and much of that time had been spent at the Fuel Up Fast. Some of the jobs had been really good as far as the work, but the pay was poor if a gal was her sole support. The first nearly three weeks I'd worked for Merrick . . . well, the pay and bonus had been generous. I'd fixed the hole in my roof and had the house painted, and I'd even splurged on some air-conditioning units, which anyone in Virginia in the summer would understand what a joy those were to have. The money I'd been paid for my most recent stay with Merrick had covered a few bills, but mostly it had gone into my savings for a car. Something reliable and cheap. And now that money had gone for the security system so that I could return to Emerald Isle.

To be able to say I'd done my best to protect my home and memories—had drained most of my savings.

Susan supplying that rental car for me for the trip to Emerald Isle had been a life saver because there was no guarantee of income—possibly ever—from metal art, either my father's or what I might craft. Which meant I needed to get a paying job. But the only jobs I could get wouldn't accommodate me keeping my commitment to Merrick. I knew it wasn't a legal commitment, or maybe even a moral commitment, but it was absolutely a commitment of the heart. Merrick needed me. It was just that plain and simple. Susan providing a vehicle again made the trip possible, and I had enough money left to cover gas for the trip, so that was good. The security system took some of the burden of watching out for this place off my friends' shoulders.

But there were still expenses. And when the money ran out? It wouldn't be the first time I'd been a little slow in paying some bills. I always came out okay on the other side of those times. One way or another.

The leased car was much like the one I'd had before, but this one was a lovely shade of blue that reminded me of the evening sky over Cub Creek and of the deeper, way-out parts of the ocean near the horizon.

So I packed my tote bags—seriously, one of these days I would have to buy an actual suitcase. Maybe even a matching set of luggage. For now, I made a pile of the assorted totes beside the front door.

I dialed the phone, and Merrick answered. I said, "I'm leaving first thing tomorrow morning. Friday. Be ready."

"I'm always ready," he grumbled. Then, in a different tone, he asked, "Ready for what?"

"It's a surprise, Merrick. I can't tell you."

"Well, if you didn't intend to tell me, then why'd you mention it? Just to aggravate me?"

"Maybe. Mostly, I wanted you to wonder."

"Wonder?"

"Wonder is good for everyone. It's almost as good as joy and hope."

"Wonder? Okay, I'll play. But it better be worth wondering over."

"That will be for you to decide. See you tomorrow afternoon. Get rest."

"Huh?"

"See you tomorrow." I disconnected, and smiled. A little teasing and wonderment would do him good.

I carried a couple of the totes out to the car that evening. I double-checked to make sure the car was locked up tight for the night because I had something special in it. Joe had crafted a box, lightweight but roomy, for Merrick's gift, and together we'd carried it out to the car and slid it into the back. I was hoping that when I reached Merrick's tomorrow, between me and Ms. B, we could manage to get that box inside the house. We'd have to hire someone to hang it after Merrick decided where he wanted it.

⊂ℛℬ∽

It was Friday and time to hit the road again. The trip down in the newly leased car—as it had been in the rental car—was so different from the first drive I'd made to Emerald Isle. My first trip ever to the beach. And now this was my third. My old car had worked pretty good, and I was grateful for that, but to have air-conditioning in the South in the summer meant my clothing wasn't drenched through with sweat and my hair didn't frizz up like crazy. It meant no one gave me odd stares as they passed me on the interstate. I swear, it seemed like when I stopped at a convenience store to hit the restroom or buy a soda, I was treated better. And then I remembered that I'd assessed arriving customers based on things like what they drove and how they dressed—and I was embarrassed. Of course, once I got to know them, it was all different. We knew each other. I knew what to expect from them as customers. Still, I wondered if I'd ever made people feel *less than* . . . I hoped not.

So the trip was smooth and cool, and I drove up to the private subdivision gate guard like we were old buddies, and he smiled and waved.

Knowing people—yep, it could make a difference.

I pulled into the garage like it was an everyday thing. I went directly to the kitchen. Ms. B heard me arriving and started to speak, but I shushed her. "Is he sleeping?" I whispered. I gestured to her to follow me.

We stepped out to the garage.

Ms. B asked, "What's going on, Lil-li? Got a problem?"

"Brought Merrick a gift, but it's heavy. How's your back? I was thinking that between the two of us, we can carry it in. But I don't want to risk you getting injured."

"Back's fine. Let's see what you brought. He's excited, I'm telling you."

I opened the hatch. "It's in the box. But it's sharp and awkward, so we'll need to carry it in the box. I'll have to hire someone to hang it after he chooses where he wants it." I touched the metal gently. "I hope he'll like this one."

She reached out carefully and tentatively touched the sharp flanges. "Is that a face in there?"

"Might be. It is, for you, if that's what you see."

She ran her fingers along the smooth metal rim and the chain links. "Yeah, I think he's goin' to like this."

"I hope so."

"Yeah," she said. "Like him. Sharp and rusty outside. The real him inside alone."

I couldn't help another glance at the sculpture. Had I seen the same? No. Maybe . . .

"Let's get it done," she said.

Between us, we managed. We tried to be quiet as we navigated the foyer with the heavy, awkward box. In the foyer opposite the study door, we set the box so that the bottom edge was on the foyer floor and the box was almost upright, leaning back against the wall. Merrick's study door remained closed. No sound came from inside.

I stepped back to stand near the foyer table in the center of the large space. I crossed my arms, then uncrossed them and put my hands on my hips, all the while taking in the sculpture and the gleaming furniture and the antique vases and so on. I'd expected a clash.

Ms. B whispered, "What's wrong, Lil-li?"

Shaking my head, I looked at her, saying, "Not a thing. I expected it to clash with the rest of the decor. But honestly . . . maybe it's just me—I'm biased, I guess—but it looks like it was meant to be here."

She nodded. "Yes. Maybe. But how am I going to dust that scary thing?"

I smiled at her and gave her a one-armed hug, saying, "Very, very carefully."

"Oh, get on with you. Listen to you . . ." She walked away grumbling, but good-naturedly.

Rubbing my hands together in delight, I peeked inside the study. Merrick was napping in his desk chair with his feet propped up on an ottoman. I watched him until he gave a soft snore and his hand twitched. Satisfied, I left him and went to fetch my bags from the car.

As I walked through the kitchen, Ms. B said, "Not the usual room. Mr. Dahl told me to keep it free for the others. You got the room across from that now."

I stared blankly. She added, "Up the stairs and first door

on the left."

"Okay. Thanks." But I felt odd. I'd found comfort in the familiarity of my visits before, apparently not realizing how much I wanted that routine to continue without change. Feeling more subdued, I gathered my tote bags, and hanging them from my arms and hands like I was a coat tree, I climbed the stairs and opened the door on the left.

This had been Merrick and Marie's suite. It was huge. Windows filled the wall that faced roughly northwest, and the view of the dunes and the series of wooden crossovers moved to the right and took in the ocean—a wide swath of ocean clear to the horizon. The bags fell from my grasp, hitting the floor and spilling some of their contents, but I didn't notice. I was drawn forward hypnotically toward that window and that view, into the wide, rounded alcove graced by that window. I could see clear up the coast. How far? Far enough. Light-headed, I sat.

Luckily, a chair was there to catch me.

Still staring, I picked out the area of the beach where I'd spent time with Miranda. The path from there to the road disappeared pretty much immediately behind dunes and green growth. Farther up, the colorful beach houses, one after the other, were strung like beads on a gemstone necklace. As I watched, a flock of birds sailed high overhead, suddenly swooping low and catching a wind gust to scatter and swirl, yet maintaining formation.

My face was wet. It brought me back to myself. I mopped at my eyes with the tail of my shirt. The rest of the room was nice enough. A king-size bed. The furniture was clearly expensive, mahogany was my guess, but the surfaces were almost empty. The previous occupant, Merrick, had moved out some time ago, when he no longer wished to bother with climbing the stairs. When he'd moved down to the room that adjoined his study.

I asked myself, *Does that bother me?* No, it felt anonymous. Might have bothered me if he'd moved *because* of me. But I did feel uncomfortable because it implied . . . it felt . . . familial. Like how you'd treat family.

*Friendly* family. I reminded myself that as far as I knew, Merrick had no family left. I'd be coming and going. Made sense that it would be less disruptive for me to use this room and leave the other room for the aides—the job that, as a full-time gig, I'd already made it clear I couldn't accept because I had obligations back in Cub Creek. Which, when I really thought of it—right here and now—if the aides were going to sometimes overlap with me, how would we manage that interaction? And then I told myself to stop. Stop borrowing trouble. Just roll with events as they came. I wasn't so important that anyone's household should revolve around me. We'd figure it out as we went along.

And this room was very, very nice. This window was beyond all expectations.

Finally in motion, I gathered up my scattered belongings and set my things on the bed. I'd sort through them later.

I saw Davis had left me a voice mail. We were playing message tag again. I'd left him a voice mail on my drive down. I sat on the edge of the bed—a lovely bed—and listened. *"Talk to Ms. B. I'll be there on Tuesday for our date. Sooner if I can manage it."*

CR80

Merrick was in the foyer. He'd wheeled his desk chair out there and was sitting and staring at the sculpture, much as I'd done.

"What do you think?" I asked. "Will it do? I have a fourteen-day return policy. No questions asked. No restocking fees." I walked across to where he sat. "In fact, I also offer a free exchange if there's an item you'd like better."

Even though he was seated, he was holding his cane in front of him, with both hands cupped over the top of it. He was hunched forward. His chin hovered low over his hands, almost resting on them.

When I started to speak again, he raised a hand to silence me. I waited. He nodded. Then nodded again. Finally, he said, "What do you think, Lilliane?"

"I think I want you to have the one you like. If this isn't it, I'm happy to switch it out."

"It's not the one I remembered most. And yet . . . it strikes me that it thinks it belongs here. I'm trying to decide why."

"Why the *sculpture* thinks it belongs here?" I stopped short of making a wisecrack about maybe its brain needing some WD-40 or more dusting. Instead, I said, "Or maybe why it looks *to us* like it belongs?"

"Either or both."

"Do you really want an answer, or do you just want to mull over the question?"

He cast a quick look at me. "I've been mulling all the while I've been waiting for you to come down."

I grunted. "Nice view from that window up there. Hard to pull myself away from it."

He squinched his face up, still staring at the sculpture. "Nice, yes. It's convenient for you and less coordination called for from Ms. B."

"I figured as much."

"Great minds."

"Think alike?"

"Indeed." He waved his hand toward the metal art, moving it in a circular motion. "See how the rounded part of the hubcap is semireflective?"

"Yes."

"Reminds me of that Vermeer painting. I have a copy of that painting in my study."

"Really? I hadn't noticed."

"And that chain." He pointed a scrawny, big-jointed finger at the sculpture. "The broken link makes me think of mystery. Not easy to break a link that heavy duty. How did it happen?" He sat back in his chair, his back straighter. "And those flanges, twisted and flaring out, make me think of the wings of birds, soaring on the ocean breeze."

"Or across the valley looking down from the cemetery."

He looked at me again. "Where your parents are buried."

"Them and more. Generations."

He went silent. He needed a nudge. I said, "When I stared at that hubcap, I could see depths. Like worlds. All the worlds from generations behind to generations to come. Continuity. I saw the curve of the waves in the flanges and change—changes in lives and loves—in the broken link."

"Like the two of us," he said. "And those we've lost."

"Or yet to find."

"Just so."

I took his hand. Surprised, he clasped it back.

"You are a poet, Lilliane. Did you know that?"

"I am not. I'm a storyteller."

"Just so," he said. "Lucky thing we're both so ornery. We can relish our wit together and save our kindness for the rest of the world."

"Indeed," I said back to him, squeezed his hand gently, and released it. I handed him his cane. "Let's have a snack. I have a plan for after supper, and I hope you're of a mind to play along."

"What?"

"You'll find out soon enough." I winked at him. "It's a surprise."

☙❧

I remembered seeing a DVD player in his study under his television. It was a nice enough TV—better than mine, for sure—and Joe had given me a DVD he had, hoping Merrick would autograph the case. I had no idea how

Merrick would feel about that, given that he'd made it clear that the directors had told his stories badly and that he never watched them. But today, I wanted to do exactly that.

"What's that?" he asked roughly. "No."

"Yes. Please. And would you mind autographing it for a friend?"

"Throw it out."

"I want to watch it."

"Then do so, but not with me."

"I've seen it before. I want to watch it this time with you so you can tell me what those awful producers and directors and screenwriters did wrong."

A light sparked in his eyes. He laughed.

"Like a critical screening."

"Very critical."

He squinted at the DVD case and held his hand out for it. A little reluctantly, I gave it to him. "It's Joe's," I said.

He grunted, looking at it. He began to poke at it savagely with his index finger. "I remember. Oh yes, I remember what they did to my book. A perfectly fine story, and they sliced and diced it."

"It was a good movie, I thought, but I never read the book."

"All right. Fire up the electronics, then, and get yourself a comfy seat. Close those blinds, too, for better viewing. Where's that remote?"

I retrieved the remote from beside the TV. "This one?"

"No." He fidgeted with a wall switch. A screen descended from the ceiling. It had probably been ages since it had been brought down because a hinge squealed.

If he got too agitated or angry, I'd pull the plug on the movie, but I was pretty sure he'd love it—being able to express himself—and I'd make sure there was plenty of laughter. Genuine, kind laughter was, indeed, the best medicine. Laughter beat an apple a day *every* day.

CRISO

I'd waited to unpack my stuff until after Merrick had gone to bed. I was up here in this room with the glorious view—and the view kept giving even as the sunset bloomed and the moon rose and the stars arrived, first one by one, and then in bunches.

That odd feeling about being in what was clearly not a hired hand's quarters lingered. This was the nicest bedroom I'd ever seen. Did it come with strings? Maybe. Did that matter? Not for one visit, surely.

I curled up in the chair in front of the window and watched the lights play along the moving surface of the ocean—the ocean itself so dark that it seemed even more like a living, inscrutable force than it did during the day. On the horizon, there were tiny lights. Ships, of course.

Didn't most gifts and favors come with strings? Pretty much, but those strings were easier to break than the ones that came with emotional attachments. Like friendship. Like love. Even death didn't break those ties. How much more strongly did they bind you when the person was weak or vulnerable?

There wasn't much that I wouldn't do for Merrick—if it was in my power to accomplish it. That was just how I felt.

It had been easier before when he was a client and I was the hired companion/aide. Friend stuff was trickier. But it was also more rewarding—or more devastating when it went wrong.

CRISO

On Saturday morning, over breakfast, I said, "I arranged another meeting with Mr. Forbes. Kirk. Scheduled for Friday. You are welcome to join us, if you like. I've asked him to show me more safety measures, equipment information, maybe actually weld something . . . That kind of thing." Never mind that I couldn't afford the costs right now. Once I got a job, I could at least begin buying the tools and trying out this crazy idea in the evenings—assuming I'd have evenings off, of course. For now, while I was visiting Merrick, this was the perfect time for preparing. I couldn't mention all that to Merrick. As for Kirk Forbes—I'd offered him payment, and he'd answered with a big *no* right up front. Said it would be his honor.

Merrick said, "Ugh. August. Too hot this time of year for me. Are you sure you can find your way?"

"Oh, yes. I have a great sense for, memory for, directions and places. Thanks for the car, by the way."

He nodded. "It was important."

Was safety important? Of course. Did he want to make sure I had few barriers to making this trip as often as possible? Probably. I felt the weight of that a little. I'd only ever been responsible for the well-being of myself since I'd been an adult. True, I'd taken care of my great-aunt during the last two years of her life—but I'd not been responsible for her. I'd accepted this companion role as regarded Merrick, but that was just here and there. Not a consistent or permanent obligation. And yet, that seemed to be changing. It was like being in unknown territory. I reassured myself that if serious decisions ever needed to be made, Susan would do that on his behalf. I would simply play the supporting role and enjoy . . . *mostly* enjoy the friendship with Merrick.

I said, "One more thing."

"What's that?" He hardly looked up.

"I don't want a lot of remarks and such when I tell you."

He looked up. "What?"

"Davis is arriving on Tuesday."

"Oh." He sounded a little disappointed.

"For me. To pick me up. We are going on a date."

His brows soared upward, deepening the creases across his forehead, and his eyes gleamed. "That so?"

"It is. Nothing fancy. Just the two of us."

He grinned.

"Ms. B will be here. Hope you don't mind if he and I leave for a couple of hours."

"Not at all."

He'd done well. I was impressed. I wanted to move on before he messed it up. I asked, "Do you play cards?"

He got that blank look again—the one that came over his face when I changed subjects too quickly. "Cards?"

"Yes, like rummy or such? Maybe canasta?"

"You play canasta? Or were you wanting to learn how?"

"I played with my great-aunt. She taught me. Pretty canny when it came to playing cards, she was."

Merrick spoke slowly, thinking as he did. "I haven't played canasta in I don't know how many years. That's how long it's been."

"Want to give it a try?" I grinned. "The worst you'll do is lose."

"Humph."

"Which means I'll win."

He looked around the room. "I think I've got cards around here somewhere."

"No worries. I brought some with me, just in case. They're well used but not too marked up."

"The ones you and your great-aunt played with?"

"Yes, indeed." I shook my head. "Shame. She would've loved meeting you and taking you on card-wise or conversation-wise."

"You should tell me about her."

"Happy to. Will you put her in your next book?"

"No next book, so don't worry about it."

"Pity. She would've loved that too. She had adventure in her heart but never got to take it very far." I turned away.

"Where are you going?"

"Time to see what Ms. B left us for lunch, and I'll get the cards, too."

# Chapter Twenty

I'd awakened early on Sunday. Merrick didn't like to be disturbed before eight a.m., so I tiptoed out to walk on the beach just before dawn. As the fog lifted and the sun lightened the sky, I walked toward the sunrise. I tried a few photos. I hadn't learned much from the library book, but the framing part made sense—like how what I saw through the viewfinder should be framed as if I were planning to put it on the wall. The seabirds were skimming the waves for breakfast. I snapped their pictures as they dipped low into the waves to catch their breakfast. A couple of fishermen were out with their poles in the water. I saw other people, distant, strolling along the water's edge too, and I guessed they were looking for shells. And there, right at my big toe, was a small but perfect twisty shell, cream with brown and tan stripes. Careful to keep the camera dry, I grabbed the shell and held it in the palm of my hand, the seawater and sand particles still clinging to it. I tried to imagine the creature who'd called it home.

I dropped it in the little bag I'd learned to carry on these walks for just such treasures. This small beauty would join my little collection of shells back home. I'd gathered them the first time I'd come here and kept them on a shelf next to my jar of sand. Sand from The Point.

And thinking of collections, I'd discovered after I'd gotten home that at least two of the photos Sam had sent me were missing. I'd received them before going home the last time and didn't have them when I returned to Cub Creek, so . . . I didn't think Ms. B would've "collected" those for herself. Davis might've asked for one, but he hadn't. So I knew who *did* have them. He must've taken them from the table while I was down at the beach. When I'd discovered they were missing, I'd considered asking him about it when I returned. But now that I was back? I couldn't ask him, of course. I did think I might buy a couple of frames and give him a big smile when I put the empty frames on his desk. I'd think of something clever but kind to say. He'd like that.

And then there was the upcoming official first date with Davis. During my first trip here I'd seen Davis almost every day—and it had been Davis who had driven Merrick up to Cub Creek to see me and ask me to return. I'd seen him a few times on my first return trip, but not since I'd been back this time. Of course, he was traveling—handling commitments related to his new, first book. Plus, he was working on the next book. He was busy. I understood that.

But our date was planned for Tuesday and I was curious. It would be just the two of us—planned ahead and not a meeting or walk on the beach. It should be interesting.

໕໓

Merrick found that approaching first date interesting too. When I came downstairs on Tuesday before lunch, Merrick eyed my outfit. "Thought you were going out with Davis," he said.

I looked down at my shirt and shorts. "I am. He said casual. This is casual."

He made a noise. "Humph."

"Seriously, Merrick."

He said, "I haven't been on a date in a decade, maybe two, so what do I know?" He spoke as if he didn't have much interest. But he didn't stop there. "In my day, I would've called that casual with friends. I always suspected you and Davis had more in your future than friendship. Maybe you feel differently?" He shrugged. "And that's fine too. Comes down to the message you're sending, I guess."

I shook my head and gave my own *humph*. "It's different now, Merrick. People don't dress up so much. It's simpler and more honest."

"Never saw much good about *honest* in dating. Might be different now. Don't know. Shame, really. Takes away a lot of the guesswork and the fun of figuring out the other person. If it's *honest* you're looking for, stick with friendship and marriage. Skip the fun part of getting to know each other in that way. As I said, it's about the message one person is sending to the other."

I glared at him, annoyed. Frankly, I didn't have much of a wardrobe to choose from. Jeans and denim shorts and one dress that I'd brought as a *just in case*.

He added, "Plus, you and Davis aren't kids when it comes to the dating thing. You two are practically middle-aged."

"Seriously? I beg to differ."

"Differ about what qualifies as youth, if you wish, but take my advice. After all, I am certainly old enough to qualify as a sage of some degree."

I said, "You'd better be right. If I put a dress on and he shows up in cutoffs, I'm blaming you directly."

Merrick grinned, with a sly look on his face. "Blame, perhaps. Or you'll be thanking me later."

"If he gets here before I'm ready, you'd better not tell him about this conversation. Promise."

He held up his hands in mock surrender. "I promise. I'm not one to interfere. Never have been."

I ran up the stairs to my room.

Aunt Molly had given me several of her dresses as she was divesting herself of belongings. They were old enough that they were pretty much back in style now, years later. At the last minute, I'd decided to bring one with me. It was colorful, and I'd told myself it looked beachy. It was what they called a sheath dress. It had short, capped sleeves and a dropped princess neckline. I pulled it on and stood in front of the mirror. The neckline dropped enough to show the pendant. I almost removed it but paused. Maybe the pendant deserved to be shown.

Objective or not, and even though Merrick had decided to call me almost middle-aged, I did look very good. On impulse, I pinned my hair up loosely, so that the strands fell in curls that looked almost accidentally casual.

One moment of doubt tried to derail my fun, but I'd heard voices funneling up from the foyer, and I shoved the doubt out of my way. It was time.

My face was warmish, my cheeks flushed, but I felt caught in a glow—kind of like I'd seen in those photographs Sam had taken. Light and glowy and owning the space around me. I couldn't remember ever having felt that way before. I was myself, just Lilliane, but myself energized. Happy.

Davis was standing below in the foyer with Merrick. He looked up, fastened his eyes on me, and smiled, ignoring whatever Merrick was saying to him. He was wearing shorts, but tailored ones, and the shirt he'd paired with them made his look one that could go either way—dressed up or dressed down. Prepared to match whichever way I'd chosen, I realized.

As I neared the bottom step, Davis was there, his hand extended.

Merrick caught my eye. And winked.

CRISO

Later, I told Davis that I wore dresses so rarely that he might never see me in one again. He smiled, perhaps with a slightly wicked gleam in his eyes, and replied—totally gratuitously and totally over-the-top schmoozing—that I was beautiful in anything and everything and he was grateful I'd agreed to come out with him.

"Grateful? That sounds odd."

He said, "At the risk of sounding smug, I know you like me . . . but I always feel like you're ready to . . . take flight, maybe."

"I'm sorry. Sending mixed messages, I guess. My life feels up in the air."

"Is that all it is?"

We had dined on the deck of a lovely restaurant that faced the ocean. We'd left the table and were leaning against the railing as a boat went past. A short while before, a school of dolphins had made themselves known and put on a show. I was staring out at the ocean, hoping to see them again.

Davis said, "At times, I've sensed you were trying to keep distance between us."

I looked away from the waves and faced Davis. "You aren't wrong. I've avoided commitments through the years. Largely, I think, because I felt so much responsibility for things at home."

"Maybe in part because of how it was with your parents?"

"What do you mean?" I shook my head. "They adored each other."

"How they left, I meant."

"That's a strange thing to bring up on a date."

He grimaced slightly and looked aside. When he spoke again, his tone was different. "Touched a nerve. I'm sorry, and you're right."

I'd spouted off because I didn't want to discuss my parents. We were here on a date, weren't we? But maybe he was a little right too. I tried to shift the focus.

"There are different kinds of commitments, I think. Some are unavoidable, but others—others are invited into one's life. I'm careful about those because I don't want to let anyone, including myself, down. But I'm here with you right now, aren't I? I'm not running yet." I tried to smile. "What about *your* family? You don't say much about them."

"I don't know what to say. I had a privileged childhood. Had whatever I needed, most of what I wanted, took a few summer jobs, but not to earn money to support the family . . . and I'm not complaining. But there's good stuff that comes along with the messiness of life. I saw it in my friends' homes. Tears. Angry words. Worry, even. But also lots of making up, cementing relationships. My best friend argued with his brother all the time. And yet, if anyone ever messed with him, his brother was right there to have his back against all comers. I never had that. I never had a pet. I wanted a dog, but my parents said no. So I never experienced the loss of a beloved pet, but I also never experienced the adoration that only a dog can give. Sorry to run on. My family, my life, was fine. Safe. And bland."

"Your parents are still living, right?"

"Yes. I think I already told you I grew up in Florida. My parents are well and busy. They spend most of the year in Florida but since Dad retired from his firm, they go to upstate New York during the hottest part of the summer."

Giving him a serious look, I said, "I almost feel sorry for you with that bland life, but then I remember you had it all. All except the mess. And you miss the mess." I thought about seeing Miranda's garage with the evidence of lives being lived in that house. "I would miss the mess too." I smiled. "But I wouldn't have minded having some of the other benefits."

"Lilliane," he said, taking my fingers. "This may surprise you. Perhaps not. Sometimes your ability to read someone, to anticipate what they're about to do or say, is uncanny. While I have you all to myself and you're feeling reasonably warm toward me . . ." He cleared his throat. "You know I don't have firm dates yet for the book tour—looks like we're targeting sometime in late September or early October—but I hope you'll consider going with me." He held up his hand, signaling me to please listen. "I'm not asking for promises from you, and I know it would be a big thing, especially being so far from home for what looks like several weeks. But consider it. Hopefully, the problem of the workshop and your father's art will be resolved by then. We can't know that yet . . . but please consider the invitation. That's all. Just consider it."

"Okay." This was unexpected, and I was confused by my reactions—dueling threads of feeling flattered, alarmed, and resentful.

"Okay, what?"

I tried to smile because I could tell he was disappointed by my lack of enthusiasm. "I'll consider it."

"Thank you." He touched my hair. "I know this is something you have to think about. No pressure. I'd love to have you there, and it would be a trip to remember—for both of us."

The rest of our date was quite nice, and we were civil, sometimes teasing, but it wasn't quite the same.

He didn't get it, that was apparent. I suspected he thought my lack of enthusiasm was a commitment thing. But my reaction was about more than a relationship that might move too fast, or about my responsibilities back home, or even about leaving Merrick, because, yes, he'd become one of my responsibilities too. The bottom line was that I couldn't afford a trip to Europe. Any trip was too costly for me. My accounts were nearly empty. But if I said that, he'd offer to pay. Might even suspect I was manipulating him in that direction. Money *was* an issue for me. As well as time. Because I needed to work. Whether I earned money as a companion to Merrick or by working the counter at the Fuel Up Fast—I needed that paycheck. I had a home and bills. But accepting his money was not an option. It wasn't how I rolled. No charity.

For my entire adult life, I'd worked hard and been proud of my independence. It hadn't been easy, but I'd managed. Sometimes with a little help from my friends, by virtue of their skills and talents, but never by taking their money. And

I'd held my head high when richer people had looked down on me. Their opinions didn't matter because they weren't my people.

I didn't blame Davis, though, for not seeing that on his own. How could he? Plus, he'd helped me choose the phone that Merrick had paid for. He'd known about the car rental, and now the leased vehicle.

My face heated up. I turned away so he wouldn't see my blush.

"Are you okay?" he asked.

"I'm fine. Just a little overheated, I think. It's hot." I pushed away from the railing. "It's been lovely. The food was excellent, and the company was even better. Thanks. And I'll think about what you suggested."

"But it's time to get back to Merrick?"

I nodded. "I think so. He and Ms. B may need me."

"I'm sure they're fine. One or the other would call."

"Probably, unless something went seriously wrong and then maybe they couldn't."

He looked across the outside dining area, but I didn't think he was seeing the people. He said, "Are you sure it's about them?"

Speaking softly, I said, "Mostly."

An expression that suggested hurt or confusion crossed his face, but was swiftly replaced by one of acceptance.

I added, "I hope you understand."

He took my hand and said, "I'll understand better if we can stop for ice cream on the way home."

Frowning, I asked, "Ice cream?"

We walked back to the table to collect our things. I was glad to see his mood had lightened. He didn't deserve to be hurt by me. He was one of the last people I'd *want* to hurt.

He said, "Sure, ice cream. And I bet I can guess your favorite flavor."

Laughing, I said, "I doubt it. But I'm pretty sure you're a cookies 'n cream fan."

"Seriously? Well, sometimes. Mint, too. Or chocolate chip." He smiled and put his arm around me as we left the restaurant together. "You, Lilliane . . . I'm thinking you are a rocky road aficionado all the way."

# Chapter Twenty-One

The next morning, Merrick invited me to stay for a chat after breakfast. I suspected he was going to ask more questions about the lunch date I'd gone on with Davis. He'd asked yesterday after I'd returned, but I'd kept the details to simple responses like the food was good, the view was nice, and yes, we chatted. Finally, he'd given up, but I expected him to ask again and thought this was it. I was surprised when he said, "I need to speak with you about a serious matter." He pointed toward my usual chair. "Please sit and hear me out."

No grunt. No gravelly voice. This was a tone I didn't recognize. Immediately, I thought of illness. When he'd said the matter was serious, my brain heard it as *I need to break the bad news to you.*

"Merrick. What is it? What's going on? Are you ill?"

"No, but I'm anticipating resistance from you. I wish I could put this off, but it's too risky to let it ride. Even if you get angry . . . it's still better that we discuss it. You have good sense, but you are also the most stubborn woman I've ever met. I'd rather not argue, and I am most sincerely hoping you'll go along with my wishes."

So he wasn't dying. That was good. "What is it?"

"I changed my will."

Or maybe he *was* dying. Anxious, I asked, "Why? Has something happened?"

He fastened me with that impatient glare I was familiar with. It reassured me. Nothing dire was in the offing.

Annoyed, he said, "Why must something be wrong? Just because of the word *serious*? No, indeed. It's possible things finally come right. That could be true, correct?"

"Of course."

"Sit down, please."

I sat. "Okay. What is this about? As Susan says, suspense is good in books, but not in real life."

He frowned, interested. "Is that what Susan says?"

"Not exactly. Something like that. As for me, I'd rather say it straight out than to front-load it with suspense."

"Is that what you were doing when you teased about bringing me the sculpture?"

"Gifts are different."

With a *humph*, he said, "I hope you'll be good enough to remember that over the next few minutes."

"Go ahead."

"You may know that I don't have close family. In fact, my distant relations are so very distant that I haven't heard from them in years. Likely, they think I'm already deceased. Or perhaps the ones who knew me have, themselves, passed. Either way, my will is already set up to fund some charities and fellowships and such."

His will? Changed, he'd said. I thought of the new sleeping arrangements—the lovely room with a view that seemed more appropriate for family than for employees or even visiting friends. My heart rate started ticking up. I felt it in my chest and in the pulse points of my neck. The pushback force was rising strong within me.

Merrick said, "Calm down. Get that look off your face. No one's dead yet, and the charities and such are still funded. In fact, most have been funded and operating for several years. More will be upon my passing."

I sat back in the chair, more relaxed. He wanted to tell me something he considered serious. The least I could do was to be civil and let him get the words said. The sooner he was done explaining, the sooner we could resolve whatever this was about.

"Recently," he said, "I requested my attorney to add a

new provision and a new bequest." He gave me a long look, then added, "For you."

"No, Merrick."

"I asked that you listen and consider. You said you would."

I sat back again, but my hands were clenching the armrests of the chair, and my chin was stubborn and stuck out, ready to argue.

"There is a bequest for you after my death, but I hope that won't happen for some time yet. Certainly, I prefer not to die to accomplish my purpose. I want to share some of my good fortune with you now. I owe you more than I can ever repay. You won't understand that because you're young. But I'm hoping you *might* understand because you've experienced deep losses and loneliness yourself.

"I cannot give you much now, not outright, without incurring tax liabilities for you, but my attorney has set up a trust that will pay out on a regular basis—"

Interrupting him, I stood. "I don't take charity. I'm here as your employee. Being your friend is incidental—"

He interrupted me back. "And I hope you will continue to be so. This is not charity. This is a business arrangement. You will work full-time at the metal art—at least for as long as you wish—and this stipend from the trust will pay your expenses."

"It's too much, Merrick. Way too much. I accepted the bonus checks, the phone, the car . . ."

"Those were for *my* convenience, Lilliane. I appreciate your courtesy in accepting them since it makes it easier for me to be in touch with you."

"But now you're adding in these other things."

"What I'm proposing is no different from arts patronage through the centuries, whether funded by universities, governments, or wealthy patrons. The time and tools of crafting art can be costly. I fund your ability to create, and in turn I shall receive satisfaction and some of the items you produce, at your discretion." His manner and tone were increasingly intense and reached a scary peak as he said, "As my friend, would you deny me this joy?"

His face was now deep scarlet, and he was standing hunched over his desk like it might need to catch him. His voice and hands were shaking.

I dialed my own anger back. Or was it my pride?

I reached across to touch his shoulder, speaking gently. "Take a deep breath, my friend. Deep, slow breaths and sit down, please. I wouldn't dare take your blood pressure right now. You'd probably blow the machine into a million little pieces."

He sat, and I continued evenly, "You've already done more for me than any human alive or dead—except maybe my parents, though . . . maybe not. I loved them and still do, and I don't want to sound ungrateful or disloyal. They brought me into this world and gave me all that they could without exception. My former husband, Joe, is the greatest guy—it may sound funny for me to say that, but it's true. He has always helped me, and with a glad heart. But you, Merrick, take the cake. You gave me a love of reading. You let me consult on your book. Who in their right mind would ever have allowed Lilliane Moore of Cub Creek to do that? You gave me the chance to experience the ocean and to do so without conditions. Through you, I met Miranda, Davis, and Susan. I have an article about me and my family written by a famous photojournalist, for heaven's sake, and photos that make me look almost glamorous." To soothe him, I added, "As for the rest of this—these financial things you've mentioned—you'll have to allow me to think on it. Anything remotely like this . . . was far from my mind."

He looked aside.

"Merrick," I whispered. "If I was ever going to have family—family I could pick and choose for my own—it would be you. I know that my parents are pleased that fate, or providence, brought us together." My eyes stung. "And now, I'm going to get us each a snack. Something restoring. I feel . . . overwhelmed."

He nodded, still not meeting my eyes.

I said, "At home, I don't often eat snacks. Did you know that?"

He didn't answer. I waited him out, staring at his averted face. Finally, he responded. "No, I did not."

"I don't enjoy snacks at home because they are almost always eaten alone." I stopped there and let the words speak for themselves.

Merrick said, "Tea. Hot tea, if we have it."

"Dandelion and honey tea, coming right up." I added, "Stay seated, please. This has been . . . stunning . . . for us both."

I walked away with a deliberate display of composure, but as soon as I was sure he couldn't see me, my shaking knees took over. Regret. Guilt. I was his paid companion and also his friend; I'd almost done him in with my offended reaction. My pride. Shame on me. I could have said a simple *no thank you*, and I could've done so without turning his attempt at kindness into the opening round of a nasty alley fight.

Abruptly, in the kitchen, I sat on the nearest stool and leaned my arms on the island counter.

Had I reacted like that out of surprise and shock because I'd never expected any such offer from him? Or because, with the money having been offered, the temptation was so heavy, so compelling . . . I could honestly say it had never occurred to me that he'd make such an offer, but when it came to refusing his generosity . . . I wasn't sure why it would be such a dreadful gift to accept.

But what would people think? My friends, that is. Maybe strangers. I'd never worried too much about the judgment of others, had I?

My face heated up, and I waved my hands in an empty room. *Stop it,* I told myself. *Stop now. Think about it later.*

*When my temper has cooled. After I've gotten Merrick settled again.*

Forcing myself to move, I put the water on to heat and prepared the tea bags in the cups. As I laid the biscuits out on the plates, I saw my hands were still shaking. It made me more concerned for Merrick. I hurried back to the study, almost forgetting the tea, and found him fine. He was slightly subdued, perhaps, but calm and seemingly focused on his email. When I walked in, he closed the laptop lid easily, as if nothing was troubling him. I knew better. But if he could pretend so convincingly, then maybe he was doing okay.

It felt awkward sitting there with him sipping tea and nibbling cookies. I could see he felt it too. I was watching him until he looked at me, and this time I looked away. It struck me how uncannily alike we were. Not just in stubbornness and self-reliance, but in how we nibbled our cookies and how we avoided reigniting conflict with each other. Being careful—not of each other, but of each other's feelings.

"Merrick," I said. "May I propose a cessation of hostilities?"

The corner of his mouth quirked up.

I shrugged. "I heard that phrase somewhere. It sounded eloquent."

Now his lips curved up on *both* sides.

"I propose," I said, working hard to keep it calm, "that we table our earlier discussion for forty-eight hours. At that time, we can reassess."

"Counter proposal. Twenty-four hours." He surveyed my expression, then added, "Time waits for no one. It's up to us to mind our minutes."

I stared at him. "Feels like I should cross-stitch that on a sofa pillow."

He frowned, but in an interested way. "Do you cross-stitch?"

"No. My momma did. I expect I could learn, if need be."

"I expect you could, Lilliane. In fact, I don't doubt it for a minute."

CR&SD

I sat at the table by the pool. I'd put on my swimsuit with a long T-shirt over it, so if Merrick noticed he'd assume I was going for a dip. I needed my emotions to get out of my way so I could think clearly. What he'd said to me weighed heavily on my mind. I was confused. I didn't have many friends, as such. Joe was a friend. Gwen was a friend too, but . . . I knew what she would say. I'd never take this to Joe because, before the sun rose, he'd have everyone in five counties thinking I was an heiress. Davis? No. I already had a sneaking suspicion that Davis was slightly jealous of my relationship with Merrick. His remark about being kept at arm's length . . . He didn't see that in my actions with Merrick, but he was right about himself.

That left Susan. She was almost a friend. And I knew where her primary loyalty lay. With Merrick. Merrick had surely involved Susan in this idea of his. Yes, she was the one I should talk to. Yet, I hesitated. Why?

This matter felt like it was just between Merrick and me. The two of us. As if we'd reached a new level of . . . I searched my brain for the right word and couldn't find it.

*Personal.* It felt personal and . . . like family.

Maybe that was it. This was a personal level we hadn't really touched before. Before, when it had come to all things money and job related, Merrick had told Susan what he wanted, and Susan alone had discussed it with me.

Yes, this was different. Personal. For now, I'd keep my own counsel even though more than twenty-four hours had passed without mention of our deadline to revisit the subject. I guessed he was as reluctant as I was to wade back into that discussion.

I ditched the T-shirt and stepped down into the pool.

Semifloating, I watched the moon and the stars. Somehow, I was sure I'd know what to do about Merrick—and maybe Davis too—when the time came.

And in two days, on Friday, I had a date with Kirk Forbes—in a manner of speaking. I smiled at the night. He was going to show me some basic ropes of metalworking, and I was very likely to sweat out a lot of pent-up angst like I'd never done before.

Might be a good thing.

And it should be interesting."

# Chapter Twenty-Two

Thursday passed unremarkably. Neither of us brought up touchy subjects. The truce was holding despite the passing of the agreed deadline, but the contention was there around us like an ever-present shadow, kept subdued in a corner only by our unusual courtesy. We were so very polite.

We were polite because we cared, of course. But such civil interactions between us weren't natural and couldn't last. Which made me edgy. Him too. So when we met over breakfast on Friday morning, neither of us was feeling relaxed or easy.

I reminded him of my plan to meet with Mr. Forbes, and he grunted in approval as he ate his fruit. I greeted Ms. B when she arrived in the morning and told her too.

"I'll be gone for a few hours in the middle of the day. I hope you don't mind."

"No problem. I'll get his lunch for him. Got plans? Another date?"

Did she wink at me? I thought maybe she had.

"Not with Davis this time. I have a date with metal."

"What? Please?"

"A metalworker. He is going to show me how to handle metalworking tools."

"Oh, of course." She nodded but then looked at me again as if I'd grown a second nose. "Why?"

"The metal sculptures my dad made?" I gestured toward the foyer. "I'm thinking of trying it myself."

Ms. B gasped, then scoffed, then outright laughed.

I stared in amazed wonder as she regained control of

herself. I'd never heard her laugh that I could recall. Everyone else had been supportive. *Of course you will, of course you can,* they'd said. I wondered if her reaction might've been the most honest of them all.

"Sorry. So sorry, Lil-li. I'm thinking you need to eat better. Eat more. You need to build up more muscles for that kind of work."

In exaggerated fashion, I did a couple of bodybuilder poses. Ms. B wailed in laughter this time. Of course, we drew Merrick's attention. We heard his cane tapping in the hallway, and we looked at each other—which made her laugh all the more as she covered her face, trying to stop.

"What's wrong with you two?" he asked. "Ms. Bertie, are you okay?"

She nodded, pressing a cloth to her wet eyes. "Fine. Fine, Mr. Dahl."

I smiled at Merrick. "She thinks I should work on building more muscles if I'm going to work with metal."

"She has a point. But if you do that sort of work, I suspect you'll build those muscles over time, whether you want to or not. *If* you have the right tools. *If* you have the workspace you need."

*And it all costs. That's what he's saying.*

I couldn't resist responding. "True. And I may not get everything I need overnight, but I can use what I have as a start. I may not even stick with it, so there's no need to invest in a lot of expensive tools yet." I waited, and he said nothing more, so I added, "I'm leaving for Kirk Forbes's place in an hour or so. Anything I can do for you before I go?"

His words came as almost a non sequitur, but I understood his message clearly when he said, "Some gifts are for the convenience of the giver. Some gifts—sometimes the costliest ones—aren't about present gain at all, whether for wealth or convenience, but about a promise for the future, and about the mark we made . . . or didn't . . . while here."

CRSO

Kirk and I had already agreed that this meeting was about tools, their usage, and safety measures. And it was now August in North Carolina, so yes, it was hot.

"Stay well watered, Lilliane."

"No worries."

He reached into a cardboard box and grabbed a clean cloth from the top. He offered it to me. "Tuck this into your pocket or waistband. You'll need it."

He'd already made printouts of the tools he thought I should start with in my own shop, then he took me through his tools one by one, explaining them, firing them up, and letting me have a go with them.

After forty-five minutes, I was flagging.

Before the hour was done, Kirk said, "Time to break."

"Yes." I suspected I might need more than a break. I was done in. I plucked the rag from my waistband and wiped my face for the gazillionth time. When I looked up, I saw Davis.

He was standing in the open doorway, watching Kirk and me. The overhead fans blasting air at us were not enough to dry up the sweat. My clothes were clinging to my body and dripping, and the salty perspiration that trickled down my face stung my eyes. I grabbed a fresh rag and mopped my face with it, then picked up my bottle of water, drank what was left, and craved more. When I was done, I spoke to Kirk and motioned toward the doorway. He saw Davis too and nodded. I left him there and walked over.

I said, "I wasn't expecting to see you here. That's maybe some kind of understatement, but my brain is too tired to figure it out. How'd you know where I was? Must've been Merrick."

"Ms. B, actually. Merrick was napping. I never expected . . . this."

"Well, you did say that you'd always know where to find me. Maybe that includes knowing who to ask."

GRACE GREENE

"I remember. I said it on the beach soon after we first met, and more recently on the phone."

I mopped my face again. "It's a famous line from that movie, *The Last of the Mohicans*."

"In fact, you are correct."

"It's a good line. A very romantic line."

Davis grinned and moved toward me. I held out my hand with the sweat rag dangling from it to stop him.

"No. I'm sopping wet with hot sweat and gritty with salt. Probably smell like a fired-up furnace too."

"You wear it well. It's an intriguing scent. And, frankly, Lilliane, if you don't mind me saying so, there's something rather sexy about you standing over that forge with a flamethrower."

"There's no forge here, and that's not a flamethrower."

"I write fiction, Lilliane. Allow me some leeway."

"Leeway? How about answering a basic question? Why are you here? What was so important that you couldn't wait until I returned to Merrick's?"

"A gift. I have a gift for you. I went to Merrick's to find you and . . . you weren't there, so I just kept going."

"Well, don't stop now." I smiled. "Follow me a little farther. You found me, but I know where to find some cooler air." I headed to the porch.

⊂⊃

Davis followed me onto the porch and pulled the door closed behind him. He paused and looked slightly awkward, as if realizing he was entering someone's home with no more than my invitation. I'd already sat, all but panting. Mrs. Forbes came out to the porch with two bottles of water and a plate of cookies, then went back inside.

"Thanks," he said to her retreating back.

"She doesn't say much but is very kind. I wonder how she feels about strangers showing up on her porch like this?"

I was hoping she'd come back out with chocolate cake, but she didn't. I smiled, thinking to myself, *We'll make do,* and bit into the cookie. I was feeling much better by now, and frankly, I didn't care how I looked. It was August and hot. Davis had shown up without fair warning. He'd have to take me as he'd found me.

He sat in the nearest chair and picked up a cookie. After he finished it—possibly giving me a minute to recover—he said, "You are really going to do this, aren't you?"

"Maybe. I think so. Might dabble with it. Even if I might give it a real effort, I could still decide I don't want to spend my time with torches and blades and bolts." I took a long swig of water, recapped the bottle, and said, "But I'm enjoying doing something different. Feels good." I laughed about the word *feels.* That word had a heck of a lot more dimension than it got credit for. I added, "But I suspect I picked the wrong season for it."

Kirk was approaching the house. His face was beet red, and he was as sweat-soaked as I was. He joined us on the porch.

He said, "Calling it a day?"

I nodded. "I think so." I gestured toward Davis. "This is my friend Davis McMahon. He's a writer like Merrick. Has a book about to come out and is writing another."

Davis looked surprised. I took some satisfaction in that.

Kirk smiled broadly. "That so?" he asked, looking at Davis. "What's it called?" He sat in the empty seat. Mrs. Forbes appeared again with another bottle of water, which she handed to her husband.

Davis told him the book title.

"I'm going to buy a copy when it's in the stores. Maybe you can sign it for me?"

"Happy to."

"Kirk," I said, "I think it's time I got back to Emerald Isle. I left the list I was making in the shop. I'll go grab it. You stay here and cool down. Thank you so much for all your help."

"My pleasure," he said. "I'm excited to see what you turn out, working in your daddy's shop."

"Me too," I said softly. And now the warmth I felt was in my chest. "I'm looking forward to that too."

I left them on the porch. It was still hot in Kirk's metalworking shop, but I'd cooled off enough that the wind from the overhead fans felt good to me now. I found my list beside the soldering coil and the small torch that would melt it. Kirk had discussed the main tools with me and had advised which ones I should buy, including brands and models. I was close to being ready to take this on. But it *would* cost. Even Joe couldn't pull off everything in trade or as a freebie. I left the metal shop and stood in the shade of a large, sheltering tree.

"Did you sigh?"

Davis had come up behind me.

"Maybe a little."

"What's wrong?"

I shoved some stray hairs out of my face, except they were stuck to my skin and wouldn't move. I tried to pull them free. "Nothing, really. It's just a big undertaking."

"And Merrick? How is he doing?"

The mention of his name, just as I was thinking about the expense of taking on this . . . hobby? Or would it be a real, actual thing that I would dedicate my time to? But how could I do it, whether as hobby or career, without the updated tools?

All that effort just to let down my friends and give a whole bunch of others an excuse to laugh at me.

"You look upset. Is something wrong? If I spoiled things by coming out here, I'm sorry."

As we approached the cars, I shook off my personal worries to answer his question about Merrick. "Merrick's fine. Why do you ask? Have you noticed anything with him?" I did have concerns. Davis, not being around as much these days, might've noticed something I'd missed. "At least that awful bruise is gone."

He reached over and touched my hair, unsticking a strand I'd missed freeing. I stood there wishing I didn't look so bad, but he said, "You are more beautiful every time I see you."

I didn't know what to say. My initial response was to joke it away and make some self-deprecating remark, but it wouldn't, couldn't be said this time. I might look a mess, but I felt . . . beautiful . . . vital . . . and that might've been in part because of the gleam in Davis's eyes.

There was a long moment of silence between us, but though it lacked words it was full of promise and fear and possibilities. One of us must break it, but neither seemed inclined to. Then Kirk called out, "Hang on. The missus has something for Mr. Dahl." We looked, the spell broken, as Kirk crossed the yard carrying something in his hands. He said, "The wife wants to send this with you, for you and Mr. Dahl." As he handed me the foil-covered plate, he added, "He was taken with that chocolate cake of hers, you know."

"He was indeed. Please thank her for us." I looked over at the house, and even though I couldn't see her clearly, her form was just visible on the porch. I smiled and waved. "And thank you again, Kirk, for everything."

"My pleasure," he said and stepped away.

Davis opened my car door for me. I appreciated the gesture, then remembered what he'd said.

"You have a gift for me? You said that, right? Unless my overheated brain imagined it."

"I do."

"Well, then?"

"It's in my car. Don't leave."

In fact, not only didn't I leave, but I continued standing beside the open door, curious.

He was back in a moment with a small package wrapped in paper. I knew what it was before it reached my hands.

Davis said, "It's the ARC . . . the trial run, so to speak, of the printed book."

"Your book?"

He nodded. "The fact of its existence is mind-blowing to me. I never expected this day to arrive."

I held the book close to me. "May I open it?"

"Please do. But remember it's not the final edition. Might be a lingering error or two in there. All that's getting corrected now, but the final edition won't be out until the tour. I wanted to share this with you now."

With me. No wonder he'd been so excited and eager. Feeling shy, I removed the wrapping. The cover showed a landscape scene of distant snowcapped peaks, and in the foreground, a small village. *All the Days Yet to Come* was written across the blue sky, and *Davis McMahon* was printed in large letters across the bottom.

A surge of happiness swept me, and impulsively, I reached up, put my hand behind his neck, and pulled his face toward me. I kissed him before suddenly remembering how filthy I was. And I laughed.

His eyes glittered.

I said, "Thank you."

He said, "I'll follow you back to Merrick's, but I can't stay. I have a meeting to dial into later that might go long."

"I understand."

All the way back to Merrick and Emerald Isle, the cake rode safely on my passenger seat, and judging by the size of the covered plate, there was plenty for both of us. Maybe for all of us.

CRSO

Davis did come in, but only for a moment, he said. After a quick peek in the study to check in with Merrick, I left Davis with him and headed straight up to my room for a shower. I stood under that amazing spray and let it sweep all the salt and perspiration away in rivulets to be banished down the shower drain. I tried to hurry because Davis was downstairs, and I wanted to thank him again—looking more like my usual self—and make a fuss over the book and all that. But even so, he was already gone by the time I was done and in the study.

Merrick said, "He said he was sorry. A meeting. He said you knew."

"I did." I shook off the disappointment. "Did he tell you what he brought me?"

"No. What?"

I showed him the book. He took it into his hands and held it like a delicate work of art as he stared at the cover for a long moment. I watched his face and thought it might be how a man might look when seeing his first grandchild.

Softly, I said, "Davis said it's not the final edition. It's the . . . what did he call it?"

Without looking up, he said, "An ARC. Advanced reader copy." He looked up slowly, saying, "It takes me back, Lilliane. Back to long ago."

"Memories?"

He nodded.

That same rush of impulsiveness that had come over me with Davis filled me again. I walked to stand beside Merrick and put my hand on his shoulder. I gave him a gentle pat, and his hand came up to cover mine, while he continued holding the book with the other.

I said, "Ms. B left a baked spaghetti casserole for us. I'll get things started for our meal."

Not moving, Merrick said, "Wait." A few seconds passed before he continued. "You never did say much about the date with Davis. It's been several days."

"Four days. And, as I already told you, our date was lovely." I wouldn't mention Davis's invitation. It would lead to either speculation from him about Davis and me, or into Merrick's money discussion that I'd so far avoided. I didn't want to get drawn into discussing either. Merrick had allowed the twenty-four truce to extend to forty-eight hours and counting, likely because he didn't want to press me until he felt surer of getting the answer he wanted.

"You two going out again?"

"I believe so. But as you know, he's very busy these days. Not like when I was here before."

"And you have big plans on your mind too."

"True." I stopped there, not sure where to go with it.

"How'd it go at Kirk Forbes's shop today?"

"Hot. So hot. But interesting." In fact, I was sagging a bit after my stint in the metal shop, and Merrick . . . he seemed a little lost.

"Why don't you look at the book while I get supper together. We can talk about it over our food."

He nodded.

CRSO

He seemed less engaged during the meal. Not even distracted, as he sometimes was. I thumbed through *All the Days Yet to Come*, and he made noises and comments that were appropriate, but . . .

Then he went to bed but didn't join me poolside for a snack. I checked on him, and he seemed fine. Just tired, he said. His laptop was turned off and in its place on his desk, so the reason for his withdrawal wasn't because he was sneak-writing in bed again.

I was worried/not worried. But I was watchful as ever.

But the next morning, he decided not to get out of bed.

# Chapter Twenty-Three

The next morning, I had his breakfast in his study at eight a.m., as usual, but he wasn't there, and his bedroom door was still closed.

I knocked lightly. "Merrick?"

Faintly, he responded, "Come in."

He was in bed. The first thing I did was to place my hand on his forehead.

"I'm not sick."

"Then why aren't you up, dressed, and eating breakfast?"

"I'm old. Ninety. I've earned a lazy morning."

I frowned and sat on the side of the mattress. He quirked an eyebrow up at me. I asked, "Do you hurt anywhere? Did you fall?"

He sighed. "Last night."

"What?" I exclaimed, alarmed, all set to check him for injuries.

"Fell right into bed and pulled my covers up snug. Slept soundly."

"Wretched man. You scared me." I shrugged. "It's fine to stay in bed. I imagine your back will be hurting soon from it. But if this is what you really want . . . I'll leave you alone, *if* you'll have a bite to eat first. I'm not dealing with low-blood-sugar spells if I can avoid it."

He all but spit the words at me. "What is the deal with low blood sugar? You have some kind of strange fixation on *low blood sugar*."

Without expression, I said, "Because you are prone to

low blood sugar. You and I eat lots of small meals and snacks because of your *tendency* to low blood sugar." Just to be annoying, I stayed with the theme. "In fact, low blood sugar, for those with a tendency *toward* low blood sugar, can be very serious."

"I surrender. You win." And he did, indeed, sound weary.

"Let's compromise. I'm going to prop you up in bed and bring you the tea and fruit from your breakfast. After you eat and drink, then you can go back to sleep if you want."

He nodded.

I helped him sit up and scoot back, then tidied his covers. His hair was bedhead crazy, but I resisted going for a comb. I brought the tray of food over to him.

"You said fruit and tea. That's a whole meal."

I set it on his lap. "Don't move or you'll have it all over you and the bedding. Then you'll have to get up so we can change the sheets and blanket. You don't have to eat it all. Only eat the fruit and drink the tea. The rest is optional and up to you." I went over and opened the curtains and blinds.

"It's too bright," he said.

"Vitamins C and D, delivered handy-dandy and free of charge. Be grateful."

"You are bossy."

I ignored that. "Would you like the TV on? Maybe something mindless or an oldie-but-goldie in black-and-white?"

He ignored me.

I found the remote and turned the TV on. "Oh, look," I said. "*Perry Mason*." He didn't answer. "Okay. Oh, look here. A movie. *The Maltese Falcon* with . . . what's his name?"

"That'll do. Stop switching those channels around. It's aggravating."

"At your command."

He grunted. "I know you're worried. That's why you're

hovering. I'm fine, Lilliane."

I collected the empty fruit bowl and pushed the oatmeal toward him. "A couple of bites, please." I added, "I was wondering if I should call Dr. Barnes to come by. I'm trusting you, Merrick, to tell me the truth. How do you feel?"

Softly, he said, "Blessed." He grinned and added, "But lazy. And I'm fine, so don't worry over me."

"That's what I do best, Merrick." I checked his nightstand for his phone and his alert pendant. As I turned away from him, this time my eyes caught what they'd missed before.

Two framed photos were hung on the wall opposite his bed. They were beautifully framed and matted as if intended for an honored place in a museum. In one, I was seated on the cemetery wall and staring down across the meadow. In the other I was laughing at something Sam and I had been discussing. Both were remarkable photographs. Merrick had had them framed and displayed where he would see them daily.

He'd fallen utterly silent. I turned to face him.

He cleared his throat. In a croaking voice, he asked, "Do you mind?"

My eyes burned and I was worried I'd lose control. I managed to say, "No, not at all." But true to form, I couldn't help adding, "As with my father's metal sculpture in your foyer, these look like they are exactly where they are meant to be."

Softly, he said, "Thank you."

Shaking off the emotion, I said gently, "You have your alert pendant, and your phone still has a charge. I'll leave you in peace. Call if you need me." I added, "I'll be nearby."

I left him then with the door cracked open a bit, just in case, and I understood it was now time to call Susan.

CRLED

"I must've been thinking about you too loudly," Susan said, laughing. "If I believed in psychic connections, I'd swear we had one. I was just reaching to push the call button when you rang."

Rarely did she show that much emotion in her voice, and she never joked.

"You sound happy," I said. I'd just stepped out the door to the pool area, and the bright light hurt my eyes. I brought up my hand to shade them as I said, "I apologize for bringing negative news—"

She cut me off. "*I* have news. *Very interesting news.* News that could make all the difference, Lilliane."

"But—"

"Wait. Let me get it said, okay?"

"Go ahead."

"I just got off the phone with a producer who's done some of those shows. You know, like the Picasso in the attic, odd inheritances found in unexpected places, those antiques and vintage items that people find in Aunt Maisy's closets and want appraised—those shows. He called me *after* the print mag called to ask if we'd be open to this project. They are talking about doing a short publicity segment that can cross-promote the special-edition issue and the cable show. Frankly, they want you involved too. They saw Sam Markham's photos, and the combination of story, words, visual, and you could be *the* winning difference—*per them.*"

She waited, but not for long. "I'm hearing silence from you, Lilliane. Are you stressing? You should be celebrating. This won't be any different than what you did in the magazine interview, and you enjoyed that, right? I could tell you did. And it's just a one-shooting deal—not a series or a long-term commitment. They'll need your cooperation, so you'll be in the driver's seat." Her voice changed as she dropped it to an excited whisper. "*You*, Lilliane Moore, *will* be able to have your cake and eat it too."

After a long minute, she said, "I'm *still* hearing silence."

"I'm stunned. That's all. I don't know whether to faint or throw up."

"Don't do either. Run down to the ocean like you do when you need to think. If you can, tell Merrick first. I haven't mentioned this to him. It's your business, and I thought you might want to be the one to share it with him. I know he'd love to hear about it from you."

"This is so . . . awesome. It's kind of overwhelming, but like a fearful awe, and also exciting, like generating so much awe inside me that I might actually be able to fly."

"Best reaction I've ever heard to good news. Now, listen—I know that you've been tinkering around in the shed. Please tell me you haven't changed too much."

"No, not much. Moved some tools around on the workbench. Tried to reduce the dust. It was thick as a blanket and probably filled with allergens and mites and such, so that's necessary. I took down two of the pieces. One is in my house, and I can put it back up. The other is in Merrick's foyer. Should I ask him if I can take it back temporarily?"

"Hmm. I just had a flash of an idea about that. Give me the afternoon to think on it. And listen, best not to mention this around yet. Wait until we're signing the papers. Never know who might overhear or know somebody who knows somebody, and then things can get complicated or can even kill the deal. Frankly, Lilliane, I don't have numbers yet, but I believe the monies we can get for you out of this deal will fund you for quite a while and could lead to more. If you must tell someone, tell no one but Merrick. He'll understand the discretion that's required."

"About Merrick . . . I don't want to dampen your high, Susan, but I need to talk to you about what he's suggesting."

"You mean about the will and the trust he wants to set up?"

I was stunned on top of already being stunned. I sat in the nearest pool chair, my back to the house. "You knew about that?"

"Of course. He probably could've managed the arrangements directly with his attorney, but better for it to be done with my help."

I was hearing *business-business-business* in her voice. The adrenaline already fueling me from worry about Merrick, from the crazy-good news she'd shared—it all twisted into an ugly, irrational resentment. My voice changed, growing cold and calculating, and loud, too loud, as I stood, saying, "I always said I don't take charity. Guess that's not true anymore. I'm being bought—and allowing it. That's it, short and simple. I'll take Merrick's money and give up some of my life and walk away all the richer for it."

This time *I* heard silence. That emptiness reminded me of that struck-dumb look people who had it all would give you when you actually opened your mouth and spoke up for yourself. And I thought of my father, who'd joined the service only to be bossed around by people who knew less than he, who probably couldn't even change the oil in their own cars.

He'd left. I felt that need to run, too, but I didn't want to leave. It made me feel . . .

Sarcastically, I said, "You pay handsomely, I give you credit for that. You more than make it worth my while to hang around here." As if I wouldn't otherwise? The warring thoughts jarred my brain.

Susan said, "I am trying to figure out how we got to that from where we were."

If I'd ever heard hurt in Susan's voice, I was hearing it now.

Were those noises behind me? From the house? It was hard to be sure over the roar in my ears and the racing of my heart.

Agitated, I had to move. I fled the pool area and headed for the gazebo. I sat on the bench there in the shade, and after a few deep breaths, the sound of the ocean began to penetrate my . . . distress, its song soothing the ragged emotions.

More calmly, I said, "Susan, I don't take charity. I stand on my own. I never had much, but I always had pride in my self-reliance. My independence. I've already accepted so much. I feel . . . like a leech. A parasite." Tears were suddenly streaming down my cheeks. "The cars, the phone . . . and now . . . what will people think, Susan? They'll think I've gotten close to Merrick for his money. I'm not that person. I can't be that person."

"Oh, Lil. Honey. If I were there, I'd give you a hug. And I never hug anyone, except my own kids. But I'd give you one for sure. Where are you at?"

"The gazebo."

"Good. A good, quiet, private place. Did Merrick ever tell you the gazebo was his wife, Marie's, idea? She considered it a portal, a sort of magical door between the land and the sea. She was rather fanciful. So breathe it all in and close your eyes. Feel the ocean breeze and listen to me."

But she stopped speaking.

I asked, "Aren't you going to talk?"

"Just wanted to be sure I had your attention. So here's the thing, as far as my rational mind and objective eyes can see it. Take it for what you will and make your own decisions. Here goes: I am fully aware of Merrick's intention, that this is what he wants, and I fully support his wishes."

"But it's like receiving pay under false pretenses. Call it charity or whatever else you will, it's not right."

She countered, "But is that really what's happening? Or is it that a woman without a family found a man who needed a family, and each one gave to the other the gifts each had to give and to share? What else is this but the completion of that circle? It benefits them both. Merrick is generous to charities and other organizations, but receiving the opportunity, the gift of being able to directly benefit someone he cares about, is one that can't be manufactured. It is personal for him and for you. And for people like you and Merrick, that's hard.

You are private and stubborn and proud. But that gift of love, of being able to pass on some of what you've created during your life and being able to pass it on to someone who loves you enough to see the value and to cherish it? To be able to do that and see the growth of that in your lifetime? That is a connection that's the most awesome and completing of all."

After a pause, she added, "It can be satisfying and fulfilling for both of you, if you can drop your pride and defenses and not worry about the opinions of others. That is a selfless act. An act of love to be commended."

And she stopped. Wow, I thought. No wonder she was good at her job. Not because she was insincere, but because she could . . . find the right words and arrange them such that they communicated her heart's intent.

"I understand," I said. "Other than needing to earn an honest wage, this has never been about the money for me."

"Of course not. No one who knows you would think that."

"Thank you. I'm . . . sorry. I don't remember exactly what I said, but I think some of it was meant for others—people not here—and not for you. You just happened to be in the crossfire."

"Not a problem, Lilliane. Now a question from me: Will you tell Merrick?"

"I will."

"What will you tell him?"

"About the possible deal. As for the rest, I'm not sure."

"Fair enough."

I grunted Merrick-style.

"Now, as for *your* business, shall I tell them you're a *go* for this? When do you expect to be back in Cub Creek?"

"Whenever they need me there."

"Excellent. I'll be in touch. And, Lilliane?"

"Yes?"

"If you start worrying over any of this, talk to Merrick. He's pretty savvy about things. He's had a lot of years, not to mention lots of successes and failures to learn from. On the other hand, if he's being annoying, go down to the beach and commune with the ocean. Do what works for Lilliane, because she's got some truly exciting stuff coming up, and we want her happy—tip-top and not wrought up."

"Thanks, Susan. One more thing. The negative thing I mentioned. Merrick stayed in bed this morning. He's seemed a little lethargic over the last few days, except for when . . . well, like when I was choosing what to wear for lunch with Davis or things like that. He perks up then. I'd like to call Dr. Barnes and ask him to drop by. Merrick forbade it. What do you think?"

"I trust your instincts. Call Dr. Barnes, and when he arrives, just let him in. Don't bother with explanations to Merrick. He's not stupid. He knows."

"Thanks again."

"My pleasure. And as for the date, what *did* you wear?"

"What Merrick suggested."

She laughed. I could still hear her laughing even after the call disconnected.

*Humph.* It was all well and fine for Ms. Susan Biggs to laugh. I was the one Merrick was going to be angry with.

CR80

The call with Susan had done me a world of good. I continued sitting in the gazebo for a while, emotionally spent, knowing my eyes were red from crying but also feeling clearheaded and optimistic about the future. What was the old saying? About pride going before a fall? I thought that maybe my pride had been offended today. And unnecessarily. Apparently, my pride had a temper.

I had a whole new respect for Susan, both for her professionalism and her kindness. I watched the waves roll in for a few minutes—I'd be back for more—but before I left the gazebo, I placed that call to Dr. Barnes.

Merrick and I would also discuss the issue of the will and the trust, as I'd told Susan. But that would wait until after the doctor's visit.

Back in the house and suddenly thirsty, I stopped in the kitchen for a tall glass of something refreshing. I found iced tea in the fridge and poured a glass. And felt eyes on me.

Ms. B was standing in the doorway. Staring. But when I looked her way, she shifted her attention, turning away and moving to stand at the counter. But she wasn't *doing* anything. Just standing there with her back to me.

I said, "I wasn't expecting you today. It's Saturday, right? Is everything okay?"

She mumbled words about forgetting something or other and coming back for it, but she continued to stand with her back like a wall. My sense of being shut out was overwhelming.

"Did you mind that I'm taking some iced tea? You weren't saving it for someone in particular?"

She hunched her shoulders a little and kept her back to me. "Fine. Whatever you want. Just take it."

No words had ever been spoken so obviously at odds with the intent of the speaker.

"Have I done something? Offended you in some way?"

She ignored me.

I knew her. We were friends. If something was wrong, I was supposed to ask, right? I moved closer. Her hands were empty. Had she found what she came for? Was it an important item? I hesitated, my hand hovering near her shoulder, before it finally landed. It felt awkward, but after a second my hand settled more comfortably.

"Ms. Bertie. Please talk to me. What's wrong?"

Her hands became fists. "You. Why did you say the awful things?"

When I'd first met her, I'd caught the slight accent that reminded me of Ms. Nachek, one of my longtime Fuel Up Fast customers. Now Ms. B's accent was much more pronounced. "What? What are you talking about? Please tell me."

"You were his friend. We believed so. You want his money? He would give it. You could ask and he would." She sniffled. "You will break his heart."

"What are you talking about?"

Despite myself, I gripped her shoulder too hard. She shook my hand off and faced me squarely.

"Oh, I know. I heard. And not just me. I heard the words. I wish not."

"What did you hear?"

"You said you weren't his friend. You said, *staying for money like a bought person.*"

She was upset, but it was my heart that was racing. Running away racing. If people who knew me could hear or see one little thing—and so easily believe awful things . . . I broke off and stepped away.

"You eavesdropped, Ms. Bertie. You overheard a private conversation, only a very few words, and instead of asking me about it—and asking about the parts that you *didn't* hear—you jumped to conclusions. Mean, hurtful conclusions about me."

"No, not just me, Lil-li. We *both* heard you say the terrible things."

"Merrick did?"

She shook her head. "No, not him. Mr. McMahon was there. He heard too."

It was as if my fire had been doused by a bucket of ice. "No one was here except me and Merrick. And you, apparently."

"He came. He heard."

"And he believed? The same as you?"

"He heard what I heard."

Now I saw doubt in her eyes.

"If you say I heard wrong, then maybe . . . I don't know. I want to be wrong."

"You *are* wrong, Ms. Bertie. Wrong to listen in to someone else's business, and wrong to assume the worst. Please excuse me." I left her in the kitchen.

My legs were shaky. Oddly, even my jaw felt shaky, as if my teeth were about to chatter. I hugged myself. I'd wanted to ask her why Davis had been there and where he'd gone, but I couldn't trust myself, my ability to hold myself together.

If he truly believed I was a monster, then wouldn't he confront me himself? He'd been my friend. We'd kissed. He had invited me to travel the world with him for the book tour. And because of a few overheard words, he and Ms. B had believed ugly things? Was I so contemptible now that he could just walk away? Leaving me hanging here? Feeling . . .

My heart was breaking as I walked back to the kitchen. I stopped at the doorway. Ms. B was standing there with her hands clasped and looking thoroughly miserable.

I asked, "Where did he go?"

"Mr. McMahon?"

"Yes."

Was that alarm I saw in her eyes?

"Never mind, Ms. Bertie. He seems able to find me when—if—he wants to." I left her there.

⚮

I stopped at the door to Merrick's study. He was working at his laptop, intently focused as his fingers pecked at the keys. For the moment, my anger lessened, and my heart warmed in the hope that he was writing again. It didn't matter if he ever finished another novel, but the act of writing soothed him and invigorated him at the same time. I'd seen it and believed it.

I remembered I was looking for Davis.

"Merrick?"

He looked up.

"Sorry to disturb you. Have you seen Davis? I heard he was here."

Nodding, he said, "He dropped some papers off for me, then went looking for you. I haven't seen him since. I take it he didn't find you?"

"We missed each other. Thanks." And while I was here and he was attentive, I said, "By the way, I called Dr. Barnes. I want him to check you out. Something's not right with you."

"I don't need to see the doctor."

"Yes, you do. And after he clears you, we'll have that talk . . . the one about the will and such. But not until after, so please indulge me. Meanwhile, I need a walk. Can I get you anything first?"

I had his attention now. He stared at my face, no doubt seeing my frown and my mood.

He asked, "What's wrong?"

"Nothing I can't sort out. One way or another."

"Something with me? Did I do something wrong?"

"No, not you."

He breathed a loud sigh. Relief? He said, "Thank goodness for that. Anything I can help you with?"

"Not at the moment. I'll let you know if that changes."

"Be careful, Lilliane."

"What does that mean?"

"Just what it sounds like. Take care. Sometimes the smallest things done or not done, like that road we talked about, can have the most enduring consequences."

"I'll keep that in mind."

"Lilliane, I don't know what you've got on your mind or what you're looking to sort out, but take an old man's last-gasp advice. Go looking for fun instead. Let the lesser stuff take care of itself."

I restated, "Remember what I said about the doctor. If he comes by, cooperate with him."

"Yes, ma'am."

"Call me if you need me."

CREO

I left Merrick but came to a stop again in the middle of the foyer. Dad's metal sculpture was still standing against the wall. In point of fact, I'd only been here for a week and a half thus far, so it wasn't too lackadaisical that we hadn't gotten it hung. And yet, today alone felt almost like a lifetime.

Where was Davis? I'd never been to his home. Should I track him down there?

I didn't care what he thought of me—not one little bit. From what Ms. B had said, he'd proved himself unreliable and a poor judge of people, especially of me.

He'd eavesdropped, made assumptions, and then had run away. I should just let it go and let him go.

At the far end of the hallway and backlit by bright daylight flooding in through the pool door stood a figure, still and waiting.

Not Davis. Ms. B. She stepped forward but didn't come all the way to the foyer. Instead, she backtracked and scurried into the kitchen.

I had every right to be angry at her. Every right. I crossed my arms, rocked back and forth a little, and then gave it up.

She was in the kitchen, standing there, hands clasped. I stood in the doorway, not knowing what to say.

Ms. B averted her gaze and shook her head, saying, "I know what I heard." She threw up her hands, more agitated than I'd ever seen her, and this time met my eyes. "But I must've heard wrong. Just wrong. Lil-li, I don't know what you were talking about or who with, and I didn't mean to listen. We walked out 'cause we saw you there—not to spy. But then it was too late, and I should've just shut my ears, should not have said anything. Not my place."

This was wrong. I said, "I disagree with that."

"How?"

"If you thought someone was trying to take advantage of Merrick, I'd expect you to speak up. The problem is that you believe *I* would ever do anything intentionally to wrong him."

"Oh my, yes. I know. I was so upset, my brain . . . kept saying it heard what it heard." She hit her forehead with the butt of her hand.

I moved forward and stopped her. I took her hand in mine, saying, "Don't."

"Sorry, Lil-li."

"It's okay. It's all good."

"Good?"

I forced a smile. "We're good. And now, please excuse me. Keep an eye on Merrick? Thanks. I need to take care of something."

She whispered, "Something or *someone*?" She added, "Be kind."

☙

I left the kitchen but got stuck spinning my wheels in the foyer again. I was hurt and angry, with no one to vent my ire and frustration on. Not on Merrick, certainly. Not on Ms. B. Our brief unpleasantness had been excruciating. I'd never felt like such a bully ever in my life. I remembered that first meeting between us in the kitchen—the very first meeting— and how intimidating she'd seemed to me as she'd worked at the kitchen counter and the flash of the sharp knife in her hand. I'd *worked* on her, getting closer to her, just as I'd done with Merrick. And had discovered the kindness in them, and sweetness. The friendship.

Too much anger and energy had its grip on me, and all that negative energy was at war with what Susan had told me. So much exciting stuff—TV shows, even. I should be celebrating. But she'd said not to tell anyone until she gave me the go-ahead, except for Merrick.

But Merrick was busy with his own thing, and just at this moment, and not being one to pout, I had words—strong words—that had to be said to someone. That someone should be Davis. And after I found him and spoke my mind, I'd likely be telling him goodbye.

Rather than allow my inner war to drive more, and unnecessary, mistakes, I went upstairs. I had to sort out my thoughts—not run away or run about like a mad person. As I stood at the window, staring at the ocean, I wished it could give me comfort today. I needed it badly. Instead of tracking Davis down, maybe that's where I should go—down to the beach and chase fun, per Merrick's advice. I should chill and reenergize in a positive way. In fact, there was Miranda's striped canopy far below and up the beach a ways in its accustomed spot.

Her granddaughter must've set her up down there today. I'd like to see Miranda.

Anything I had to say to Davis could be said later. Might even be better said after a cooling down period. Pride might precede a fall, but someone had also said that some harsh words were best served cold . . . or something like that.

I hurried down the stairs, paused in the kitchen for cookies and bottles of water to repay her kindness from the last time we'd sat and chatted, and then I went out the side door to the crossover. At the end, I kicked off my flip-flops and turned due east, seeking Miranda.

Her voice carried on the breeze. In the shade of the canopy, I couldn't get a good view of who was with her, but someone was because his voice carried too, indistinct but unmistakable, over the sound of the waves and the breeze, as I moved toward them.

Miranda said, "Hey there, Lilliane. Look who's keeping me company?"

Davis was seated in her other chair, leaning forward with his forearms on his thighs, and he refused to meet my eyes.

"Uh-huh. I see." The water bottles and cookies were suddenly heavy in my arms. If Miranda hadn't been there, they might've become missiles. Maybe not, but I was glad not to be put to the test. Plus, now that I'd found Davis, even by mistake, I truly wished I hadn't. No logic there.

Miranda was speaking. "You and he have something in common."

I made a sour face. Couldn't help myself. "That so? What?"

"Found him sitting in the water in his shorts. No swim trunks. Nice shorts but not made for swimming." She was teasing and all but laughing. "You'd think a smart, handsome fella like him would know to wear a swimsuit."

"And that's what we have in common? Swimsuits?" I switched my gaze from Miranda to Davis. "It would be especially nice if we had trust and faith in common too. If we could give each other the benefit of the doubt. That would be really great."

Miranda was now eyeing us both now, switching her gaze back and forth between us. Her expression indicated she was teetering between interest and alarm.

Davis was now looking at me. I gave him my best make-my-day stare. Could I forget? Pretend that what had happened didn't really matter? He should've stayed and spoken with me directly. If I couldn't count on him to stay, to have my back, to be there when things went wrong, then—bottom line—I couldn't count on him at all.

And that changed everything between us.

I said, "I have some things to say to you. It's up to you whether it's said here with an audience or privately. Now or never. Choose, because I'm not inclined to patience at this moment."

He stood. "I have a few things to say too." He turned to Miranda and said politely, "Thanks for the water and the conversation. It's been a pleasure."

"You're welcome," she said, but she was frowning. "Y'all are gonna take this dispute up the beach, I hope? Maybe to a nice lonely stretch of sand?"

"Yes, ma'am," he said. "If you're sure you're fine here alone?"

"I have my book." She patted the jacketed novel sitting on her lap. "I'm good for a long while yet."

He smiled at her. "Yes, ma'am. I believe you are." Then he turned to me. "I'm all yours, Lilliane. Lead the way."

Miranda said, "Hold up. Are those goodies for me? You can put 'em in the cooler, if you like."

As I leaned over to lift the lid and began placing the items into the ice, she lightly pinched my arm. I turned toward her. Her face was surprisingly close to mine.

She whispered, "Choose wisely."

I stood up and stared at her. Choose what? My words? My course? She didn't know anything about any of the things that were presently rocking my world.

Miranda gave us both a stare and then a smile. She said bluntly, "You can choose to fight the ocean and be swallowed by the tide, or you can choose to dance with the waves." She picked up her book and spoke as if to no one in particular, saying, "I know which way I'd go if I had the option for do-overs."

Davis was standing there only a few feet away. I nodded at Miranda and then took off walking back up the beach. West, toward The Point. It seemed appropriate.

By the thin sound of his bare feet kicking up sand as he walked, I knew Davis was catching up fast.

CRLED

I walked with speed. We needed to be away from Miranda and anyone else who had any idea that we were connected to Merrick before we started speaking. To casual eyes, we were just two anonymous people on the beach who happened to be moving along at an energetic pace.

I kept to the wet sand near the water's edge where the footing was better. Davis's legs were longer, and he had no trouble matching my pace. He tried to talk a few times, but I wasn't ready yet.

The beach was wide here, and the houses were distant from the water, especially as we neared The Point. The other beachgoers were scattered and in family groups attuned to each other. No one was paying attention to us, and they weren't close enough to hear, even if they were casual observers.

I stopped abruptly and shouted at him. "Why? Why would you eavesdrop, hear a few words of a private conversation—and that being only *my* side of the conversation—and think the worst? Poor Ms. B . . . she was distraught, thinking . . . Why did you take off and leave her thinking she was right in those thoughts? The two of you—" I took off again, almost running. Maybe I could break into a run and leave them all behind. Not Merrick, though. Not Miranda either. And therein lay an important part of my problem. Was I going to allow my pride or my hurt feelings to drive me away? Whether it was right or not, Merrick needed me.

Davis got ahead of me, then spun around. I would've collided with him, but he caught me.

"I didn't believe it, Lilliane. Okay, maybe for a moment I wondered—a split second of doubt. We heard those words, and your tone of voice was like nothing I'd ever heard from you before. I told Ms. B there was bound to be an explanation. But then I thought of Merrick and you, and it hit me that it didn't matter. I've seen you with him—your kindness, your patience with him here and at Cub Creek— all those things. But already I was ashamed that I'd thought it, even for the space of one breath. And that does matter, and I apologize."

"Are you saying you don't care if I'm mercenary? That

I might be deceiving Merrick, and you're okay with that?"

"What? No, don't be absurd. I'm saying that I know you aren't. Everything you've done for him has been beneficial. I had that one split-second of doubt because you sounded so hard, so cynical. So unlike yourself. And then I realized that you were reacting to something to do with Merrick that upset you. Merrick again. It was no longer about doubt. It was about jealousy because . . . this, as with everything these days, was connected to Merrick. There is something that ties you two together in a special way. Sometimes I resent it, and I admit that. And I'm embarrassed because I'm not a four-year-old. I'm forty. I understand he comes first."

"What will you say when you hear he wants to give me money and even put me in his will?"

His grip on my arms tightened, his dark eyes grew darker and the flecks of topaz glittered, his brows narrowed, and the vertical lines formed between them. I held my breath. And he laughed.

I frowned and tried to shake his hands off. He simply slid his arms around me.

"Please, Lilliane. I'll release you, if that's what you want, but please don't run off again."

And in that moment, the wave came—the one we totally weren't prepared for because we'd forgotten we were standing on the edge of the Atlantic Ocean. It hit our legs at the knees and swept the sand from beneath our feet. We gripped each other now, staggering. If one stumbled, we'd both fall.

And we did.

By the time we hit the water, we were laughing. We tried to get back to our feet, our arms still entwined, and we almost beat the next wave. Almost. We were kneeling in the sand when it came, and we held on to each other all the tighter.

We kissed. A bit sandy and gritty, but a real kiss, and if another wave rolled in while we were busy, we didn't notice.

Then we heard the giggle. It came right after a plastic

bucket bumped our legs.

A child, maybe five or six, was standing a few feet away. She was staring at us as we knelt there in the sand, still with our arms around each other. She seemed delighted with the show we were putting on. Fortunately, the audience only included her and a woman who was running toward us, presumably her mom.

I smiled, saying, "Hello," as Davis helped me to my feet.

She giggled again. The woman took her daughter's hand. "Come on, honey. Sorry!" And then the momma giggled too. As they walked away, Davis and I faced each other.

He asked, "Is that what Miranda was advising?"

At first, I frowned. What did he mean? Then I remembered. "Maybe. But maybe we took the dancing part a little too literally? The ocean seems to move to its own tune."

Davis kept holding on to me. He spoke close to my ear. "Do you hear it?"

I felt the onshore breeze, I heard the crash of the waves and felt the sand and salt, but I didn't think that's what he meant. "What?"

"The music. The energy in the rhythm. No wonder this is where you come when you're hurt, worried, or angry. That's why I came down to the beach."

"To find me . . . but . . ." It made no sense because he knew where I was when he left.

He shook his head *no*. "You went to the gazebo, and I didn't want to interrupt, but I was . . . well, you know. Conflicted. So I came down here because it always seems to work for you. I was hoping to find some of that magic for myself too. I don't believe, and never could, that you'd put your personal gain above Merrick or anyone's wellbeing. I'm sorry I let you down, even for a moment."

Together, we walked slowly back along the beach, but we stayed where the waves could reach us, could find us, and wash over our feet and ankles.

He said, "I apologize for laughing when you mentioned Merrick and his money. I was relieved—so relieved you weren't telling me to get lost that I couldn't help it."

"You know I didn't ask him for any of that."

"Of course you didn't. It's all Merrick. I knew he was planning something, though not specific details. He was worried he'd make you angry and lose you." He laughed softly. "A lot like me."

Lose me. They didn't want to lose me. I already knew that in my heart. Hearing the words spoken aloud made it sound like a fact—and a promise.

Davis said, "Soon after we first met, way back . . . oh, three months ago, maybe? I told you that Merrick didn't do half measures. That you were either *his* or *not his*. He adopted you back then—in his heart and mind." He squeezed my hand.

"What did you say about being jealous?"

"I was. Am. I confess."

"Truly?"

He said, "I envy his relationship with you. Juvenile of me, perhaps, and I've never acted on the feeling, but I confess to being a little envious of the connection between you. And the reality that, for you, Merrick comes first."

"Please. He is my employer and friend. And much more dependent on me."

"The heart knows no logic."

"Sounds like another line from a book. Or maybe an interesting book or movie."

He smiled. "It's true, but also ironic. Because I'm pretty sure Merrick has been trying to set us up almost from the start."

I nodded. "I agree. Didn't realize you'd figured that out too."

He shrugged, laughing a little. "Per his style, he was just cementing the relationships around him. Merrick likes to tidy up loose threads."

"Is that some sort of inside writing joke?" We both smiled, and I said, "I do remember that first conversation we had on the beach—that first day on the job. I thought *you* were mercenary—perhaps up to no good with Merrick. I suspected you were trying to take advantage of him by befriending him for your own gain."

"Did you? Seriously?"

"Guilty," I said.

"I kind of wish you hadn't told me."

"Hurts, I know."

"It does," he said.

We stopped again and faced each other.

"Yet another irony because if not for Merrick, his help, his influence . . . would I have been able to interest an agent, a publisher? Would the book tour be happening?" He touched my cheek. "Should I have refused? Should I walk away now from all the good that has come from it?"

"Of course not."

"I'm sorry for what happened today," he said. "I wish I'd stayed to talk to you after the . . . after overhearing your conversation. I was embarrassed. I needed to think things out. Then I found myself at the same place where I've always found you when you are upset. The salt water wrecked my shorts, for sure. Then Miranda came over, making remarks and waving her cane. What is it with Miranda and Merrick and those canes?"

"I think Miranda likes to entertain us. She surely does know how to deliver a line. But mostly, she's brave and wise. Talking to her relaxes me."

"Works that way for me too," he said. "So you forgive me?"

"You'll need to forgive me too."

"I do. Absolutely."

"Something else—I meant what I said about Merrick wanting to put me in his will. He's already been generous to me with the paychecks and the rental car, even the leased car. I can't stop him from doing what he wants to do with his will, and maybe I shouldn't. Maybe I should just say thank you to him. But if you hear anyone calling me a money-grubber or saying I took advantage of an old man, I expect you to stand up for me."

"Now I'm hurt that you feel the need to tell me that."

"Too bad," I said, shrugging. "Hey, just being honest here."

"I think you should apologize for suggesting I'd fail to have your back."

"I apologize."

"Not good enough. I think we should kiss and make up."

"Not so fast," I said. "First, we have to discuss the book tour. We each have things to take care of over the next few months. We've managed our lives without each other for a long time. We can manage for a few more weeks, can't we?" A rush of anxiety hit me, and I stopped walking again. "We can, can't we?" What if this moment might be the *one moment*—the one where the good was there to be seized—and lost forever if the opportunity was allowed to pass?

Instead of answering, Davis kissed me. It was a brief kiss, and even after we stopped, he kept his arms around me.

"*What if this is our one chance?*" I whispered.

"Don't be superstitious. I've never known you to be."

I shook my head. "I'm not. Truly." I drew in a deep breath. "In fact, a short time ago I . . . I was prepared to say goodbye to you forever, or so I thought. But is that it, Davis? Not being superstitious, but is it about finally having someone—my someone—that I care enough about to fear losing? Was that why I kept you at arm's length?"

He slid his hands, his arms, around my back and hugged me closely. "We feel the same, Lilliane. We aren't kids who think we're invulnerable. We know too well we are. But you are never going to look back and wonder if you should've tried this metal art thing you've decided to do, and I won't either regarding the book tour. We'll take this time to do our work and plan for the future. The *near* future."

We were standing so close that it was easy to whisper in his ear, "I haven't even told you the newest news. My *big* news."

"What's that?" he whispered back.

I grinned. "Can't tell you. It's a secret."

He frowned. "Not fair."

"Fairness doesn't enter into it. It's a secret. Per Susan."

"Susan? So it's about . . ."

"*Shhh*." I pressed one finger to his lips. "Mustn't say it aloud, or even think it too loudly, because someone might overhear."

"That makes no sense. We're alone here."

"No? Well, before I left Cub Creek for that first time, I'd been wishing for a change and feeling alone. Loving Cub Creek, yes, but so very lonely and tired of the sameness and feeling my days slipping away. And then, on one unexpected June day, I met Susan and was offered and accepted a job that should never have come my way—and then I met you."

CR80

Back at the house and alone with Merrick, I said, "I'm going to be fine. Susan gave me some news about our . . . our quest to do something positive with my father's work. It's great news, and I'll share it with you, but first I want you to understand, I'll be okay financially. You don't have to worry about me. I've always managed and always will."

He spoke evenly. "Money brings both good and ill. Ask the person who has none and the person who has too much— they both have complaints. And yet there are always people who want what the other guy has. I know you aren't that way. But I want you to be able to pursue your dreams—"

I almost laughed. *Dreams? Me? But yes,* I thought, *I do have dreams. Fine dreams. Bold dreams.*

Merrick was saying, "I think that applied to your parents. Especially your father. They had dreams but didn't like what came into their lives from the outside as part of that. They pulled in closer together and tried to keep the . . . outside out. They preferred their world, small or not."

"True enough."

"While I care about your financial solvency and such, I plainly admit that my primary concern is much more basic than that." He paused. "More personal to me."

I fought the desire to interrupt him. *Let him speak, Lilliane.*

"You are not, in fact, my family. Not by law or by blood. If I suggested adopting you, you and the world would laugh at me as a doddering, demented old fool. But the heart doesn't hear what the world speaks." He tapped his chest. "The heart knows its own truth. You are the closest thing to a child, a daughter, that I ever had. I knew it almost from the first. I wanted it to be different. You and I are too alike. We see ourselves as lone wolves. We avoid commitment. Look at my marriage—late and poorly done."

"Mine was too early, but also poorly done."

He nodded. "No family to speak of otherwise."

"True."

"Then why not?" He tapped his cane against the floor. "Why not, I ask?"

I didn't know what to say.

"Why can't you and I be family? This is your second home, as it would be to any biological child who grew up and moved away and who visits when possible. You don't have to give up your home in Cub Creek. This isn't an all-or-nothing deal. I can advise you on life, business, and how to dress for dates. You can advise me on life and on how to be . . . gentler with other people and insist I see the doctor even when I don't want to." He tapped his cane again. "Again, I ask, why not?"

I shook my head slowly. My eyes were stinging, and my

throat was tight. I was afraid to speak lest I get the waterworks going. But Merrick needed a response from me.

My voice was raspy as I spoke. "I can't promise what comes next. I don't know what tomorrow looks like, Merrick." I stopped abruptly, drew in a deep breath, and then released it slowly.

Merrick reached over and patted my hand gently. "Take your time."

I tried to reassure him with a smile.

He said, "Every family has its ups and downs. Disagreements, disappointments —as well as celebrations and triumphs. It's what bonds us together and keeps life interesting. And that's true whether we're biological family or close, dear friends."

"Oh, Merrick. You are persuasive, and I'm reminding myself that words are your profession. But it doesn't necessarily make them any less true." This time *I* reached over and touched *his* hand. The flesh was thin and spotted, the knuckles were large and bony, but the hand was warm and alive. Nothing about tomorrow was promised, and commitments could never be perfection, but maybe it was only about trying my best, whether here or in Cub Creek. I heard Miranda's whisper, "Choose wisely."

I squeezed his hand gently. "Yes, Merrick. We are family. Not really a choice at all, is it?"

He nodded. "Trust me, Lilliane. We've got this."

Merrick stood slowly, and I was right there with him. As I hugged him, I sensed we had company. Not only my parents, who'd wanted the best for me but had fumbled the execution, but others who'd loved and lost—and were cheering us on in the hope of second chances and so much more.

# Epilogue

In Cub Creek, the TV crew came first, and then the stars who hosted and headlined the show arrived on the scene. The makeup crew even fixed my face. I looked rather glamorous, I had to admit, but I drew the line at them getting crazy with my hair, though I did allow some hairspray. Merrick had come up to Cub Creek with Susan, and he offered advice on what I should wear. I appreciated his interest, and told him so, but I decided to follow the dresser's guidance instead.

Susan had had a professional photograph done of the sculpture that I'd given Merrick. She'd had the image blown up and printed full size on metal and hung in the empty spot on the workshop wall with directed lighting hitting it just right. All the metal art sculptures were given the same lighting treatment—so subtle that you hardly even knew your eyes were being directed there on purpose. The tools, especially the old ones that were too fragile or too valuable to use, were hung on the walls in and among the metal art sculptures.

*Oh, Dad,* my heart cried silently, *I can't even begin to imagine what you'd think of all this, but you'd love it. You and Momma both.*

Instead of going off the confines of the map, my smart, talented, caring friends and I had found ourselves *on* the map. At least for a brief spurt of fame. And brief was quite all right with me. I made sure inquiries of any kind, including through social media, went directly to Susan. That was not my strength, but hers. Much like the magic of the cross-promo she'd arranged. Because many people did ask—as she'd anticipated—*Why is that one metal sculpture hanging on the wall as a picture?*

Susan's idea had been genius. Not only did it continue the theme of *yesterday and today across time*, but it was that extra dollop of icing on the cake that gave the rest of the works a sense of being fine art. So when visitors, including the TV crew, asked why that metal art sculpture was displayed as a picture, I could say . . .

*Because the real one is hanging on Merrick Dahl's wall.*

*Who? Did you say Merrick Dahl? The author?*

*You betcha.*

*Is he still alive?*

*Oh, sure. He's alive and kicking—and writing. Did you know that Merrick Dahl's newest release is coming out soon? After a hiatus of years. The novel's title is* The Book of Lost Loves *and . . .*

Oh yes. And that cross-promo even extended to Europe, where Davis was on his book tour and Merrick's face followed him everywhere on a bigger-than-life-size standing image that displayed an updated photo of him, cane included, holding the new book, and below that was his old author photo with his bestsellers of the past surrounding him.

*Job well done, Susan.*

After the day's shoot was over and the crews had dispersed, Susan took Merrick to a hotel for a badly needed rest. I treated Joe and his bride to dinner out at a local restaurant. Across the dining room, I spied Gwen and Bobby. They were sharing a cozy corner booth. In town, no less. Bobby looked so well put together and respectable that I was thinking we'd have to drop that pesky, undignified *-by* and start calling him *Robert* or *Bob*. Now that I thought of it, what *did* Gwen call him? *Mr. Harrin* when she'd been at my house, but I suspected she called him something friendlier when they were alone. At this moment, public or not, they were so fascinated by each other, they never spared the rest of us a look.

*Job well done, Gwen. Keep keeping that eye on Mr. Harrin. He may yet shape up to respectability after all.*

And me? I had a fresh burn on my arm. A small thing. Only first degree, and it wouldn't leave a scar, or not for long. It would be a passing souvenir of my first completed work of metal art. An experiment, really, that might actually turn out to be something—something to prove to myself that I *could* do it, and to show Davis, currently on his book tour, that I'd missed him. We were both following our individual paths for a brief time, but those paths would lead the two of us back to Emerald Isle and to Merrick.

Which would suit Merrick just fine.

Meanwhile, I was splitting my time between home and home—it *was* possible to call two places home, at least for a while. And the *now*—the present—was really all I needed to handle. One day at a time. No borrowing trouble. Leave the unknowns for tomorrow and enjoy today, today. And I was doing exactly that.

After the TV shoot and interview stuff was done, we were well into October. And on this particular autumn evening, I was standing at the ocean's edge. The sun was setting, and the long days of summer were behind us. In Emerald Isle, the air was still mild and touched with warmth, but the occasional onshore gust reminded me that the Atlantic Ocean also had a colder nature.

Merrick had told me I was silly to come down here. That after Davis's flight landed in Wilmington, he'd still have a two-hour drive up the coast. Ms. B had agreed to stay late and keep Merrick company, so I went.

After full dark had fallen, I stood under the moon and the gathering stars—the same moon and stars that had graced Davis's nights in Europe and were even now in the skies over Cub Creek. I remembered the loved ones we'd lost, and I touched that small burn on my arm, realizing I no longer felt left behind. Certainly not forgotten. I was part of it all, including the fringe of the incoming tide that occasionally nipped at my toes. I adjusted my position, almost as if engaged in a private dance, but I stayed.

Because Davis always knew where to find me.

And this was where he'd come first.

I heard a voice and turned toward the dunes. A man, lit only by the same starlight that also touched me, had called my name. He was waving as he moved toward me over the shifting sand.

And I was delighted.

## The End

I hope you enjoyed *A Dancing Tide*. A full list of my novels and novellas is on the last page. I hope you'll check them out

# Author's Note

*Beach Rental*, the first book in The Emerald Isle, NC Stories series, was published in 2011, but it wasn't the first novel I wrote. That first novel, *Cub Creek*, set in Louisa County, Virginia, was not published until 2014. *Beach Rental* had a delightful beach setting and was mostly romance with a little suspense, while *Cub Creek* was set amid the forests and rolling hills of rural Virginia and had more mystery and suspense with a little romance. *Beach Rental* led to *Beach Winds* and *Beach Wedding*. *Cub Creek* grew to include *Leaving Cub Creek* and other single title books that share the setting: *The Memory of Butterflies* and *The Wildflower House* series, and *The Happiness In Between*.

I love both settings and the characters in each.

After writing *A Light Last Seen* in 2019, I was ready to work on a new beach book, but 2020 had arrived and unhappy things had happened and the virus was upon us. The book I was now trying to write kept going very dark. Meanwhile, a new character was whispering to me—Lilliane Moore—but she was in Cub Creek, not at the beach.

For several months I persisted with that first manuscript, but finally put it aside and got to know Lilliane. Guess what? She'd never been to the beach. She'd never seen the ocean. I took her to the beach in *A Barefoot Tide* and had the joy of experiencing the ocean and shores of coastal Carolina right along with her for the first time all over again. It was wonderful.

Lilliane works as an aide for the elderly Merrick Dahl, though she isn't a skilled nurse and considers herself more of a companion. Many of the qualities I found in her were those I found and respected in most of the aides who cared for my mother during her journey through Alzheimer's. I admired their willingness to do whatever was needed for the fragile and oft confused elderly residents, and the best of them managed their jobs with grace, kindness and practical assistance. My mother was blessed to have the same core caregivers for most of her years in the memory care facility. I will never forget them. Lilliane's job in this fictional story is less intensive than what most aides experience in real life, but you'll see many of the best qualities shown by these strong women in Lilliane as she interacts with Merrick.

*A Barefoot Tide* is my 2020 story—written during that year of struggle. Writing Lilliane's story gave me comfort. Because of readers like you, *A Dancing Tide* joined it in 2021. It was a gift to me to write it, and I hope it will be the same to you, the reader.

One last note: You can't drive on The Point during beach season, and even during the months that you can, a permit is required. Just letting you know so you don't get into trouble. As Merrick might say, *Fiction allows for a flexible representation of life ~ not a literal retelling.*

Thank you for sharing the ride with me.

*~ January 2, 2021 Grace Greene (updated September 2021)*

# Questions For Discussion

1.  When Lilliane's perceptions about her childhood and her present life changed, she never discounted the memories and values she'd cherished before. Why is that?

2.  Lilliane's future, at least the possibilities of futures she might pursue, opened up for her at the end of *A Barefoot Tide*. Now, in *A Dancing Tide*, Lilliane must make choices regarding what she values, and about new opportunities. She is concerned about making the right choices. Why?

3.  Lilliane struggles with wanting her relationship with Davis to grow, while being wary of commitment. Her life had been filled with commitments that became anchors. Is that why? Or does she sense her future lies in a different direction and fears being held back again? Or is she afraid of becoming emotionally dependent on someone else who might leave her behind?

4.  What path do you think Lilliane will choose for her future beyond this book? Why?

# About the Author

*Photo © 2018 Amy G Photography*

Grace Greene is an award-winning and USA Today bestselling author of women's fiction and contemporary romance set in the countryside of her native Virginia *(The Happiness In Between, The Memory of Butterflies, the Cub Creek Series, and The Wildflower House Series)* and on the breezy beaches of Emerald Isle, North Carolina *(The Emerald Isle, NC Stories Series)*. Her debut novel, *Beach Rental*, and the sequel, *Beach Winds*, were both Top Picks by RT Book Reviews magazine. This newest release, *A Barefoot Tide*, represents the merging of two worlds—that of Cub Creek and Emerald Isle, through the eyes of a new character, and continues in the sequel, *A Dancing Tide* released in October 2021.

Visit www.gracegreene.com for more information or to communicate with Grace and sign up for her newsletter.

# BOOKS BY GRACE GREENE

BEACH RENTAL   (The Emerald Isle, NC Stories Series ~ Novel #1)

<u>RT Book Reviews</u> – TOP PICK

"No author can come close to capturing the awe-inspiring essence of the North Carolina coast like Greene. Her debut novel seamlessly combines hope, love and faith, like the female equivalent of Nicholas Sparks. Her writing is meticulous and so finely detailed you'll hear the gulls overhead and the waves crashing onto shore. Grab a hanky, bury your toes in the sand and get ready to be swept away with this unforgettable beach read." —*RT Book Reviews TOP PICK*

<u>Brief Description</u>:

*On the Crystal Coast of North Carolina, in the small town of Emerald Isle...*

Juli Cooke, hard-working and getting nowhere fast, marries a dying man, Ben Bradshaw, for a financial settlement, not expecting he will set her on a journey of hope and love. The journey brings her to Luke Winters, a local art dealer, but Luke resents the woman who married his sick friend and warns her not to hurt Ben—and he's watching to make sure she doesn't. Until Ben dies and the stakes change.

Framed by the timelessness of the Atlantic Ocean and the brilliant blue of the beach sky, Juli struggles against her past, the opposition of Ben's and Luke's families, and even the living reminder of her marriage—to build a future with hope and perhaps to find the love of her life—if she can survive the danger from her past.

A LIGHT LAST SEEN ~ *When Jaynie Was…*

(Single Title/Standalone)

Brief Description:

Chasing happiness and finding joy are two very different things—as Jaynie Highsmith has discovered. Can she give up searching for the one and reclaim the other? Or is she fated to repeat the mistakes her mother made?

Jaynie Highsmith grows up in Cub Creek on Hope Road acutely aware of the irony of its name, Hope, because she wants nothing more than to escape from it and the chaos of her childhood. Desperate to leave her past behind and make a new life, she is determined to become the best version of herself she can create. But when she does take off, she also leaves ~ and forgets ~ important parts of her past and herself.

CUB CREEK  (Cub Creek Series #1)

Brief Description:

*In the heart of Virginia, where the forests hide secrets and the creeks run strong and deep ~*

Libbie Havens doesn't need anyone and she'll prove it. When she chances upon the secluded house on Cub Creek in rural Virginia, she buys it. She'll show her cousin Liz, and other doubters, that she can rise above her past and live happily and successfully on her own terms.

At Cub Creek Libbie makes friends and attracts the romantic interest of two local men, Dan Wheeler and Jim Mitchell. Relationships with her cousin and other family members improve dramatically and Libbie experiences true happiness—until tragedy occurs.

Having lost the good things gained at Cub Creek, Libbie must find a way to overcome her troubles, to finally rise above them and seize control of her life and future, or risk losing everything, including herself

## THE WILDFLOWER HOUSE SERIES

### WILDFLOWER HEART (Bk 1)

~ Love and hope, like wildflowers, can grow in unexpected places. Kara Hart has been tested repeatedly during her first thirty years. She's recovering, but is she resilient enough to start her life over yet again? When her widowed father suddenly retires intending to restore an aging Victoria mansion, Kara goes with him intending to stay until the end of wildflower season.

### WILDFLOWER HOPE (Bk 2)

~ Kara is building a new life at Wildflower House - but will digging in to restore the old mansion not only give her a sense of belonging, but also restore her heart?

### WILDFLOWER CHRISTMAS (A Novella)

~ Kara is expecting a quiet Christmas ~ just like she'd always known ~ but if she's lucky she'll have a very different Christmas experience ~ one worth building new traditions to treasure.

*Please visit www.GraceGreene.com for a full list of Grace's books, both single titles and series, for descriptions and more information.*

# BOOKS BY GRACE GREENE

**Emerald Isle, North Carolina Series**
Beach Rental *(Book 1)*
Beach Winds *(Book 2)*
Beach Wedding *(Book 3)*
*"Beach Towel" (A Short Story)*
Beach Walk *(Christmas Novella)*

**Barefoot Tides Two-Book Series**
A Barefoot Tide *(Book 1)*
A Dancing Tide *(Book 2)*

**Beach Single-Title Novellas**
Beach Christmas *(Christmas Novella)*
Clair *(Beach Brides Novella Series)*

**Cub Creek Novels ~ Series and Single Titles**
Cub Creek *(Cub Creek Series, Book 1)*
Leaving Cub Creek *(Cub Creek Series, Book 2)*
The Happiness In Between
The Memory of Butterflies
A Light Last Seen

**The Wildflower House Novels**
Wildflower Heart *(Book 1)*
Wildflower Hope *(Book 2)*
Wildflower Christmas *(A Wildflower House Novella) (Book 3)*

**Virginia Country Roads**
Kincaid's Hope
A Stranger in Wynnedower
www.GraceGreene.com